MW01224245

Other books by
Margery Reynolds

One Summer at Ril Lake
One Winter at Ril Lake

By D. M. Rutherford

Reflections From Doteaga
(A compilation of poetry and recipes)

One Winter at Ril Lake

Published by

The Golden Pencil ✎

Copyright 2023 Dale Margery Rutherford

(aka Margery Reynolds)

All rights reserved.

This book is a work of fiction. Names and characters are the product of the author's imagination and are used fictitiously. The incidents are not real and are not meant to replicate any person living or dead. Some places mentioned existed at the time of writing and the businesses mentioned have given their permission to be used in this series.

Library of Canada Archives and Publication
ISBN: 978-1-7386767-5-0 (paperback)
ISBN: 978-1-7386767-6-7 (e-book)

by

Margery Reynolds

www.margeryreynolds.ca

Cover designed with Canva,
by D. M. Rutherford and Jennifer Merivale

One Winter at Ril Lake

A Muskoka Cottage Novel

By
Margery Reynolds

In Gratitude
Enjoy
Margery Reynolds

For
my granddaughter,

Aline Rose

who will always be,

my girl

Part One

Annie

Chapter 1

There were exactly three renters at the lodge that week, and Annie Taylor knew before opening the door which one had dragged her from her bed before six that morning. She pushed her feet into a pair of old winter boots kept just inside the back door, pulled her housecoat tighter over her nightgown, and opened the door to a rush of December cold.

"Good morning Mr. Gibson. What is it this time?" she asked, gasping at the bite in the air.

"The space heater isn't working," Mr. Gibson said, kicking one foot against the other.

It was the third day in a row Mrs. Gibson had sent her husband up to the house with a complaint. Annie had offered them one of her all-season cottages at a heavily discounted winter rate, but the Gibson's couldn't afford it. They'd opted for a one-room fishing cabin instead, which had baseboard heating, but apparently wasn't good enough for Mrs. Gibson.

"Why didn't you tell me sooner? I would have fixed it or brought you another one." She might have argued that the baseboard heating in the cabin should have been enough to warm the single room, but she let that go. It would have fallen on deaf ears, anyway.

"We didn't notice it until we got up this morning and saw ice on the inside of the windows." He glanced toward Cabin One, where his wife huddled on the front porch, no doubt expecting his successful return.

"So, you weren't cold during the night. Only when you got up this morning?" Annie shoved her hands under her armpits and tapped her feet to keep them from freezing.

"Well, yeah, I guess. We had loads of blankets on, but that isn't the point. The heater isn't working. Didn't you say each cabin had working heaters? My wife thinks we should have a refund."

The third day, the third complaint and always the same request—he wanted his money back. She hadn't given him a refund for the first two days, so what made him think she was going to do it today?

"I'm sorry, Mr. Gibson. That's not possible."

"Not a full refund. Just for one night. On account of it was so cold."

"You just said you weren't cold."

"But the heater wasn't working."

"But you didn't notice it until this morning."

Mr. Gibson slapped his gloved hands together and looked at her with a stare so icy it could rival the temperature. He sent a noncommittal shrug toward his wife, then looked back at Annie. "So, do we get a refund?"

Annie sighed. "No. But I will provide you with a working heater for the rest of your stay. As soon as my dad is up, he'll look at it. Will that do?"

"No refund, eh?" His gaze drifted toward his wife again and he shook his head. Mrs. Gibson sent a disgruntled huff into the morning air, then went inside, slamming the cabin door hard so it echoed off the lake like the crack of a whip.

Annie shook her head of auburn curls and gazed at Mr. Gibson through discerning eyes. It wasn't his fault his wife was a miserable so-and-so. "What about breakfast on me? Will that help?"

Mr. Gibson shrugged his shoulders. "I suppose. We passed that place in town, that's advertised in your brochure. The wife was kinda counting on eating there."

So that was it. He needed the money for breakfast. A twinge of sympathy pinched at Annie's generous nature as she stared into the worn face, looking back at her, waiting, hoping. "You mean *Around the Corner Diner*? Let me call Brent and set it up."

Mr. Gibson looked down at his boots, then sent a glance toward his cabin, as if unsure that was going to satisfy his wife.

"Well?" Annie said, just as eager to get out of the cold as Mrs. Gibson had been when she slammed the door a minute ago. In a sudden, unexpected burst of authority, Mr. Gibson shook a finger at her.

"Alright. But I want the heater repaired or replaced by the time we get back."

"Not a problem. Good morning Mr. Gibson. I hope you have a pleasant day."

As she reached for the door handle, Annie had another thought. What if she was in his shoes? What if her children were hungry, and that cold, and they were homeless? She turned back, just as he reached the bottom step.

"You know. The local theater group is rehearsing for the Christmas pageant at the church today. They'll be serving hot soup and sandwiches at lunchtime and it's all free, because it's a dress rehearsal."

He gave a slight nod before making his way toward the cabin, his shoulders stooped, his steps measured like those of a troubled man. Annie knew something about these worries, too. The pile of notices from the bank she'd shoved into her desk drawer had been weighing on her for days. Her shrinking bank account and the cupboards that were nearly as sparse as Old Mother Hubbard's were also a problem. She wasn't begging yet, but if she didn't find some answers soon, she might be the one knocking on someone's door begging for a refund or a handout.

"Trouble in Paradise?" her father asked when she went inside to start the coffee.

Sam Taylor had come to live with Annie and the kids after her mother died. It was an excellent arrangement. He helped around the lodge and she and the kids were company for him. Violet, her mother, had been a nurse devoted to caring for the sick. It seemed madly ironic that someone who took care of others would have been so ill herself. Cancer was a horrible thing and her death had touched them all, but mostly it had left Annie's father without the woman he'd always said was his soulmate.

It bothered Annie that her father had been disturbed by Mr. Gibson's insistent pounding at the back door, but there was little she could have done about it. Sam's bedroom was on the main floor of the house, and not far enough away from the door to sleep undisturbed, especially by an angry renter. She told him about the faulty heater and the previous two days' complaints.

"I hate to see people struggling, but I can't let them stay here for free. As it is, I'm paying for their breakfast at the diner. Four breakfasts! What was I thinking? I should have just refunded him the money for a night's stay."

Sam sipped his coffee, eyeing her as she started getting their breakfast together. "You know Brent won't charge you full price," her father said.

"I know. But it's still cash I just don't have."

"I could help you out. If you need some money."

"No Dad. Your pension is all you have, and you already do so much around here." He looked about to protest, so Annie rested her hand on his shoulder. "If I'm desperate, okay?"

"Okay. I'll go look at that heater while you get the kids organized. Speak of the angels, here they come." He turned as Ali raced into the room to give him a hug,

"Morning Grandpa!" she cried, clinging to his neck.

"Morning little Sweet Pea." When Ali unwrapped herself from him, he nudged Noah's shoulder. "Cat got your tongue this morning?"

Noah grunted and slid into his chair.

"Guess so." Sam laughed, then gave Annie a whiskery kiss on the cheek, which made her squirm and put her hand up to rub his jaw. "I'll shave later," he promised with a laugh. "After I check the Gibson's heater."

When he'd left, Annie used the last of her flour, sugar, and eggs, to make pancakes for their breakfast and when they were ready, she slid two short stacks, slathered in maple syrup, across the kitchen table to her son and daughter. Six-year-old Ali eyed them suspiciously, her arms crossed over her chest and a deep frown creasing her forehead.

"I wanted waffles with whipped cream and strawberries," she said, pushing her plate away.

Annie tucked a strand of auburn hair back into her messy bun and sighed. "I'm sorry, Pumpkin, but we don't have any strawberries, and I used the last of the flour." She pointed to the clock. "Even if I had some, there wouldn't be time. You've got twenty minutes to eat, get your stuff together and be at the end of the driveway for the bus."

Noah, who had a voracious appetite, eyed Ali's plate as he dove into his own stack of pancakes. "I'll have Ali's," he said, wiping syrup from his mouth, across his sleeve.

"Oh, Noah!" Annie cried. "Now you'll have to change your shirt."

"It's just a little syrup, Mum. Chill."

Annie sent him a disapproving frown, then nudged Ali's plate a little closer to her daughter. Ali stabbed at her pancakes, idly swirling her fork in the syrup, while Annie poured herself a cup of coffee. When she returned to the table, Ali's pancakes were still untouched.

"If you're not going to eat them, don't mess around. How about a banana or an apple?" Ali's face lit up, and she nodded. "Fine, I'll peel and slice an apple for you while you put your lunch and library book in your backpack." Better than no breakfast at all, Annie thought as she got out the peeler.

Ali slid off her chair to get her backpack organized. "But can we have waffles tomorrow? It's Saturday. We can sleep in, so we won't have to hurry so much."

"That's true, but I'd still need time today to get groceries, and we have three families checking out in the morning," Annie said.

Noah groaned. "What about my hockey game?"

"I can take you." Sam came back into the kitchen then and settled into his place at the head of the table. He reached out to Ali, who was struggling with her backpack. "Bring that here, Sweet Pea, and let me help you."

"Thanks Grandpa." Ali sidled up close to Sam and opened her backpack wide so he could drop her library book and lunch into it.

"There, all done." Sam patted Ali's back and pulled her close for a hug before she scampered away to find Frank, her beloved teddy bear, to put in her backpack, too.

"Don't know what I'd do without you." Annie set a second cup of hot steaming coffee and a plate of pancakes in front of him. Then she slid Ali's apple slices into a plastic bag so Ali could nibble them on the bus, and she whisked Noah's empty plate into the sink and sent him upstairs for a clean shirt.

"Come on Noah. Let's go," Annie called over her shoulder, as she shoved her arms into her winter coat. "You're going to miss the bus."

"I'm coming." Noah swooped down the stairs and scooped up his backpack in a smooth Spiderman kind of move. Then he pushed his feet into his boots, pulled the hood of his coat over his head without putting his arms into the sleeves, and headed out the door. At the bottom of the porch steps, he flew past Ali, making fresh tracks in the new snow that had fallen overnight as he hurried up the drive.

Annie followed him out the door and found Ali about to drop into the snow to make a snow angel. "When you get home, sweetheart," Annie said, urging her daughter toward the bus stop.

"But if I make one now, it means an angel will watch over you and Grandpa all day."

"I'm sure the angels already have a close eye on Grandpa. Don't you worry about him." Annie reached out to take hold of Ali's hand. "Come on. Let's run the rest of the way and see if we can beat Noah."

Ali giggled and raced past Annie to catch up with her brother. "I hear Ted," she called out, and sure enough, in the distance, they heard the whine of the engine and saw the yellow roof of the bus cresting the hill.

The door swung open as Ted pulled up and stopped. "Morning Annie, Noah, Aline." Ted was the only one who could use Ali's full name without getting a wince from her. Annie kissed her children on the forehead as they pushed past her up the steps and inside the bus.

"Morning Ted," Annie shouted over the din from the children already inside.

Ted had been driving the school bus since he retired from the mill; the same year Noah started Junior Kindergarten. All the kids called him Turtle Ted, because Ted loved turtles and had them all over his bus. Plush toys, stickers, water bottles with turtles, ninja turtles from the cartoons, pictures he'd taken of turtles. Ted had no children of his own, which always seemed a shame to Annie, since he loved the kids who rode his bus. When Ted learned Noah wanted to be a stand-up comic, he started telling him a new joke every day. Noah wrote them in a notebook and when he got home, he always told Annie the joke of the day, and Annie always laughed, even if it wasn't that funny.

"How's it going, Annie?" Ted called back while the kids found seats. "Are you booked up for Christmas?"

She shook her head. "No. But I always hope for a miracle."

"There's one just around the corner. I'm sure of it." Ted reached for the handle to close the door and gave her a reassuring nod. "Everyone sitting down?" He glanced up at his mirror as he pulled the door closed.

When Annie backed away from the bus, she found Ali's face pressed to the window a few rows back and blew her a kiss. Then, with a roar of the engine and a puffing cloud of diesel fuel, they were on their way.

Annie headed back to the house, pulling the flaps of her jacket tighter against the cold while scrolling for the diner's phone number.

"I'll come in later and pay for it," she said when Brent, the owner, answered and she told him what she wanted. It wasn't the first time she'd sent customers to him for breakfast, and it wasn't the first time she'd sprung for their food. "Just make sure they don't order the most expensive thing on the menu, please."

"Four specials," Brent said. "Two eggs, three slices of bacon, toast and hash browns." Brent had sighed into the phone. "You know Annie, I could…"

She knew what he was going to say, but she stopped him there. It wouldn't be the first time he'd offered her a job at the diner, but Annie strongly suspected Brent wanted more than just a waitress. Besides, working there would mean having to hire someone to run things here because her father couldn't manage on his own, even in the slower winter months. Working somewhere else and paying someone to work here made no sense.

"Gotta go, Brent. Thanks again."

In the kitchen, she poured herself another cup of coffee and warmed up Ali's mostly untouched pancakes in the microwave for herself. Wasting food was not in Annie Taylor's vocabulary, and all this early morning confusion had left her famished.

"Heater's fine," her father said, when she sat down at the table.

"What was wrong with it?"

"Nothing."

"Nothing?"

Sam added milk and a generous teaspoon of sugar to a fresh cup of coffee and stirred. "He hadn't even turned the damn thing on."

"You're kidding." Annie rolled her eyes toward the ceiling. "You mean I dished out for free breakfasts for nothing?"

"Looks like it." He reached out to pat her hand. "But you know, Karma has a way of fixing things. It'll come back to you."

She let out an exhaustive sigh and set her fork down as they heard a vehicle coming down the drive. Sam stood to look out the kitchen window.

"Speaking of Karma, that's Luke's truck pulling in."

Luke McCann was their occasional handyman, who Annie had hired a couple of years ago, when she and her father couldn't keep up. The problem was, Luke had more than just repairs and maintenance in mind once he'd gotten to know Annie's marital situation. Admittedly, she hadn't discouraged him most of the time, but lately he'd wanted more than Annie was willing to give. His most recent marriage proposal had set their relationship and Annie's teeth on edge. She liked his company, but she didn't feel *that way* about him and he wasn't taking no for an answer.

"Will you speak to him, Dad? He's going to want his pay and I haven't got it."

"Annie. You've got to work something out with him. You can't keep stalling."

"I know, but you know what it's been like. One decent season wasn't enough to turn things around after the covid fiasco and now it's winter."

"Then let him go. I can manage without him."

"You can't. There's too much to do. Besides, he's got a daughter to support and an ex-wife who wants alimony."

Sam threw his hands in the air. "But you can't pay him, so how is keeping him on helping?"

Annie's face scrunched into a grimace. "Point taken. But just for today, could you talk to him?"

"No! This is something you have to do. I'm going to shave." He left the room, taking his coffee with him, while outside, Luke's pickup truck was pulling up to a stop. The door slammed shut.

"Fine," Annie called down the hall, loud enough for her father to hear her. But when she slipped her coat over her shoulders and pushed her feet into her boots, it was herself she was blaming. It wasn't her father's fault. It had been a blessing having him live with them, helping with the kids and with the lodge. The man was a saint!

No, this was not her father's fault. It was hers for letting this thing with Luke go on for too long. Maybe it was a bit Luke's too, for sticking around, even though she'd made her feelings clear months ago. But she owed him money, and that was something she would have to deal with. That, and this morning's trio of, a harsh bank manager's foreclosure letters, a disappointed daughter's demands for strawberry waffles, and an angry customer's petitions for free meals.

Annie wanted to be grateful for what she had and not dwell on what troubled her, but it was hard to ignore the worries sometimes or the fact that everyone seemed to want something from her. She felt pulled in a hundred different directions, and each tug seemed to exhaust her more than the last.

"Just once," Annie whispered to the ceiling. "I'd like to hear someone say, *Let me take care of you, Annie.*"

Chapter 2

To call Annie's Lodge a resort was extravagant for what the place really was—a dozen cozy, winterized cottages on one side of her century-old farmhouse, and an equal number of rustic fishing cabins on the other. There was also the main lodge that consisted of a huge room with an enormous stone fireplace and cozy couches for gatherings around it, a second, smaller meeting-type room, and a fully equipped kitchen. Acres of woods surrounded them on all sides except for the north, where the boundary of her property met the shores of the beautiful and breathtaking waters of Ril Lake.

Buying a place in the Muskoka Region of Northern Ontario had really been her late husband's dream, but when they found this place, Annie had instantly fallen in love with it and his dream, too. It wasn't long before Noah was born, followed by Ali a year later, and their lives seemed complete. But then they'd received the terrible news of her mother's illness and not long after she'd succumbed to cancer. As if that weren't enough the following winter, an accident took Annie's husband's life.

Some people said she should remarry, that her children needed a father figure in their lives, but they didn't seem to understand that no one could replace the love of a soulmate. Felicity Pierce and Annie's father were the only ones who hadn't encouraged her to find someone. Perhaps because her father had lost his own soulmate, and, after a difficult first marriage, Felicity had finally found hers.

Annie didn't know about getting married again, but she knew it wouldn't be to Luke, despite his persistence. He had that look now, as he came towards her and Annie dragged her feet down the back stairs.

"Hey," she said, casting her eye out over the frozen lake to the shadowy tree line on the opposite shore.

"Hey," he said back, reaching out to caress her hand.

She ignored the playful smile on his face and nodded toward his truck. "What's in the back?"

"Just a few things for the kids for Christmas. I was hoping you could hide them in the attic."

Annie's heart sank right to the bottom of her chest, knowing he would have put these gifts on his credit card, expecting his pay. "You shouldn't have done that, Luke," she said, following him down the steps to his truck. He pulled back the cover to reveal a box of brightly wrapped gifts, trimmed with bows, ribbon and nametags.

"It's just a couple of things. Where can I put them?"

"Luke. I…" Her heart ached for the kindness in this man. He cared about her kids, and he could fix just about anything that needed repairing around the place, but Luke couldn't fix her and she could not return his love, not in the way he'd like her to.

"What's up, Annie? You've got that look again."

"What look? I don't have a look." She let her eyes wander out over the lake, avoiding his gaze.

"You do. It's that look that says you've got something to say, but you don't want to say it. Like when I asked you to marry me. That look."

She turned back to face him and twisted her fingers until a knuckle cracked and he reached out to stop her from doing it again.

"Whatever it is, it has to come out. You can't keep stuff bottled up inside you. I keep telling you that." He pulled her into his arms and tucked her head under his chin. "You know whatever it is, I'm still gonna love you, don't you?"

There it was. The biggest problem of all. He would still love her, but she just couldn't love him back, not the way he wanted her to. But that's not what she needed to talk to him about today.

"It's bad, Luke. Really bad."

"Double shot latte bad?"

"Worse. You want to come inside for coffee?"

"Better had." Luke pressed the lock button on his key fob and the beep echoed across the lake and into the distant shadows. Scooping the box of presents out of the bed of his truck, he followed her up the back stairs and into the kitchen, where he settled into Noah's chair and nodded to Annie's father.

"Morning Sam. How are things?"

"Things are good Luke. Well, I'm good anyway. Sorry I can't stay, but Noah and I marked a couple of Christmas trees the other day. One for here and the other for the lodge."

"I'll help you with that," Luke offered, half rising out of his chair.

"That's okay. I'll get them one at a time and use the big sled and some rope. It'll be fine." He disappeared out the back door, leaving Luke and Annie alone.

She pushed a cup of coffee in front of Luke and set her own cup on the table. "Be right back," she said, and went to her office. When she returned, she put the letters from the bank on the table in front of him.

"They're going to foreclose at the end of January, if I don't come up with three months' mortgage payments by then. I'll pay you the money I owe you, I promise, but Luke, I can't afford to keep on paying you."

Luke frowned at the letters, then looked up at her, a worried expression spreading across his features. "Why did you wait to tell me this?"

"I'll get you the money. I just have to take a cash advance on my card." She didn't tell him it would max out her credit card and there would be little left after she bought groceries. She might eke out some Christmas presents for the kids once her guests checked out in the morning.

"Annie." She couldn't tell by his tone if he was angry or hurt or scared. He reached for her hand. "Annie, for goodness' sake. You don't have to pay me. Not now. Not ever. I only agreed to getting paid because you insisted on it. I've got a bit stashed away and other people pay me for odd jobs. Besides, I can get a regular job, if I have to."

"I thought..." She turned her head to the wall, unwilling to let him see the tears in her eyes. Was he just being kind?

"This is my fault. I thought I was helping you. You thought you were helping me. What a pair we are." He pulled her chin back to face him and flashed her one of his irresistible smiles.

She caved and smiled back, but only for a moment. Then she put her head in her hands and began to sob. "But even if I don't have to pay you, what am I going to do about the bank?"

"I think the obvious answer is to sell the place. I've told you hundreds of times this place is too much for you and it's a sinking ship. Jump Annie, before it takes you down with it."

"But I love that my kids get to grow up here, and the values they have from living in a small town with good people around them. What would my father do? He loves it here too, and he works hard to help me keep this place going. I can't believe you would suggest I sell it."

"You could make a killing, buy a smaller place in town and your kids can still grow up here, but you won't have the headaches." He took her hands and pulled her gaze to meet his. "Or we could get married, and you and the kids could come live with Chelsea and me. I have room and you know I love you."

Luke's daughter and Ali had become inseparable friends. They were less than a year apart. They doted on each other and were great playmates. There was no question Ali would have loved having Chelsea as a sister, but that wasn't a reason to get married.

"What would my dad do? And don't tell me he could go to some senior's place. He's not that old yet, and he'd hate it."

"We'll add a couple of rooms onto the back of the house. He can have his own in-law suite and see the kids whenever he wants." He kissed her hands and rubbed the back of them with his thumbs.

Once, in those early days of knowing Luke, his touch would have sent warmth running up her arm, but lately she felt none of that.

"Really, Annie. It's not that big a deal. It's doable."

Not a big deal for who? She wondered. It was for her. It would be for the kids and it would be for her father, too. If Luke were being realistic, it would be for him and Chelsea, too. He was suggesting a life-altering change for all of them.

She could, perhaps, learn to feel something more than just friendship for him. There was much to love about him, but there was no spark, no fire, no passion. She'd known him for two years and not once in that time had they made love. Didn't that say something about this relationship? She could curl up with him on the couch and sip wine and watch old movies and feel comfortable in his arms, but something was missing and she would not marry Luke or any man, just to solve her money problems.

"We've discussed this before."

He dropped her hands, then he templed his fingers and pushed the tips into his lips in thought. "Then sell this place and move into town. You could rent something until you figure out your next move, but at least you won't be worried about creditors."

She nodded. "Maybe you're right. Maybe that's what I need to do."

His expression changed then. "Yeah, maybe it is. Because it's pretty clear you're never going to marry me, are you?" He slid

his untouched coffee to the middle of the table. "Will you ever, Annie, or am I fooling myself? Because lately, I feel you pushing me
away, despite my loving you more every time I see you."

She bit her bottom lip and looked across the table at him,
tears welling in her eyes. "I can't marry you, Luke. You know I
can't. Nothing has changed. At least not for me."

He nodded. "Doesn't get any plainer than that, then does it?
But I'm not giving up. You'll need me one day, and when you do,
I'll be here." He bent to kiss her on the forehead and slipped out the
back door.

Chapter 3

Ali and Noah's bus pulled up to the top of Annie's driveway, at twenty-eight minutes after three, just as it did every school day. Ali and Noah clambered down, their arms laden with things they'd been asked to bring home over the holidays, including a note to all parents that they should please check the lost and found next time they were in the school. Annie waved to Ted as Ali handed her a bag of artwork.

"Just one more week before the Christmas break. Want to put this up in your room?" she asked. But Ali was already scampering away out of earshot, leaving Annie to walk down the driveway on her own. The wind sent a mysterious whisper through the overhead pines that drew her attention to the clouds. They were puffy and light, like giant pillows you could lay your head on and sleep the winter away. The lodge windows seemed like a pair of pleading and sad eyes. *Don't sell*, they seemed to say, and Annie thought that the whole place didn't want to be sold any more than she wanted to let it go.

When they'd first bought the place, they'd held holiday gatherings there, for their guests. The local Canada Day car rallies had started and ended there with a big barbeque or a pig roast. There were fish fries every weekend, and a Labour Day picnic to round out the end of summer season. That was followed by a Thanksgiving turkey dinner and then Christmas and New Year's parties. It had been fun, and Annie had become more energized with each event.

It was the pandemic that sealed the fate of these gatherings and it held on just long enough that people had stopped asking and she stopped trying to organize them. Now she was getting bookings again, but they weren't coming in fast enough to keep up with the bills.

Ideas percolated as she headed back to the house. What if she offered the use of the lodge to yoga retreat goers, or maybe other kinds of retreats? Writer's groups, company bonding weekends, or religious getaways. Could this be something that kept her going until the seasonal cottagers started coming again? Maybe it was time to come up with some enticing package deals and revamp the website.

Ahead of her, Noah and Ali were tossing snow into the air and catching it on their tongues. Their giggles made Annie smile and brought back memories of her own childhood. How could she possibly consider selling this place? It was home. For her, for her father, and her kids. Somehow, she had to make this work.

"Hey Mum," Noah said, when they'd had enough of making snow angels and attempts to make a snowman proved impossible.

"Yes, Noah?" She waited patiently, knowing he was about to tell her the joke Turtle Ted had passed along that day. It had become their routine now. She set their boots by the radiator. Their mitts, scarves and hats, she draped over it and the coats she hung on the hooks on the opposite wall. Mudrooms were a wonderful place to leave behind the outdoors you didn't want inside—mud, snow, leaves, all kinds of things. Annie closed the door behind them and went to the kitchen, watching Noah scrunch his face into a bright smile while he rehearsed the joke in his head.

"What's a Christmas tree's favourite candy?" he finally said.

"I don't know. What's is it?"

"Orna-mints. Get it?"

Annie laughed. "I get it." She tousled his fly-away hair that stood up straight with static. "Hey, now *there's* something funny. Go look in the mirror."

Noah put both hands on his head to flatten his hair. "It always does that. I hate it." Seconds later, his unruly hair was forgotten because his stomach growled. "Can we have some hot chocolate with our snack?"

"Sure. Help Ali with her backpack and I'll get organized in the kitchen. We have your favourite cookies. Chocolate chip."

"Yummy!" Ali said, dragging her backpack into the kitchen behind her. "From the dough we put in the freezer last weekend?"

"The very same," Annie said, setting a pan on the stove for their hot chocolate and glancing out the window. Her father's truck was in its usual parking place behind the house, now. Earlier, he'd gone into town to get a new axe, after breaking his old one, when he went to cut down their Christmas tree. She'd been busy most of the day, and couldn't recall when he'd come back.

Maybe when I was vacuuming, she thought, or doing the laundry. "Yes, that must be it," she said half out loud.

"What must be it, Mummy?" Ali asked, climbing onto her chair.

"Nothing sweetie. Just wondering where Grandpa is, that's all."

"Can he have hot chocolate too?" Ali asked.

"Of course. He went out to cut down our Christmas tree and one for the lodge."

Noah sat down at the table, a cross look on his face. "He was supposed to let me help. Why didn't he wait?"

"Maybe he wanted to surprise you," she placated. "Tell you what. Drink up and have a couple of cookies and if he's not back by the time you're done, we'll go find him, okay?"

Annie was about to join her kids at the table when her phone pinged with an email notification.

"Customer," she told the kids. A smile crept over her face as she read the booking dates. The customer wanted a cottage for ten days over Christmas and didn't even quibble about the seasonal premium. The money would be a huge help.

"I've got to take care of this. You two okay for a minute?"

"Sure Mum." Noah nodded. Ali shoved another cookie into her mouth and nodded, too.

"Good thing I made those bite-size," Annie said, patting her daughter's head as she headed across the hall.

Annie loved her office. It was a small room tucked into a corner of the house that the previous owners had used for storage. The original house was a square box type; four rooms up and four rooms down, but renovations over the years had added a family room, which was now Sam's bedroom, a powder room, and her office. The mudroom, and shifting the back door to its new location, had come later, along with a second-floor balcony off her bedroom.

Annie loved the spectacular view over the lake through a bank of north-facing windows in this room, and that she could see the front door of the lodge and the east and west paths that led to the cabins and the cottages. It was the perfect place to spend her days, when she had work to do, if she could keep her mind focused on that, and not the breathtaking views outside. Like now, with the sun glistening off the new fallen snow and the tiny flecks of silver and gold dancing in the glow of early evening.

At her desk, she opened the reservations app on her computer and checked the booking. One adult and one child, and one dog, it said, checking in tomorrow around two in the afternoon and staying until the day after Boxing Day. Annie breathed a sigh as her phone pinged again, this time with a notification that the full amount had been deposited into the lodge's bank account. It was rare to get anything more than a deposit with a booking. This was a nice surprise. It meant that once her current guests checked tomorrow, she should have enough for one month's mortgage payment, the money she owed Luke, and a little something left over for Christmas. A few more reservations like this and she might ward off the vultures until spring.

"Alright, Mr. J. Hewitt and child, and your dog, Moose Cabin, awaits." She sent back the confirmation along with a thank you for the payment in full and closed her laptop.

The kids were already putting on their boots and coats when she returned to the kitchen. "Ready Mum? Can we go now?"

"Sure. I'm just going to get a thermos of hot chocolate and some cookies for Grandpa."

When she was ready, with a thermos tucked into one pocket of her coat and a small baggie of cookies in the other, she took Ali by the hand and headed down the path towards the woods. Noah ran ahead, shouting that he knew exactly where to find Grandpa because he'd helped pick out the tree.

"We know that already," Ali said with an annoyed hiss in her voice. "It's all he ever talks about. He says it's his tree. Not mine. Not yours. His and Grandpa's."

"It's everybody's tree, Ali. Don't listen to him when he says things like that. He's just trying to get your goat."

Ali looked up at her mother matter-of-factly and frowned. "I don't have a goat."

"It's an expression. It means he's teasing you. He wants to see a reaction from you."

"He's horrible. I hate him."

"You don't. You just don't like him very much when he's being a pain. That's not the same thing. You shouldn't say hate, Ali. It's a horrible word."

By the time they reached the woods, she'd lost sight of Noah. As they passed the last cabin, she spotted two sets of tracks in the snow. The small set was Noah's and a larger set she knew belonged to her father. When the snow got too deep for Ali, Annie scooped her up and wiggled her onto her back in piggyback fashion.

"Is that easier, Pumpkin?"

"Yup. The snow was getting in my boots. Look, Mummy. There's Noah He's coming back."

Tears spilled over Noah's cheeks as he came running up to them. "Hurry. It's Grandpa. I think he's… he's…" He took a gulping big breath. "I think he might be… dead."

"What?" With Ali bouncing on her back, Annie took off at a run, doing her best to keep up with Noah. "Dad! Dad!" she shouted.

Dead? He couldn't be dead. He was only sixty-seven years old and more fit than a lot of men half his age. At least that's what his doctor had said at his last checkup.

She came upon two huge fallen trees which had crossed over each other and blocked the path. Climbing over them on all fours, she set Ali down on the other side where the snow wasn't as deep, so Ali could manage on her own.

Noah led them to a circle of small pine trees, where Sam's shiny new axe was embedded in one of them. The sleigh was propped up against another tree, ready to be useful when the time came. Her father, much to Annie's horror, lay face down in the snow.

"Dad!" she screamed, rushing to him. She rolled him over and brushed the snow from his face. "Dad. It's me. Annie." No response, but when she put her cheek to his nose, she could feel warmth there. Her fingers, pressing at his neck, found a weak pulse. She looked up to see Noah, his arm around Ali's shoulders and tears flowing down both their cheeks.

"He's not dead," she said. "But we have to hurry."

Ali went into immediate hysterics. "I should have made snow angels," she cried. "I should have made snow angels. You should have let me, Mummy."

"It's alright Pumpkin. The angels will always watch over Grandpa, because he has a good heart. Don't you worry."

When Ali settled into her brother's arms, Annie pulled out her phone, but as she suspected, there was no reception that far into the woods.

"Okay, here's what we have to do. Noah, bring the sleigh here so we can roll Grandpa onto it and pull him back to the house. Got it? Come on, kids, we can do this." Tears filled their little faces as Ali and Noah helped, and together, they got Sam onto the sleigh.

Annie took hold of the rope. "Noah, run ahead with my phone and as soon as you get reception, dial 911, okay? Remember how we practiced it, for emergencies?"

"Got it, Mum." Noah took off like a shot, while Ali and Annie tugged hard on the sleigh. They were doing well until they came to the two fallen trees.

"Damn!" Annie exclaimed. "How are we going to get him over those?"

"Don't say bad words, Mummy. Now you have to put a looney in the swear jar."

"Right, Pumpkin. Sorry."

Annie stopped and considered how she was going to do this. A ramp would be useful, but she didn't have one. Maybe if they could get the top of the sleigh over the logs, they could slide him down the other side. She bent down to lift the front of the sleigh, but it slipped out of her hands and Annie ended up on her backside. She wasn't strong enough to do this.

"Please. Please. Please." She made herself refrain from saying *shit, shit, shit*, which is what she would have said if Ali hadn't been hovering over her.

As she stood up to try again, she was surprised to see Luke heading their way, with Chelsea and Noah trailing along behind him. Under any other circumstances, she wouldn't have wanted to talk to him so soon after this morning's conversation, but now she couldn't help thinking how lucky they were that he was there.

"I got him, Annie," Luke said, pulling the sleigh up and over the fallen logs and down the other side.

"I sent Noah to call for an ambulance," she explained as they hurried toward the path by the cabins. "Did he call?" They were pulling together now, the kids racing down the path ahead of them.

"I told him not to bother. By the time the EMTs get all the way out here, and then back to the hospital, it might be too late. If you help me put him in the truck, it will be faster. Then you and the kids can follow in yours."

"What's wrong with Grandpa Sam?" Chelsea asked when they reached the trucks.

"He's going to be just fine," Luke assured her. "Just go with Annie. I need to lay Grandpa Sam down on the back seat and strap him in."

"Okay, Daddy, but I need my car seat."

"Geez, I hadn't thought of that," Luke said, wrenching her seat out of the back and handing it to Annie.

She set it on the ground and leaned in to help. "Here. Let me…. Got him?"

Together, they lifted a motionless Sam into the back seat of the truck and laid him down. Luke pulled both seatbelts over him and clicked them into place. "Bracebridge is the closest. I'll see you there."

"I'm right behind you. Just got to find his wallet, for his health card." Annie fitted Chelsea's car seat into their truck as Luke sped down the driveway. In the glove box, she found her father's wallet, right where she knew it would be with his health card inside.

"Alright kids. Everyone buckled? We need to catch up with Luke."

In the emergency room at Bracebridge General Hospital, the charge nurse, in teal green scrubs with a pink, feathered pen dangling around her neck, took Sam's details from Annie. Then she asked them all to wait while they assessed him. They found places to sit in the busy waiting area, in uncomfortable, unyielding beige and brown chairs lined up in rows of six. When Chelsea spotted a round table with toys and colouring books in a corner, she squirmed to get out of Luke's lap.

"Can we, Mummy?" Ali asked.

"Sure," Annie said, glad they had something to keep them busy. Noah stayed next to her, trying to look brave. He was too old for colouring books, or so he'd told her the last time she'd tried to get him to sit with her and Ali. But, at the same time, he was too young for something as traumatic as finding his grandfather in the woods like he had. She put an arm around his shoulders, gave him a squeeze, and told him everything was going to be fine, hoping she was right.

It seemed hours later when a nurse came into the room and stood next to them. Other people had come and gone, and now there was only one other family besides theirs who was waiting.

"Nothing yet," she said, when Annie stood up. "I just wanted to tell you there are machines down the hall if you want a hot drink or the cafeteria is on the lower level." She winked at the kids. "I have some candy canes at the desk if it's okay with Mum?" She gave Annie a quick smile.

"Sure, but only one, and remember your manners," Annie said as Chelsea and Ali raced after the nurse to get their treat. "Don't you want one too, Noah?" Annie asked.

"No. I just want to know if Grandpa's going to be okay."

"Turning down a candy cane won't get us an answer any sooner and we're going to be right here until we do."

"Well maybe. Okay then." Noah slouched out of the seat beside her and went to follow the girls.

Luke put an arm around Annie and pulled her gently toward him. "He's going to be okay, Annie. We were quick."

"I should be in there with them. What if they have questions or..."

"They will come and ask if they do. Let them do their work. You can't help him in there. You'll just be in the way."

"I know. I know you're right, but I just can't sit still doing nothing." She put her head on his shoulder. "God, Luke. What if...? No, I can't even think that."

He squeezed her shoulders and kissed the top of her head. "It'll be okay. I know it will."

It was another hour before the doctor finally came to see them. Everything about the man was small. The tiny fingers he used to pinch the bridge of his fine-boned nose, the round rimmed glasses that were too big for his beady black eyes and the short choppy sentences he used to tell her about her father's condition.

"A stroke," he said, his eyes fixed on Annie. "We gave him tPA. Tissue Plasminogen Activator. It finds the clot and breaks it up. We won't know how severe the damage is until we run some more tests."

"Is he awake?" Annie asked. "Can I see him?"

He nodded. "In a few minutes. He's weak. There is some paralysis down one side of his body, and his speech is quite slurred." He glanced toward the table where the girls were still colouring. "You might want to warn the kids. It will be a shock for them to see him."

"What's the prognosis?" Luke asked. "Will he regain his mobility?"

"It's too soon to say. He'll have physio and we'll do what we can, but you should prepare for him being like this for the rest of his life, worst-case scenario."

Annie gasped at the thought of her father, confined to a wheelchair, watching the world he loved through a window instead of being out in it. Ali seemed to sense her mother's worry. She flew to Annie and took her hand.

"Is Grandpa alright?"

"He will be, Pumpkin." He has to be, she thought. Annie looked at the doctor. "He'll be fine. I know he will. He's a fighter. My father will fight back."

The doctor nodded. "A strong will is a good thing in cases like this. He's going to need it and you will, too." He paused. Now that the information had been passed along, the man's features softened, and he smiled down at the kids. "Are you Noah?" he asked, bending down to Noah's level.

"Yes, sir." Noah stood up straight and met the man's gaze.

"He asked for you." He turned to the girls. "Which one of you is Ali?" Ali's hand shot up in the air. "Ah. Yes, the one with the butter coloured curls. I should have known. That means you must be Chelsea."

Chelsea nodded enthusiastically, then hid behind her father's leg.

"How did he know the kids are here?" Annie asked the doctor.

"He must have been cognizant part of the time, before you brought him in. It's not uncommon. He kept repeating the children's names. It took us a while to figure them out because he's slurring, but he got us to understand. He certainly seems to love the kids." He reached out to touch her arm. "You can see him now. But only for a few moments. We want to start those tests right away."

"Thank you." Luke reached for Chelsea's hand, and Ali and Noah each took one of Annie's. Together they went to curtain eight, where Sam lay on a gurney, his face as white as the sheet that covered him. Annie had never seen her father look so frail. He was not a big man, but neither was he small or fine featured, like the doctor they'd just met. He had broad shoulders, a strong back, and a sturdy frame. His legs were long and muscular, and his forearms solid and lean. His jaw was strong, his nose long and prominent and set between eyes that always seemed to sparkle with mischief. Sam Taylor was not this spindly man with a gaunt face, and eyes so full of fear it made Annie gasp a second time.

Her hand flew to her throat as she went to the edge of his bed. "Oh, Dad."

He reached out his right arm to take hold of her hand. "Aaaa. Neeee." His voice seemed to belong to someone else. His lips formed a half smile, one side not moving as he looked toward the kids. Annie nudged them closer so he could see them. "Noah," he said, as clearly as if he had not just suffered a stroke. He ruffled Noah's hair, which made Noah grimace, but to his credit, Noah kept quiet. Usually, he hated it when people did that, but this was Grandpa who could do no wrong. Sam reached for Ali, but she pulled away, and turned to her mother, frightened by the unnatural look of her grandfather with tubes sticking out of him and the machines that beeped and blipped on either side of him.

Annie scooped her up and set her on her hip. "It's alright, darling. Grandpa's had a tough day." She looked across the bed at Luke, who stood with Chelsea clinging tightly to his hand. He met her gaze, and she knew he was waiting for her sign, waiting to be useful, waiting to do whatever she needed him to do.

"Can you…?" she nodded toward the door. "I think Ali might like something from the machine down the hall."

"Of course. Come on Chels. Noah, do you want an orange pop or root beer, maybe?"

Noah shook his head. "I'm gonna stay with Grandpa."

"Okay sport." Luke gave Sam's shoulder a squeeze, the bad one, so he probably didn't feel it, but it touched Annie's heart all the same. Then he took the girls down the hall.

Annie found a chair and pulled it closer to her father's bed and set Noah on her lap. "What happened Dad? Wait. Don't talk. It's too hard. And the doctor already told us. I wish you'd let Luke help you, like he said he would."

"Caw jo." Sam waved his good hand in the air and held it up to his ear, like he was talking on a phone.

"Call who? Who do you want me to call?"

"Jo. Caw jo." Sam pulled at her arm.

There seemed to be an urgency in what he was trying to tell her, but Annie patted his hand. "Just rest Dad. We can talk about it when you're better."

A tight-lipped nurse with shoes that squeaked across the room came in to check the monitors and fiddle with Sam's IV drip.

"You'll have to go now," she told Annie. "The doctor has ordered more tests. After that we'll take him to a ward. He won't be able to have any visitors until tomorrow afternoon."

"Really? No one? Can't I stay at least until you get him settled in the ward?"

Sam patted her hand. "S'ok. Go."

Annie had no trouble understanding that. Hot tears poured down her cheeks as she bent to kiss her father's forehead. "I'll be back as soon as I'm allowed to, tomorrow," she said.

Noah squeezed his grandfather's hand. "Luke and I will cut down the tree. It'll be up and decorated by the time you get home. I love you Grandpa. Get better real fast, okay?"

Chapter 4

Saturday. No school today, Annie thought when she woke at eight without her alarm going off. No complaints from Mr. Gibson this morning, either. If only her bank manager could be placated as easily. She thought of the promised strawberry waffles and that she hadn't gone to the grocery store yesterday. Ali would have to settle for something else.

Annie slid her feet into a pair of battered bunny slippers. A gift her late husband had given her their first Christmas together. She hated to part with them because he'd given them to her, but they had obviously seen better days. Only one of the floppy ears remained intact, and, like the single eye that stared up at her, its lifespan seemed uncertain. She pulled her housecoat over her shoulders and shuffled down the hall for a peek in each of the kid's rooms. Still sleeping. It had been an exhausting day for all of them yesterday. They had so many questions when they came home from the hospital that Annie couldn't possibly answer them all. Some things it was impossible to know, like would Grandpa ever be like Grandpa again.

In the kitchen, she brewed a pot of coffee, and set the table for a cereal-and-toast breakfast. Maybe she could squeeze in some shopping before visiting her dad in the hospital. There was money in her account now that Mr. Hewitt had booked in, and there would be more when her guests checked out later that morning. The bank wasn't going to have it all. She had decided on the way home from the hospital last night that if this ended up being their last Christmas at the lodge, they would go out with a bang. The kids would have presents under the tree and they would have a full-blown turkey dinner with all the fixings. This would be a special Christmas because the thought that her father had been close to not being with them devastated her. What might have happened if he'd been out in the woods a little longer or they hadn't been able to get him to the hospital so quickly? She reached for the peanut butter and found it nearly empty. The jam jar was the same and only half a loaf of bread stared up at her from the breadbox. Annie took her coffee to the table and started a shopping list.

An hour later, the kids had eaten their breakfast, and she sent a sulking Ali to the living room to watch TV. Noah seemed as determined as Annie to make this a wonderful Christmas and set out on a mission to find pine boughs to decorate the house. Annie gathered the laundry, made the beds, and was just about to pull out the vacuum cleaner when all of her guests came to check out. Mr. Gibson was first, full of thanks for her recommendations from the day before. The cash in the envelope he handed her was short twenty dollars. He gave her a pleading look.

"I've got a job. At the diner. The one where you sent us for breakfast. I'll pay you the rest soon. I promise."

"It's fine, Mr. Gibson," Annie said, and she meant it. If Brent had hired him, that meant he'd stop hounding her about working there. "I hope you and your family have a wonderful Christmas."

Annie watched him go down the back steps and hoped they had somewhere safe and warm to go tonight. Somewhere other than here because she just couldn't manage another handout right now. The Baxters and Janet Jacobson paid their balances by credit card, which meant a one-day delay before it landed in her bank account. No worries, Annie thought. She couldn't go to the bank to make a payment until Monday, anyway.

With visiting time at the hospital three hours away, Annie ran the vacuum through the living room and kitchen, and then she tackled the fridge. There was a time when food got pushed to the back, forgotten like the lost city of Atlantis, and once unearthed, was unrecognizable for whatever it had once been. But now, with an ever-shrinking food budget and her children's growing appetites, she'd learned to menu plan much better. Also, she labeled her containers. As she took stock of what was available, she decided a bowl of leftover chili would be chili dogs for supper tonight, and there was enough stew for a meal on Sunday.

Annie sighed and rested her chin on her fist. She flicked her pen back and forth, tapped it on the table, and glanced down her list. Eventually, she decided there was nothing else she needed. "That'll have to do," she said, and estimated the cost of what she'd already written. "With just enough left over for the ingredients for our cookies."

"Who are you talking to, Mummy?" Ali, still in her pjs, meandered into the kitchen with her favourite teddy, Frank, tucked under one arm.

"The angels," Annie said. Pulling her daughter close for a hug, she brushed back Ali's hair, and planted a kiss on her forehead. "Sorry it was just toast and cereal this morning. We'll get some groceries later."

"It's okay, Mummy. Is Grandpa coming home today?"

"I don't think so, Pumpkin. We need to take some things along for him. Do you want to help me pack his bag?"

Ali nodded and followed her mother to Sam's bedroom. While she sang to her teddy, Annie put a bag of personal things together for her father. Noah came in from outside, toting his third armful of pine boughs, and dropped them on the floor, just outside the bedroom door.

"Is this enough?" he said with a hopeful look.

"Plenty," Annie told him. "We'll do that right after we get back from visiting Grandpa, okay?"

"What are we gonna do about the tree?" he asked, slipping out of his jacket. "It's not Christmas without a tree."

"I'll help and Ali will too, won't you, sweetie?"

Noah wasn't satisfied with Ali's enthusiasm or his mother's. "Ali will just get in the way and you don't know how to chop. You gotta call Luke."

"Oh honey. I don't want to ask Luke to come all the way out here. He'll be busy." Annie sighed when she saw the disappointed look on his face. It was obvious Luke had filled a gap in her son's life, but those ties had to be broken, especially since she'd practically kicked him out of the kitchen yesterday morning. And if she couldn't pay him, how could she keep asking him to help? She could get the money she owed him from the bank this afternoon. That was something, at least.

Noah was still staring up at her with that pleading look that always made her cave. "I'll call him," she promised. "But if he can't come out, you and I will figure it out, okay? Or maybe we could ask Ben Pierce, or Cam Myers."

Noah reached out and squeezed his mother's biceps. "I dunno Mum. You're not very strong. Even for a Mum."

Annie tousled his hair and laughed when he pushed her hands away. Picking up the bag she'd prepared for her father, she took it to the mudroom to set it by the door. Then she looked at her children.

"Okay. We have two hours before we have to leave to see Grandpa. Who wants to help me put away the laundry?"

Ali buried her face in Frank's and muttered, "Let's go tidy our room." Then she headed for the stairs. Noah said nothing, but made a beeline for the living room.

"Just as I thought," Annie laughed as she opened the dryer and pulled a load of clothes into an empty laundry basket.

As she stood up to take it into the kitchen to fold, a white sedan pulled into the parking lot by the lodge and a man got out and opened the back door, releasing an obviously pent-up Bernese Mountain dog. The dog instantly gave chase to an unsuspecting squirrel, much to the chagrin of the driver. A moment later, a boy about Noah's age climbed out after the dog and let out an ear-piercing whistle. In a spray of flying snow, the dog stopped, turned around and raced back to them, his tongue drooping and his tail wagging. As soon as he was within reach, the man clamped a leash onto his collar and pulled a treat out of his pocket.

Annie pushed open the screen door and called out to them. "Good morning. Are you here for a cottage rental?"

"Hello," the man called out as they approached the porch steps.

As she met his gaze, Annie found herself staring into a pair of dazzling slate grey eyes, not unlike her late husband's. She tilted her head to one side as a flicker of something familiar trickled down her spine and set gooseflesh prickling up her arms.

The man coughed, and she realized she'd been staring, unabashedly admiring this man as he came closer. Now she was embarrassed at the heat rising in her cheeks. She blinked and turned her gaze away, suddenly aware that he was looking at her, just as ardently as she'd been looking at him. Or was she imagining it?

On the bottom step of her porch, he shuffled his feet. He seemed to be expecting her to say something more, but Annie was, for the first time in a long while, tongue-tied. Finally, he handed the leash to the boy and came one step higher. One step closer. Annie gasped, but she didn't move. The resemblance of this man to her late husband was uncanny.

"I made an online reservation yesterday," he said, breaking the silence and Annie's trance. He pointed to his phone. "I have the confirmation here. The name is Hewitt. Joe Hewitt, and this is Ryder."

Ryder patted the dog on the head proudly. "He's Max." The dog sat obediently and looked up as if hoping for another treat.

"Mr. Hewitt, of course. I'm glad you're early. I was going to leave a note for you. My father landed in the hospital last night, so I would have been gone when you checked in."

There was a genuine look of concern on his face as he looked up at her. "Oh. I'm sorry to hear that. Is he going to be alright? What happened?"

Was it odd that he sounded so concerned about someone he didn't know? Maybe he was just one of those people, she thought.

"Thank you. We're hopeful. It's just that this has been a crazy morning and I haven't had time to take the towels and bedding down to your cottage."

"We can come back if we're putting you out."

"Oh no. Your timing is perfect. Why don't you step inside? If you can give me a minute to gather everything, we can walk down to the cottage together." She stepped back to hold the door open for them, and Ryder started up the steps, with Max close behind.

"I don't think Max should go inside," Mr. Hewitt said. "Let's just tie him up to the post here. He'll have fun watching the squirrels."

"Goodness no. It's freezing outside," Annie said. "I love dogs and I have two kids inside who would love him too. Please, Mr. Hewitt. Bring Max inside."

"Only if you call me Joe."

Their eyes met and something stirred within Annie's belly. As he reached past her to take hold of the door, his hand brushed her arm and Annie nearly melted into a puddle right there on the porch. Get a grip, she told herself.

A little hesitantly she said, "Alright Joe. I'm Annie. Please come in."

Noah had been hovering by the inner door, no doubt excited to see a guest with someone his own age. Max was an even bigger bonus because Noah had been asking for a dog for ages and Annie had had to refuse. Even a free puppy from a friend's litter had to have shots and needed to be fed. A pet cost money she simply did not have.

"Hey," Noah said, watching Ryder slip his boots off at the door.

"Hey," Ryder said back. The two eyed each other cautiously for a moment, obviously sizing each other up, until Noah bent down to scratch Max behind the ears.

Then he turned to Ryder. "Wanna watch Camp Cretaceous?"

"Can I, Uncle Joe?"

Not father and son, Annie quickly noted.

"I don't see why not, if that's okay with Annie," Joe said.

"Of course."

Annie led Joe to the kitchen, where she poured him a cup of coffee and invited him to sit at the table. Then she went to the office, printed out his reservation details, and got the key for Moose Cottage. When she returned, she slid it across the table. "I assume one key is enough?"

"Yes, that's fine."

Annie felt her face flush with embarrassment when Joe's eyes fell to her bunny slippers. "Oh gosh! They're pathetic, aren't they? But I just can't bear to part with them. They're so comfortable."

His easy smile stopped her flustered excuses. "I kind of like the bunny-slipper look on a woman."

Annie burst out laughing. "Okay, that was way too smooth. Have you been practicing that line?"

"Most of my life. Did it work?"

His smile was infectious, and Annie felt her embarrassment slipping away to be replaced with a little cockiness. "If you're hoping for a refund on your cottage, then no."

He smiled again. "Not the result I was hoping for at all." At the moment their eyes locked, Annie realized he was flirting with her, and she'd been flirting right back. What was she doing?

"I'll just get the linens," she mumbled, backing out of the room. She left him to finish his coffee, while she went to the cupboard in the laundry room, where she kept the fresh towels and sheets. He had definitely been flirting with her, she decided when she thought about it some more. Or maybe he was just that kind of guy, the kind who says nice things and lights up a room with smiles and... Oh, who was she kidding? They'd both been flirting, and it had been kind of fun, but it had also left her feeling like a silly teenager.

She pulled towels and sheets from the shelf, followed by a tea towel and a dishcloth, then headed back to the kitchen, resolved that this teasing had gone on long enough. She didn't even know the man.

In the kitchen, though she tried to avoid his gaze, she found her eyes met his again, over the stack of bed sheets.

"Sorry," she said, feeling a flush rise in her neck. She couldn't help blushing under the intensity of his gaze. He was probably the most handsome man she'd ever seen. Dark hair cut short and neat, a sexy two-day shadow that she guessed was his permanent look and a pair of lips that just begged to be kissed. She looked away, hoping he hadn't seen how embarrassed she was. But he had.

"It seems I have that effect on all women who wear bunny slippers." He nodded to where Ali sat in the chair opposite him, kicking her own bunny-slipper-clad feet back and forth. Max lay at the bottom of her chair, his brow twitching at every word Joe spoke.

Annie grinned and tilted her head to one side. "Or it could be the dog. Some women like a man who loves dogs. It says something about them," Annie offered, matching his teasing tone. And that, she decided, was exactly what it was. Teasing. Not flirting. The gold band on his finger suggested he probably had a wife. Someone who would show up in a day or two, or someone he and Ryder were going to see as soon as they left here.

"Ah, but Max belongs to Ryder. It has to be the slippers." When he smiled, his eyes crinkled at the corners, and dimples poked his cheeks. Annie had to turn away from the burning stare. It was too familiar, too intimate. Too much like…

She spun around to look at the clock on the kitchen wall; a corny thing with hands that were fashioned out of a knife and fork they had bought on a whim at a garage sale.

"Look at the time. I really must get you set up and then we've got to be going."

"I'll help," he said, setting his cup by the sink. "Great coffee, by the way. I'm usually a tea drinker."

"I have a collection of herbal teas, but I save those for nighttime when I don't need the caffeine infusion."

"Mummy drinks tea in her room after we go to bed." Ali slid off her chair and took Joe by the hand. "I'll show you where the cottage is."

"Why, thank you," Joe said, flashing a sheepish look over her head to Annie as he followed Ali back the way they'd come, to the mudroom.

Annie zipped up Ali's coat, then went to the living room. "Okay boys, time to bundle up. We're going to walk down to Moose Cottage to get Joe and Ryder settled in."

"Ah, do we have to?" Noah whined. "We just started watching the second episode."

Annie looked at Joe. "Ryder is welcome to stay if you're okay with it. Although I do have to leave at around one."

Joe shrugged. "It's fine by me, so long as you behave, Ryder."

Ryder groaned and rolled his eyes. "We're just watching TV."

Joe gave him a look that warned the wrath of a Tyrannosaurus rex if he didn't behave, and Ryder grinned back at him.

Ali was fascinated by Max and wanted to know if she could hold the leash. Joe handed it over to her when they were on the path to the cottages, and they took off together, Ali in a fit of giggles, Max running slow enough for her to keep up.

Moose Cottage was some distance along the lane, with other cottages on either side of it. Each had its own covered porch, front and back, a campfire pit, and a clear view of the lake. Inside the living rooms had working fireplaces with a pile of logs at the ready; one of the last tasks Luke had done earlier in the week.

"You can follow the roadway in the back and pull your car up here." Annie showed Joe the access route that led to the back of the cottages. "We keep the front walkway as a pedestrian route, and sometimes bicycles, in the summer."

They'd arrived at the cottage with a wooden sign swinging on hinges over the door that read *Welcome to Moose Cottage.*

"This is you." Annie waited while Joe unlocked the door, then followed him inside, with Ali and Max trailing behind. She switched on lights and kicked the furnace up to a comfortable temperature. "It won't take long to warm up the place." Then she pointed out the extra space heaters in each room and where he could find everything he might need. She set the towels in the bathroom and went to make up the beds.

Joe followed her into the first bedroom. "I can do these. I don't want to keep you from seeing your father," he said, taking the sheets from her.

She scooped a fitted sheet off the pile he held. "It's no trouble. I have time. Visiting hours aren't till two." She fitted the top corner over the mattress and went to the end of the bed to do the same there.

"We're early. So, it's the least I can do." Joe fitted the corners on his side of the bed, matching her moves. Annie reached for the top sheet, snapped it out of its folds, then smoothed it over the bottom one.

"It's really no trouble."

"I never got the hang of these," he said, watching her expertly form a perfect hospital corner.

"It's easy. Let me show you." She went to his side of the bed. "Fold all this out of the way, like this. Then tuck here. Then you take what you put out of the way, smooth it out and tuck. See? Easy." She stood up and smiled. "Now you try." She pulled it out and made him do it himself.

Joe struggled, repeating her instructions but making a mess of it so that Annie laughed and offered to do it again.

"I'll never get it," he said, watching her fix his mess. Then he spread the comforter that had been lying on the back of the chair over the bed. "That's what I usually do. It covers everything so no one can see what's underneath."

She grinned and held out the pillowcases. "Can you manage these?"

He laughed as she tossed him the first pillow. "That's a little cheeky," he said, tucking the pillow inside the case and flinging it to the top of the bed. "But then I deserved it, didn't I?"

When the first bedroom was ready, they went to the next. Annie leaned on the doorframe, arms crossed over her chest and put on her best schoolmarm face. "Alright cheeky. You do this one and I'll watch."

"Oh gosh. I'm not sure I can do this all alone. You better come and help."

The mischievous glint in his eye made her laugh out loud. "Oh no. This is a test and maybe if you pass it, I just might send some cookies down to you after Ali and I bake tomorrow."

"Home baked cookies? Well, then I'd better do a good job."

His attempt to get the corners right was even funnier this time and, in the end, he gave up and tucked the sheets in haphazardly. A no-no for Annie. "Let me do this before you tie yourself into knots." She took over and made the bed up for him.

"Does this mean I don't get any cookies?" He feigned a school-boy pout, which left her laughing all the way back to the living room.

"I suppose I could make an exception, if it's okay with Ali." She reached for her daughter's hand. "Time to go, Pumpkin."

Ali jumped up from the couch, with Max following right behind her. "Mummy and I make cookies every year and give them to our friends and neighbours," she told Joe. "Maybe Joe wants to help us," she said, turning to her mother.

Annie smoothed out her daughter's hair and reached for the hat she'd discarded on the table when they came inside. "I'm sure Joe's got better things to do than help us bake cookies."

"I don't, actually." He took a step closer, closing the gap between them. "But I also don't want to be in the way." He jerked a thumb over his shoulder toward the bedroom and looked at Ali. "I'm not very good at making beds. Maybe your mum thinks I can't do cookies either."

Ali giggled. "I can't make my bed right either. Mummy always fixes it for me."

"Alright, you two. No ganging up on me." Annie nudged her daughter toward the door.

As they went down the cottage stairs to the pathway, Annie pointed toward the lodge. "There is a big screen TV with a DVD player in the lodge. Loads of board games and movies. You can borrow them, or you can make use of them up there. There's also a pool table and ping pong. Your key opens the lodge, so please enjoy. You'll have to kick up the furnace if you go up there. We don't use it much this time of year."

"Except for Christmas Eve, right Mummy?" Ali chimed in, taking Annie's hand on one side and slipping her other hand into Joe's.

"Do you do something special on Christmas Eve?" Joe asked.

"We used to. I'm surprised she remembers. The pandemic sort of put the kibosh on a lot of things and we just never started again. She was really little when we had the last one."

"It's 'cause I don't have much to remember," Ali said. "Not like Mummy does."

Annie and Joe exchanged a smile over Ali's head at the wisdom of a six-year-old. "Maybe it's time to resurrect the tradition," Joe offered.

"Maybe." But how would she finance it?

Ali gave Joe a running commentary all the way back to the house about the lake and the rules about not going on the ice. "A girl named Abby drowned when she fell through." Ali's face was solemn when she looked up at her mother. "Felicity's daughter, right Mummy?"

"Yes. It was a long time ago," Annie said. "Before we moved up here. Her mother lives just one road over from us and is a friend. We always remind the kids of how dangerous the ice can be."

Joe nodded. "I'll make sure Ryder knows, too." He bent down to whisper something in Ali's ear that made her giggle at first, then she took Max's leash from Joe and hurried down the path with him.

"She's adorable," he said, as they watched her chasing Max, who was desperately trying to catch up to a squirrel.

"Thank you. I think so too, but then I'm slightly biased when it comes to my children."

"Aren't all parents?"

There was something intriguing and a little mysterious about Joe that Annie couldn't quite put her finger on. He was handsome, yes, but it was more than that. Late thirties or so, muscular, beneath well-fitted clothes. That was all true, but it had something to do with Ali, as if he'd known her all her life. He seemed genuine, no pretentiousness about him, and that meant something in Annie's book. And those beautiful grey eyes!

"Thank you for letting us disrupt your family Christmas," he said, stopping at the porch steps.

"Oh, it's no disruption at all."

"It must be. I know what it's like to run a business during the holidays. My father owned a family-style restaurant. My mother used to say, '*No rest for the wicked.*' Then she'd say we must have been terrible people because there was never a moment's peace. Especially during the holidays."

"Well then, I'm sure you're familiar with the 'everyone helps' rule of a family-owned business. I couldn't manage without my father and our friends and neighbours. I have to admit, those years during the lockdowns were hard. It was lonely, with just the kids and my dad." He didn't ask why she hadn't mentioned a husband and she offered no explanation.

"I know what a lonely Christmas can be like," he said. After a pause, he added, "This is Ryder's first Christmas without his mother. She died of cancer just after New Year's. He misses her and I'm pretty lonely without my sister, too."

"I'm so sorry, Joe."

"Thank you. We're moving on, but it's not always easy. His father has never been a part of his life, so I'm Ryder's guardian. It can be a challenge to help him deal with his loss while I work on my own. But he's a good kid, and we get along pretty well."

Annie knew time was getting on, but given the gravity of their conversation, she didn't want to rush him. They waited a while on the porch while Ali made tracks in the snow with Max. There was a long moment of silence when she wasn't sure what to say, or ask, or if Joe even wanted to talk about it anymore. Finally, he took out his car keys.

"Is it alright if Ryder hangs out here a couple of minutes longer, while I unpack the car?"

"Sure. But I have to leave at one o'clock sharp. Sorry, otherwise I know Noah would love to have him stay longer."

"I promise not to take advantage of your generosity. I'm glad he has a friend." He took Max's leash from Ali, and put the dog into the back of the car, then climbed into the driver's seat. "See you in fifteen or less."

Ali waved goodbye, then slipped her hand into her mother's as they watched Joe drive down the back lane toward Moose Cottage.

"I like Joe," she said. "You should marry him, Mummy. He makes you laugh."

Annie looked down at her daughter, thinking it was an odd thing for her to say. When would Ali have given any thought to Annie marrying anyone? She was far too grown up for her six short years, sometimes.

Chapter 5

"Come on, Noah. You can't stay in the truck while we shop. You'll freeze." Annie retrieved the reusable grocery bags from behind the back seat and closed the door with an exasperated thunk. After three turns around the parking lot, and losing two spaces to people with small cars who'd butted in, she was now operating on her last nerve.

"I know you're angry about missing your hockey game, but it couldn't be helped. There was no one to take you. I had guests checking out." She had winced when she saw the disappointed look in her son's eye. He loved hockey, and she hated that he'd had to miss it. Not even his coach had been free to come out and pick him up. Still, missing his game wasn't an excuse for not helping with the groceries.

"I'm not leaving you here. This is a big order, not a quick in-and out for milk and bread. Besides, you can pick out something for your lunches next week. You always complain about what I pack for you."

"Okay. I guess I can come. Can I get any cereal I want?"

"Don't push your luck, bud. You know I won't buy the ones with a lot of sugar in them. But we'll have a look, okay?" Annie watched Noah drag himself out of the truck and slam the door. Then he fell in line with his mother and sister, dragging and scuffing his boots in the snow.

The front doors of the store slid open as they approached it. As Annie reached for a shopping cart, Noah spotted a classmate in the produce section with his mother.

"Hey Trev," Noah called out.

"Hey Noah," Trev said back, heading in their direction.

Annie exchanged smiles with Trevor's mother. "How are you, Jill? Ready for Christmas?"

Jill shook her head and rolled her eyes. "I'm never ready," she sighed, then went back to the bin of melons.

"Whatcha doin'?" Noah asked, sidling up next to Trevor.

"Nothin.' What'r *you* doin'?

"Nothin'. I hate shopping."

"I know. Boring right?"

"Yeah, boring."

Jill nudged Trevor along. "Only a week before the boredom really sets in, eh, Annie?" She tugged on Trevor's hood. "Come on. We have to get going."

Trevor and Noah fist-bumped with their mitten-covered hands. "See ya!"

Trevor trailed after his mother and, reluctantly, Noah trailed after Annie.

Familiar Christmas carols burbled merrily out of the store's speaker system, inspiring Annie to hum along. She loved everything about Christmas, decorating, shopping for the perfect gift for people, and watching her kids' faces when they opened their presents on Christmas morning. She loved their annual holiday baking with Ali and making up the boxes for friends and neighbours. It was a little thing, she knew, but something she loved to do. She loved walking the streets on a snowy evening, when Christmas carols echoed off the walls of the shops. It was a friendly time of the year when people smiled easily, said thank you more often and the store clerks were cheery.

With cookies and squares in mind, Annie led them to the baking aisle and stopped in front of the bags of flour.

Ali tugged on her coat sleeve. "Can we take a box of cookies to Grandpa's nurses at the hospital? Because nurses don't have time to eat. They have to look after people all day and all night."

Annie smiled. "Yes, they do. They are wonderful people. Your grandmother was a nurse and you know what? I think you'd make a wonderful one, too, if that's what you wanted to do with your life."

"Maybe. I haven't decided yet. I'm only six." Ali pointed to the brown sugar and Annie nodded, trying to contain her laughter at Ali's reasoning over a future vocation.

At the checkout, with a buggy fuller than she'd expected, Annie tapped her credit card, praying there was enough left on the balance for their order. She wanted points towards a free movie that her credit card would give her. Trivial as that might have seemed to some, it was the only way they could afford to go to the movies, and she was hoping to take the kids sometime through the holidays. When the card went through, Annie exhaled and tucked it back into her wallet. She would print out the movie tickets and put them in the kids' stockings. Thank you, Santa, she thought to herself as she filled her bags and stuffed them into the cart.

In the parking lot, a familiar looking white car pulled up beside them. Annie tilted her head to one side when Joe and Ryder got out of it.

"Are you following us? Should I be worried?"

Joe grinned. "We went to *That Little Place By the Lights* for lunch." Ryder and Noah went into immediate secrecy mode, their heads bent over something in Ryder's hand. "Pokémon cards," Joe explained.

"Ah, from the game store?"

"Yes." He took a step closer, keeping his voice low. "I saw something in that store I want to get him for Christmas, so we'll go back later. I guess I'll have to distract him, so he doesn't notice."

"He could come with us, if you like," Annie offered, as Joe moved to help her load the groceries into the truck. "I'm going to see my dad at the hospital, but the kids will probably just watch TV while he and I visit. Then I'll be going straight home."

A concerned look spread across Joe's face. "Will he be alright? What does the doctor say?"

It was the second time he'd asked, and that was not lost on Annie as she set a bag of potatoes in the back of the truck. "Thanks again for your concern. I'm hoping we will have some answers today."

They both reached for the last bag of groceries and his hand clamped over hers, at first, until Joe pulled back.

"Sorry," he said, as their eyes met. He took a step back to let her put it in her truck. "I'll take the cart if you're finished with it."

"Sure. Saves me putting it in the corral."

They looked over at the boys, still hovering over Ryder's new cards. "Are you sure about this?" Joe asked.

"I am," she nodded. "Noah would love Ryder's company. And it will give you some time to get what you need."

"Maybe I could reciprocate another time. Noah could come down to the cottage or something. Ali too, but, you know, only if you're okay with that."

"Thanks for the offer, but they'll be in school next week, so I'll visit my dad during the day and I don't have much Christmas shopping to do." Just a few things drastically marked down somewhere, she thought to herself.

"Sure. I understand. But if you change your mind, or it's an emergency or something, I'd be happy to help."

If it seemed a little above and beyond, Annie didn't tell Joe that as she pressed the fob to unlock the truck's doors.

"In you get kids. Ryder, looks like you're coming with us."

"Yippee!" Both boys shouted and fist-pumped with each other, then scrambled into the back seat.

"I should be home by five," Annie told Joe as they were leaving.

"Just a thought," Joe said, lingering by her door as she got in. "How about if I take care of supper?" When she hesitated, he added, "As a thank you for taking care of Ryder this afternoon. You could spend a little more time with your dad if you don't have to rush home to make it, couldn't you?"

Annie gave him a reluctant look. "I wouldn't want you to go to all that trouble. Honestly, Ryder is no bother."

"It's no trouble, and it would be my pleasure. I also wouldn't feel so guilty about pawning Ryder off on you."

"You didn't. I offered, and I meant it. Anything that keeps Noah from complaining he's bored is just fine with me. But…" She looked into the back of the truck. "What do you think, kids? Is it okay if Joe cooks us supper?"

"Sure!" Ali said, a little too enthusiastically. "And you're going to help bake cookies, too, right, Joe?"

Annie watched Joe's face break into a wide grin, but she was sure baking cookies was not on his list of the ten best things to do in the Muskokas. "I don't really think Joe wants to help us with our Christmas baking."

"You're wrong about that, Annie. I'd love to," Joe said. "Honestly. As long as I'm not invading some private mother-daughter time."

"Alright then, if you're sure." Annie started her truck. "The lodge has a fully stocked kitchen." She smiled as he stepped away from the truck. "See you later, Joe."

At the hospital, Noah and Ryder had been content in each other's company, and Ali had her colouring books and a doll to keep her occupied, so there were no altercations or grumbling that afternoon. But on the ride home Annie had resolved six, *she touched me* arguments between Noah and Ali, three *he pulled my hair* complaints from Ali and one *you're an idiot*, from Noah, before pulling over and asking Ryder to trade places with Noah. With Ryder as a neutral territory between the warring nations, she finally had peace the rest of the way home. It left her time to consider the options the doctor had given her regarding her father's future care.

She was exhausted trying to sort out what he had said about patients recovering from strokes. As she understood it, her father might regain all of his mobility and his speech, or he might be no better than he was right now, or he might fall somewhere in between. They had discussed that he might need a wheelchair, maybe even permanently, which meant building a ramp to the back door. Doable, she thought, though where she'd find the money for the lumber, she didn't know. Likewise, how would she manage the cost of converting the main floor's two-piece bathroom into a full size, wheelchair accessible one which was a must, since he couldn't possibly manage the stairs? Somehow, she had to be prepared for anything.

"He could go to a nursing home or respite centre," the tiny doctor with the pinched nose had suggested. When he saw the look of horror on Annie's face, he'd added, "It doesn't have to be permanent. Just till he gets enough mobility back to live at home again."

"But is that likely?" Annie had asked. "You've just discussed all these different scenarios, and I'm feeling completely confused."

A pacifying smile spread across his face. "There is no way to know for sure. Anything is possible. He's already doing very well."

If doing well meant her father was no longer comatose and his eyes shone every time buxom and curvy, Nurse Donna came into the room to check his vitals, then the doctor was right. He had seemed somewhat better after a decent night's sleep, not so drawn looking, and the fear and uncertainty had left his eyes. But his speech was still so garbled she had trouble making out what he was saying. It took three attempts and Nurse Donna's help for her to determine that what sounded like, '*nesters swep pwetters*', was actually, '*never slept better.*'

How would she cope at home if she couldn't understand what he was saying?

Whatever else happened, her father would not go to a nursing home. She would call Luke tonight and ask for his help. Her conscience was eased knowing she had the money to pay him what she owed him now. For work on a ramp and bathroom renovations, she'd find the money somehow.

It was dark by the time Annie turned into their driveway and parked the truck. She switched off the engine and unlocked the doors so the kids could get out.

"Help, please. Don't take off and leave all the groceries for me to carry in."

Ali unhitched herself from her car seat and climbed down from her seat. "Mummy, why are all the lights on at the lodge?"

"Joe is cooking supper, remember?" But that didn't explain why Luke's pickup was parked right outside the front door of the lodge or why the pine boughs Noah had collected were looped over the railings and up the stairs.

"Chelsea's here!" Ali cried, hurrying toward the lodge.

Luke opened the door of the lodge and came down the steps. "Hiya Ali."

Chelsea flew down the stairs behind him and gave Ali a hug. Then she tugged Annie's hand. "Come and see," she cried, pulling her toward the lodge. "It's Christmas! It's Christmas!"

When Luke closed the door behind them, Annie stared in disbelief at the sight before her. A fire crackled in the fireplace across the room, its flames leaping high into the chimney. Shadows danced across the walls from the glow of what looked like a hundred or more candles. And on the other side of the room, between the windows, stood a ten-foot-tall Christmas tree already trimmed with lights and ornaments. All it was missing was the angel on top.

Luke would have known they took turns doing that, because for the past two Christmases, he and Chelsea had celebrated with them. The room was positively glowing, and Annie felt her heart swell with warmth and gratitude.

"You're right, Chelsea. It really does look like Christmas. It's beautiful. Thank you for doing this." She turned to him as Luke draped his arm around her shoulders.

"It wasn't just Chelsea and me. We had help." He nodded toward the kitchen, where Joe leaned on the doorframe, a tea towel tossed over his shoulder and a contented smile on his face.

The room fell silent as Annie's eyes connected with Joe's and she recalled a Christmas not so very long ago, when someone else had stood just like that with the same lean of his shoulders, and that same identical smile.

Luke gave her shoulder a squeeze, drawing her attention back to him. "How's Sam?"

Suddenly, Annie didn't want his arm around her and she didn't want him hovering or being sickly sweet toward her. She extracted herself from his hold and took a step backwards. She would hire him to do the work in the house, but he would not worm his way back into their family life. She'd meant it when she said no, every time she'd said it. Nice as this gesture was, Luke had to get that through his head.

"Maybe we can talk more about Dad later?" she said, slipping out of her coat.

"Sure. Yeah. I guess now isn't the time." Then he called the kids. "Whose turn is it to put the angel on top?"

Ali jumped forward. "It's my turn, isn't it Mummy?"

Annie nodded. "Yes, Pumpkin. It is your turn."

"K. Then I'd like to give my turn to Ryder."

Ryder grinned sheepishly and nudged Ali lightly with his shoulder. "No, that's okay, Ali. If it's your turn, you should take it."

Ali shook her head with great determination. "Nope. I want you to do it. Mummy, tell Ryder he has to."

"Well, honey, he doesn't have to. Do you want to, Ryder?"

Ryder shrugged. "Okay, I guess. What do I have to do?"

"Put the angel on top, silly," Ali said. She took his hand and led him to where the angel sat on the window ledge. "Luke will lift you up, won't you, Luke?"

Luke looked at Ryder. "Or you can use the ladder, if you'd rather."

Ryder grinned. "No, it's okay. But can you lift me that high?"

"Piece of cake." Luke hoisted him over his shoulders and when Ryder set the angel on top of the tree, everyone yelled, "Press the button." Presto! Annie snapped a picture with her phone as the angel lit up and the whole tree seemed alive with twinkling fairy lights and dancing angels and sparkling bobbles.

Chelsea pulled Annie toward a long table, set with festive napkins and a red tablecloth. "I helped," she said, as Joe came out of the kitchen with a huge pot and set it on the table.

"Yes, she did," he agreed. "Seven places, like the seven dwarfs, right Snow White?"

Chelsea grinned. "Right!"

"Let's eat!" Ryder cried, hurrying to find a spot. "I'm starving."

When they had found places to sit, Joe lifted the lid off the steaming pot of stew and reached for Ali's bowl. "How much, madam? One scoop or two?"

"Two please?" she said, beaming at her place of honour between Joe and Ryder and the bowl of stew Joe laid before her.

Chelsea had made herself comfortable next to Annie. Joe picked up another bowl and said, "For you, Snow White?"

Chelsea giggled and covered her mouth with her hand. Then she held up one finger.

"One scoop it is," Joe said, ladling out the stew.

When everyone was served, they ate and discussed how wonderful the room looked with all the decorations. Noah wanted to know how Luke had brought such a huge tree out of the woods by himself.

"I didn't," Luke said, with a nod to Joe. "I had helpers."

Annie saw Joe's head droop. He liked helping, she decided, but he didn't want praise for it. "This is such a treat," Annie said. "It reminds me of old times."

"Just like your Christmas Eve?" Joe asked.

"Except we usually have turkey, but yes. Friends and family gathered around the table."

"Well, maybe we can do it again next week, but cook a turkey instead," Joe suggested. "Then you could revive the old tradition. I could cook, so you don't have to worry about that part of things."

"Oh, I wouldn't want to impose on you over Christmas." Annie dunked a piece of bread in her stew and ate it. Her mouth was not quite empty when she mumbled, "This is delicious. Where did you learn to cook like this?"

"My father was the owner and chef at our family restaurant. I learned everything I know about cooking from him."

Annie gave a little nod. "My father-in-law was a chef too. He passed away a few years ago, but his food was always delicious."

"Bet he didn't make stew like this," Luke offered. "You've done yourself proud, Joe."

"Actually, he did," Annie said. Then she shrugged. "Well, not exactly like this. I'd say this is better." She flashed Joe a grateful smile. "Thanks for doing this."

By the time they'd eaten, and the adults had talked over a shared bottle of wine, while the kids had played a round of ping pong, it was time for bed.

"But first we have to clean up," Annie said, stacking bowls.

"I'll do it," Joe said, taking them from her. "You have the kids to see to."

"Not in your life. You did all this and you think I'm just going to walk away from the mess?" Annie protested. "Let me get the kids settled and then I'll come back. I've got a monitor, so we can hear them if they need anything."

Joe put his hands up in the air. "Okay. But honestly, I don't mind."

"I should get Chelsea home," Luke said with a hint of reluctance. "I hate to leave you with all this, though."

"Go, Luke. She's exhausted," Annie said. "We can manage. Can't we Joe?"

He nodded. "You bet."

Luke grabbed their coats from the hook. "Come on Chels. Time to go." He looked at Annie. "I'll call you tomorrow and we can talk about Sam."

"Yes, please," Annie was motioning for Ali to get her coat on. "We're going to have to make some changes in the house, and I'll need your help with that."

She knew he'd been hoping for her to say something other than what she had. Changes inside meant she was not selling up, nor was she about to accept his offer. She watched as the smile faded from Luke's face and his eyes dropped to the hat in his hands.

As the kids got their things on, Ali looked up at her mother with disappointment. "We were supposed to bake the cookies after supper and Joe promised to help, remember?"

"It's late," Annie told her. "The baking will have to wait, okay?"

"Okay," she pouted. "But is Joe still going to help?"

"Oh sweetie, I don't know. Joe might have other things to do," Annie said, tucking Ali's hair inside her hat.

"I'd love to help." Joe looked at Annie. "As long as I'm not in the way." His eyes flicked toward the door and Luke, who was halfway through it.

She knew what he was really asking, but how could she explain Luke's possessiveness was one-sided? Suddenly she wanted to, very much.

"You wouldn't be in the way," she said, nodding toward the door and lowering her voice. "Luke is our handyman. He helps a lot, but… He doesn't bake cookies." She smiled as she zipped up her coat and met his gaze. "If Ali wants you to come, and you don't mind, then we'd welcome your help." She reached for Ali's hand. "Come on, kids. Say thank you to Joe for that delicious stew."

Noah didn't wait for his mother, but sped down the steps and across the parking lot for home. Ali and Annie walked a little slower. The light from the solitary streetlamp at the top of their drive cast shadows across the snow. Everything was still except for the echo of Noah's boots clumping up the steps. Ali smiled up at her mother and though she said nothing, Annie couldn't help remembering her words from earlier that day.

"You should marry him, Mummy. He makes you laugh."

When the kids were settled; glasses of water set on their nightstands, nightlights turned on and they were tucked in for the night, Annie took the monitor with her and headed across the driveway to the lodge. Joe was stirring the ashes in the fireplace and Ryder was curled up on the couch, a set of headphones covering his ears.

"I don't believe in video games as a babysitter, usually," Joe said, helping her off with her coat. "But sometimes it's the only thing he wants to do."

"I remember my parents saying the same thing about TV when I was a kid. I don't think it did me any harm."

She was pleased to see that he'd done as she asked and left the cleaning up. It was kind of him to have made dinner for them all. Cleaning up, too, seemed wrong. She began gathering bowls and things from the table and setting them on the counter to pass them through to the kitchen. Joe followed her with another pile of bowls. There was a moment when they simultaneously reached to save a spoon from falling on the floor, and their hands touched. Annie pulled back and tucked a curl of hair behind her ear, leaving Joe to rescue the falling spoon. Just standing this close to him was sending ripples of nervous energy up and down her spine. What was it about this man that had her as giddy as a teenager?

"So. Joe," Annie said, trying to calm herself and make polite conversation, as she cleared napkins and condiments from the table. "What do you do when you're not vacationing in the Muskokas?" Small talk. Keep it simple.

"Oh, this isn't really a vacation. It's a home between homes, I guess. A couple of months ago, I bought a construction company. Maybe you've heard of it. Melville's?"

"I have. They do good work. They did a major renovation on my friend Felicity's place. I didn't know George was selling."

"He said he was ready to retire. Can't blame him. He's been in the business for thirty years. For that reason, and his reputation, I don't plan on changing the name or making any sudden changes in the people who work for me."

"So, you're moving to Huntsville?"

He went to the kitchen and started rinsing dishes, then handed them to her to load into the dishwasher. As he glanced across the room at Ryder, there was a look of uncertainty in his eyes.

"I'm not sure where we'll settle down yet. I'm keeping my options open."

"So, you're a… carpenter?" she asked, reaching past him for a bowl. Her eyes met his when he grabbed it first and passed it to her. There was a moment when she was once again, locked in a memory of another time and another pair of steel-grey eyes. She blinked once, twice, and the memory faded.

"There. That's the last of them," she said as she set the bowl in the dishwasher. "The soap is in…" She pointed to the cupboard above the sink, but Joe was already reaching for it.

As he picked one of the tabs out and set it on her open palm, a shiver ran through her, as if a current of electricity had passed between them. She could not deny the warmth that spread up her arm and straight into her heart. She bent low to put the tab in the slot and close its lid, letting her hair fall over her shoulder to cover her face and hide her blush from Joe.

"Plumber," he said, when she closed the door and pressed start.

She frowned.

"I'm a plumber by trade, but I'm experimenting with other things."

"Oh! I see." How nice to have the financial luxury to experiment, she thought. "Well, I hope it goes well for you."

If she had the money, she could hire Joe and the Melville team to do her renovations, but she didn't, so she would rely on Luke. He would do a good job, but it also meant he'd be hovering over her, pushing her, egging her on about moving in with him or at least selling, and that was the last thing she wanted to hear just now.

"This place was a bit of an experiment too," she said, leaning against the counter. "We wanted to get out of the city. Wanted our kids to experience something different from what we grew up with. Running a resort, even on this level, wasn't exactly what we'd had in mind, but when we saw this place, we fell in love with it."

"It's a beautiful piece of property," he said, standing next to her, leaning against the counter like she was, arms crossed over his chest. A frown creased his brow. "I wonder. Would you…"

A crash from the other side of the room interrupted him.

"Ryder!" he cried, racing to the couch. Annie was right behind him, but when they reached Ryder and realized he'd just drifted off to sleep and dropped his tablet, they both laughed.

"I should get him to bed," Joe said, scooping up the iPad. "I'll come over in the morning and unload that dishwasher, and put everything away."

"No. Leave it. You're supposed to be a guest here, remember?" Annie went to unplug the tree lights and snuff out all the candles, while Joe bundled a sleepy Ryder into his coat.

"Well, I guess this is goodnight," Joe said, pushing his arms into the sleeves of his jacket.

She set her hand on his arm to stop him from leaving too soon. "Luke doesn't think of doing things like this, so I know this was all your idea. Thank you. It was like old times tonight. Seeing the lodge decorated for Christmas again has brought back a lot of memories."

"All good ones, I hope."

She nodded. "Yes. Wonderful memories."

Chapter 6

Annie was awake before the Monday morning alarm sounded at six. She'd been going over the events of the weekend in her mind, feeling like it had all been a blur. There were last-minute cottage rentals to couples with snowmobiles, discussions with Luke about the renovations, and endless loads of laundry that seem to ooze out of the woodwork, all of which had left her so exhausted that last night, when the kids were settled, Annie had gone to bed too. But sleep hadn't come right away because she lay awake worrying about everything; her bills, her father, the renovations and how she was going to pay for them, and about relying far too much on Luke.

Now swinging her legs over the side of the bed, her head still woozy from lack of sleep, she went into autopilot. As she reached for her housecoat and pulled it on, her feet instinctively found her slippers on the mat by her bed. Then she made her way down the stairs to start breakfast and infuse her body with enough caffeine to face the day.

Ali had asked for waffles again this morning, and while she hulled the last of the strawberries, Annie considered the price she'd paid for the California imports. Yesterday morning when Ali had sat up at the table, devoured her plate of waffles and smiled up at her mother with a whipped cream mustache, Annie decided that this time, it had been worth the cost. However, it was an extravagance she would not indulge again. Ali would have to learn that buying food that was in-season locally was more affordable, and it helped people they knew.

But just for now, she wouldn't say anything about it because this morning, Ali had come down for breakfast, and while she was waiting for her desired waffles, she had been unusually quiet. Annie couldn't help wondering if something was wrong.

"Everything okay, Pumpkin?" she asked, pouring batter into the waffle maker.

Ali grinned. "Yup. Peachy keen. Handy dandy. Bob's your uncle. Right. As. Rain!"

"That good, huh?" Annie laughed, kissing her on the nose. Maybe she'd thought wrong.

Noah found his way into the kitchen twenty minutes after his sister and slumped into his chair. He reached for the generic cereal she'd had to buy to stay on budget, ate a bowl of it without complaint. He even set his dishes by the sink without being reminded. It might have seemed a miracle if something wasn't obviously bothering him.

"You're pretty quiet this morning," Annie said a little later, as they walked to the bus stop. "Anything on your mind?"

Noah shrugged. "Not really." He tugged at his toque, pulling it down over his ears, and looked up at her, then squinted and shaded his eyes against the glare of the rising sun. "Well, yeah. Kind of."

"What's up?"

"I was thinking of Ryder and his mum. It must be hard to lose your mum. I'm glad I have you." He looked up at her with tears brimming his eyes. "I'm sorry I'm such a nuisance sometimes."

Annie pulled him close for a shoulder squeeze. A full-on hug would have embarrassed him, even though no one was around. Then she bent down to his level, nose to nose, and said, "You're not a nuisance. You're a normal boy who's growing up and testing his wings. Sometimes we clash a little. It happens. But we still love each other." She let that sit a moment, then as they started walking again, she added, "Are you worried about Ryder being without his Mum this Christmas?"

"Kinda."

"I'm sure he misses her a great deal, but you know, a dad, or sometimes even an uncle, can love his children every bit as much as a mum does. I'm sure Joe is doing his very best to help Ryder. You really like him, don't you?"

Noah nodded. "Yeah. Except he's going to leave after Christmas, and I won't get to see him again."

"I think Joe's looking for a place to live near here, maybe in Huntsville or Bracebridge. If he does, then there is no reason why you two couldn't still get together sometimes. I'm really glad you have a new friend."

They both looked up at the sound of Ted's bus grinding its way up the road. Annie bent to kiss the top of his head.

"Have a great day, honey, and try not to worry too much. Things have a way of working out, you know."

Noah smiled. "Love you, Mum."

Ali flew to her mother, arms open wide. "Don't start baking without me," she insisted. "Bye Mummy. Love you!" She turned her smiling face up for her kiss, then hurried after her brother.

Annie waved to Ted, then watched the bus until she could no longer see it lumbering up the road. Eight twenty-five. She knew the time by heart, not by looking at her watch, but because it was the same every morning.

On her way back to the house, she pulled her phone out of her pocket and called Luke. He would be on his way to drop Chelsea at kindergarten. If she timed it right, she'd get him before he went back home.

"Luke. Hi." It was impossible to keep the hesitation out of her voice. She'd been a little cold to him last night, when they'd talked about the renovations and he'd asked once again why she didn't just sell the place. It had resulted in a heated argument, one he'd eventually backed away from.

"Hey, Annie. What's up?" Luke asked in a hurried tone.

"I was just wondering about the list of things you're going to pick up from the hardware store. I can't afford this, Luke. We need to scale back somehow. Do you have time to talk?"

"Sure." But he stretched out the word, as if he wasn't sure at all. After a hesitation, he asked, "Is the coffee on?"

"Isn't it always? But you don't have to come out here. We could talk about it over the phone."

"I'll be there in twenty minutes."

"Okay, if you think that's best. And Luke…?" He said nothing until she said. "Thank you."

"Yeah. It's all good, Annie."

But somehow she knew it wasn't, not quite.

She was just climbing the steps to the back porch when Max came bounding down the trail from the fishing cabins.

"Hey Max," she said when he came up and gave her a slurping, wet kiss on the hand. "Where's Joe? Why are you all alone?"

Max barked loudly, his leash dangling from his collar and dragging in the snow. He pulled away from her and headed back the way he'd come. At the first cabin, he turned to see if she was following and when she wasn't he barked again.

"Okay, boy. I get it. You want me to come with you?" Annie took off after Max, running as fast as she could in the old boots she'd thrown on to walk to the bus stop. Max carried on, loping his way along the path in front of the fishing cabins, his breath streaming into the air as he went. At the beginning of the woods, Annie stopped to catch her breath, her heart pounding as her mind slipped back to the other day and finding her father face down in the snow. What disaster awaited her today?

Max ran back to meet her, grabbed her glove between his teeth and pulled. "Okay, Max. I get it. I'm coming. What's wrong?" As she rounded a corner, she saw him, or at least she saw the familiar yellow toque Ryder had been wearing the day before, lying on the snow. And Ryder was a few feet away.

"Ryder!"

He turned to look back at her. "Annie! Help me. I'm stuck."

It took less than a minute to see that Ryder had gotten his foot caught between the two fallen trees she had struggled over the other day. The bark was stripped clean, and the snow had frozen over them, making them slippery.

"Are you hurt?" she asked, as she got closer to him.

Ryder shook his head. "I don't think so. But I can't get my foot out. I'm sure glad Max was here."

"How long have you been here?" Annie wedged herself on the other side of the fallen trees to see if it was possible to shift one of them. Ryder twisted himself around, trying to follow where she was going. "Don't move too much, Ryder. You might end up more stuck than you already are."

"Okay. Did you see Uncle Joe? I tried to call him, but he didn't answer." He held up his cell phone.

"I didn't know you had a phone."

"It's for emergencies. But I only have one bar."

"Yeah, we're a little off the beaten track." Annie straightened. "I'm going to go back to one of the cabins and get some rope and things." She fished in her pocket and found two mints and a broken, but still wrapped, energy bar. "Here," she handed them to Ryder. "Not much, but it's something to munch on until I come back."

"Thanks!"

She picked up his toque and set it on his head. "Stay warm. I won't be long and Max is going to stay here and keep you company, aren't you, Max?"

Max answered with a resounding, "Arf."

"Good boy."

As Annie left the woods and came out onto the trail, she looked up to see Joe hurrying toward her.

"Have you seen Ryder? He's out here somewhere. He sent me a message."

"Yes. He's okay." Annie put a hand on his arm to calm him. Joe seemed nearly frantic with worry. "He got his foot stuck between some fallen trees, but he doesn't seem to be in any pain. Max is with him."

"I never should have let him go out on his own."

"He'll be fine, Joe. It could have happened to anyone. I promise. He's okay." He didn't seem ready to believe her. "We'll need some rope. Come with me and then I'll take you right to him."

Annie slid a key from under the flowerpot on the front porch of the closest cabin and opened the door. In a closet inside, she grabbed two coils of rope, a handsaw and a shovel. "There is a chainsaw at the house if these don't work."

"Maybe we should get it, anyway."

"The trees are huge, Joe. It would take ages to cut through them. But if we can hoist the log out of the way, I think he should be able to slip out."

"Okay, if you're sure." Joe hoisted a coil of rope over each shoulder.

Annie led him back through the woods, where they found Ryder, his head resting on Max's back.

"Ryder!" Joe dropped the rope and raced to him.

"Uncle Joe!" Ryder cried. "I'm sorry. I know you said not to go any further than the cabins, but Max chased after a squirrel, and I couldn't stop him."

"Hey. It's alright, kiddo. Just as long as you're okay. Are you in any pain?"

"My foot's a little sore and I'm cold, but that's all."

"Alright. We'll have you out in no time." Joe looked at Annie. "I'm thinking we should loop these ropes around this top log, then up that hill and around those two trees, and pull it off him."

"Sounds good. I'll put one about here and you do yours about five or six feet further down." She pointed out two places about three feet apart, along the top log.

When the ropes were in position, Joe explained to Ryder that when they shifted the log, he should pull himself out and roll to the side. "Can you do that?"

Ryder nodded.

"Okay. Ready, Joe?" Annie braced her feet against a tree for better leverage, and Joe did the same behind another tree.

"Pull!" he called out when they were in position.

"Pull," she called again until they could feel the log begin to shift. "Pull. Pull. Pull."

"We need help," Joe said, when they realized it was too heavy for them. He spun around and pointed in the other direction. "Isn't the Pierce Cottage just over that way?"

Annie nodded. "How do you know that?"

"I was there a couple of weeks ago doing an inspection and we walked to the edge of their land. I'll go and see if Ben is home and maybe Felicity's son, too."

A few minutes later, Joe returned with a posse of help, Ben, Felicity's son Will, and Cam Myers, with Felicity bringing up the rear. "We were just about to help Cam put his fishing hut on the lake," she explained.

With three on each rope, it wasn't long before they eased the log enough for Ryder to squeeze his leg out of it. He rolled to the side, out of the way.

"I'm out!" he shouted.

The log slammed back into place with a resounding thud. Joe raced to Ryder to check him all over. "Are you sure you're not hurt?" he asked, gently flexing Ryder's foot from side to side and back and forth. "Does any of this hurt?"

"A little. I think I can walk." Ryder stood up and tried walking around but the first step on his left foot and he crunched down again. "Ah! It's a bit sore, but I'll be okay." He flexed his ankle again. "Not so bad. It'll be fine. Right as rain."

Right as rain, Annie thought. That's what Ali had said this morning. She knew that she said it sometimes too, but it seemed odd coming from Ryder.

"Well, that's a relief. It could have been worse." Joe looked at Annie and the others. "Thank you. All of you. Can I return the favour and help with the fishing hut?"

Ben took a step forward and clapped Joe on the shoulder. "Take care of the boy. We can manage. Cam's done most of the work already."

Ryder stepped up beside Joe and grinned up at them all. "Thank you," he said. "I thought I was going to be stuck in there forever."

They all laughed and Ben said, "It's no problem, son. We're glad you're okay."

They headed back through the woods. Annie and Joe recoiled the ropes and returned everything to the fishing cabin. They were on their way back to the house when they saw Luke coming down the path toward them, an annoyed look on his face. Only then did Annie remember their arranged meeting.

"Luke I'm sorry. We..."

"Geez Annie." He threw his hands up in frustration. "You called me, remember? We agreed I would be here in twenty minutes. I've been at the house for nearly half an hour and I've called you three times. Where were you? On a pleasure hike in the woods?"

Joe held up a hand to Luke. "Hey, take it easy. Ryder got his foot caught between a couple of fallen logs. If you're going to blame someone, blame me. Don't take it out on Annie."

Luke sent a look of disbelief in Joe's direction, but his features softened when he saw Ryder limp toward Max.

"You okay, kid?"

Ryder shrugged. "It's just a little sore." Then he looked at Joe. "Can I go work on my model?"

"Sure. I'll be there in a minute."

"Thanks again, Annie. I'm sure glad you were here." Ryder clapped his hands for Max, and headed off, slowly, toward Moose Cottage, limping on his sore foot.

Joe echoed Ryder's gratitude. "I'll tell him to stay out of the woods from now on."

When he cast a concerned glance between Luke and Annie, she wondered if he was going to say something more, but he didn't. Instead, he just followed after Ryder.

Luke stared after him, kicking one foot against the other. "There's something about that guy I don't trust," he said, half under his breath.

"He seems a nice enough guy to me." Annie led the way up the steps to the back porch.

"Maybe too nice. I don't think you should get too friendly with him."

She paused on the top step. "Luke McCann, are you jealous?"

"What? No." He opened the door. "Should I be?"

Annie unwrapped herself from her coat and slid her boots off. "No, you shouldn't. First, because he's a customer. A nice, quiet, *paying*, I might add, customer. Second, because you and I are not a thing. Remember?"

"Yeah, well, I don't like him."

"Oh, for crying out loud." She went to the kitchen and took two cups out of the cupboard and poured them each a coffee. Luke sat down at the table across from her.

"So, what's so urgent that I had to come out here right after I dropped Chelsea off?"

"It was your idea to come out here. I could have talked about this over the phone. But since you're here." Annie reached for the envelope she'd prepared the day before and handed it to him. "It's the money I owe you," she said, nudging it a little closer to him when he didn't pick it up. "I had a little windfall when Joe booked in, so this should settle my debt."

Luke took her hand in his, squeezed it a little, a familiar pleading look in his eye. He pushed the envelope back to her, a frown creasing his brow. "I told you not to worry about it. Keep it. Get the kids something for Christmas. Stock up on groceries. Pay the water bill."

Annie yanked her hand from his grasp. "What's up with you?"

"Nothing. What are you talking about?"

"You were short with me on the phone this morning. Then you criticize one of my guests and now you're acting like…like you own me or something. You can't tell me who I can talk to and who I can't. I won't stand for it."

His mouth gaped open. "No! That's not it at all. I'm just worried about you. Especially after you showed me the letters from the bank. I know you can't afford to pay me this money. You should keep it. It's fine."

"We had a deal. You earned this. I wouldn't feel right about keeping it."

Luke's glance flitted toward the row of cottages outside the kitchen window, then he turned back to her. She knew he was wondering if something was transpiring between her and Joe. She'd been wondering about it too, but she wasn't about to tell him that or that she was sure Joe had been about to ask her out the other night. Maybe it was wrong to have Luke do this work. Maybe being here was going to be too difficult for him, for them both, whether or not anything transpired with Joe.

"Really, Luke. You know I'm never going to marry you. Give this up."

"How can you be so sure about that? I love you so much, Annie. Don't you feel anything for me?" He stood then and pulled her into his arms. "Can you honestly say that these past two years have meant nothing? What has this been, then?"

Annie twisted in his arms until he released his hold on her and leaned back against the counter. "I don't know, Luke. I'm not sure what you and I have been, but this much I know. There is nothing between Joe and me. He arrived two days ago, a stranger. He's been nothing but kind. I have the kids to think about and I'm careful about who I let into their lives. You know that."

"Yeah, sure. I can see that." Luke's tone was sarcastic. "He's baking cookies with you and Ali, cooked dinner for everyone, and his nephew and Noah are practically best friends. And he's been a guest here for what? Three days? Sounds a little too cushy if you ask me."

She shrugged. "He's being kind. What do you want me to say, Luke?"

"Nothing. It's fine." He exhaled deeply and raked his hand through his hair. He was wearing the shirt she'd given him last year for Christmas and the significance of that resounded in her mind; another reminder that they had history and another attempt to solidify their relationship. She was through defending herself.

"What did you want to talk about then, if it wasn't us?" he asked with a defeated sigh.

"I told you. This is about the renovations. About what we discussed yesterday. I can't afford the things you're suggesting. We have to scale it back. Then there's this ramp and the amount of wood it will take is just far too much. Can we do something else?"

Luke went to the window to look out at the steps. "I can't make it any smaller or the incline will be too steep. When is he coming home?"

"I'm not sure. They are arranging for a physiotherapist to visit every day and a PSW will come and help with meals and bathing. They say he might regain some or all of the use of his limbs. But he also might not, so we need to be prepared."

"Sure, but it's winter now, so you just need to get him into the house, and I think you could do that through the front door. That wide cement porch is level with the ground. You'd just have to shovel the snow off it, and I'm sure you're capable of that." There was more than a hint of bitterness in his tone when he added, "or get someone to do it for you."

She knew what he meant, but she was not about to play his game. Jealousy never looked good on anyone and it certainly did nothing for Luke's demeanor just then.

"I can clear that," she said, crossing her arms over her chest. "I honestly never think of using the front. We always use the back because it's where we park the truck."

"Well, maybe you should start, because if he's still in the wheelchair by spring, he'd be able to go out onto the porch almost without help. He'd just need someone to get him over the threshold." He reached for her hand and caressed the back of it with his thumb, softening his gaze as he looked at her.

"Or you could put this place on the market, and you could all move in with me."

Annie stiffened and shot him a warning glare. "Don't go there again, Luke. I thought this was settled."

"Why, Annie? Just tell me why." He reached out to cup her face in his hands, but she pulled away.

"I can't Luke. You know why."

"I don't believe you. You say you don't love me, but I think you do. Maybe it's not the same as what you felt for your husband, but there's something between us. Who do you call when you have a problem? Who do you turn to when you need to talk things through?" He nudged her shoulder and grinned. "Who do you call when you're watching scary movies and you don't want to be alone?"

"It's not the same thing, Luke. I don't love you the way married people love each other. Yes, you're here and reliable and you're always kind to the kids. But is that enough?"

"It is for me. Just think about it. That's all I ask. Don't push me away. Just take some time. When you think it through, I'm sure you'll see I'm right."

Luke downed the last of his coffee. "I have to run. I've got a little Christmas shopping to do and I'll stop at the lumberyard to pick up those two by fours." He put his cup by the sink, then bent down and kissed her cheek. "Think about it, Annie. Don't say no, yet. That's all I ask."

This time, when he reached out to take her into his arms, she let him. There was comfort in his familiar embrace, his heart beating against her chest. Luke was her safety net. She knew that and despite being sure of her platonic feelings, she couldn't deny she felt loved by Luke. She looked up to see him staring down at her and when their eyes met, he bent his head to kiss her. There was an urgency in it, as if he wanted her to feel the full depth of his love in that single moment.

"I love you, Annie," he sighed when she ended the kiss almost as quickly as it started.

"I can't do this," she began to say, but Luke put a finger over her mouth.

"Just think about it. That's all I'm asking." He held her gaze until she nodded.

"Alright. I'll think about it."

Chapter 7

Annie cleared the snow from the front porch as Luke had suggested, then, when it was done, she realized the little patch where they once parked their car was badly overgrown by a hedge of cedars. Retrieving the clippers out of the toolshed, she trimmed back the hedges, saving the longest boughs for decorating. When it was finished, there was room to park a vehicle again, maybe even two, with easy access to the front door. Annie felt confident this would be the answer to getting her father in and out of the house. Not building a ramp at the back door was going to save her a fortune in lumber costs.

Inside, and out of the cold, she stood outside the main floor bathroom considering the plan she and Luke had come up with to knock down the wall between it and the closet giving them enough room for a full bathroom complete with a walk-in shower with a preformed seat. It would take away a closet but that had become nothing more than a storage space anyway. Everything inside it, could go somewhere else.

She located some spare totes in the attic and filled them with stuff from the closet to sort more carefully later. Her father's bathroom things she stored in his room temporarily. They would go back in the bathroom when it was finished. Then she examined the coats, first setting aside a couple of things Noah and Ali had outgrown which could go to the secondhand shop in town and then moving the rest to the mudroom. How on earth did one family accumulate so much stuff, she thought. After Christmas she would sort through it all and take another load of stuff to the shop in town, or the bin at the church.

Walking through the entire main floor of the house, Annie imagined herself pushing a wheelchair to see what difficulties they might have moving her father from room to room. They would eat their meals in the dining room, she decided, because its door was wide enough but getting to the kitchen would be a challenge. He would have to negotiate a sharp turn in a narrow hallway. Maybe he could manage it but she rather liked the idea of eating in the dining room for a change.

Standing in the doorway of the living room, it occurred to her that if she moved the furniture around, she could open up the pocket doors to the hallway. That way, her father could move easily between his bedroom and the living room without having to go all the way down the hallway and negotiate that same turn he would if he were going to the kitchen. She had rearranged the furniture, ran the vacuum over the rug and floor and opened up the pocket doors. Annie smiled to herself when she stood back to survey the job. It was all going to be very manageable for her father, once the bathroom was done and there would be no nursing home for Sam Taylor.

"I should have done this ages ago," she said out loud, recalling that the pocket doors had stayed open when they first bought the place. She couldn't recall when she had closed them up and moved the couch in front of them, or why, but she was happy she'd changed it back.

She crossed into the hallway and through to her father's bedroom, where his freshly washed sheets and duvet cover lay on the bed waiting for his return. She picked up the picture of her mother, that stood on his nightstand and sank onto the bed, running her hand across her mother's face. She should have been here baking cookies with Ali and cheering Noah on at his hockey games. They were little more than toddlers when cancer took her, but at least she'd held them in her arms.

Annie often wondered if there was some truth to the idea that our loved ones were always around, because even now, in her father's room, her mother held an undeniable presence. Her handmade blanket lay over the back of her father's chair. The favourite cardigan he always reached for was one she'd knitted him for Christmas years ago and the photo album he kept in the drawer of his nightstand, which, she knew, he often pulled out to look at, was filled with pictures of her. There was even a bottle of her perfume on her father's dresser. Once she'd offered to throw it out.

"It can't be any good anymore, Dad," she'd said.

"Don't you dare!" He clutched it close to his chest. "Every now and again, I open it and the smell reminds me of her. So just leave it right there."

"Okay, Dad. I get it." She did, because there was a closet in her room, half filled with clothes she couldn't bear to part with and shoes lingering by the back door that no one wore anymore. Little things, like clothes, shoes and perfume, kept the people we loved closer.

Annie replaced the photograph and went to the kitchen to get everything ready for baking. Ali would be desperate to get started and the baking would take hours, so she'd decided on frozen pizzas for dinner tonight, which would be easier than cooking a full meal. The kids would love it.

At ten after three, Annie wrapped a scarf around her neck, slid her feet into her boots and pulled her wool cape around herself. She was at the top of the driveway when the bus pulled up and Ali and Noah climbed down the steps.

"Thanks Ted," she called out, waving as he pulled the door closed behind the kids. He smiled back and put the bus in gear.

"Hey, Mum. Got a joke for you," Noah said, hurrying up to her. "Why does everyone love Frosty the Snowman?"

"I don't know, Noah. Why?" Annie said, taking the bait and Ali's hand.

"Because he's soooo cool." He burst into a fit of giggles. "Get it Mum?"

"Yes, I do. Good one." She tugged on the pompom on top of his toque. "Who did you help today?" It was something she'd started asking once or twice a week, instead, to get the kids thinking about ways they could help other people, instead of only thinking about themselves.

"I helped Miss Wight sharpen pencils, and I showed Alfie Gibson where the gym is."

"Alfie Gibson? The family who stayed here?"

Noah nodded. "Yup. They go to our school now."

"Oh. Well, that's great. Sounds like you were quite the helper today." Her arm was around Ali's shoulders as they headed toward the house. "How about you, honey? You're pretty quiet."

"I'm practicing my listening."

"Oh. Why is that?"

"Because Mrs. Vickers says I talk too much and I should listen more."

"I see." Annie guessed that Mrs. Vickers didn't have chatty children of her own at home. She loved that Ali had questions and wanted to talk about things. Even if it was the hundredth question asked when she was putting her to bed at night.

"Woah!" Noah cried out when he saw she'd cleared the front porch and he could see the front door. "I didn't even know there was a door there."

"I don't think we've used it since before you were born," Annie said.

"Cool!" Noah took off at breakneck speed, and when he reached the door and tried the knob, he found it locked. "Hey. What good is a door if it doesn't open?"

"There's a key inside. This is for when Grandpa comes home. For now, we use the back, same as always." Especially when we're tracking in all the snow, she thought.

When they rounded the corner to the back door, Ryder and Joe, with Max bringing up the rear, were just coming down the lane from Moose Cottage.

"Hey Noah," Ryder called out. "Guess what happened to me today?"

Noah threw Annie a question look. She knew without asking that he wanted to show Ryder his fort. "Backpack," she said, reaching out her hand. "Then you can go."

"Thanks Mum." He hurled it in her direction.

"Supper in an hour or so," she shouted as the two boys made a beeline toward the toolshed, followed closely by Max.

"His foot seems fine now," Annie said to Joe when they went inside and hung up their coats.

"Right as rain," Joe said, hanging his coat beside hers and following Annie and Ali into the kitchen.

"I don't know what Ryder's like, but the minute Noah gets in the door, he's looking for something to eat. Can Ryder have peanut butter?"

"Yes, he's allergy free." Joe helped Ali lift her backpack and Noah's onto the counter.

"We have to empty the lunch stuff out," Ali said, opening the zipper on hers.

"Oh, gotcha!" Joe opened Noah's and pulled out several plastic containers. Annie pointed to the sink when he held them up to ask what to do with them.

"I'll make peanut butter stuffed celery, apple slices and I have some trail mix for a snack."

"I usually tell Ryder to grab an apple or a banana from the fruit bowl and leave it at that."

"Well, supper is just frozen pizza tonight and so I thought their snack should be more substantial."

Ali put Joe to work sorting out bowls and cookie sheets and then instructed him on their system of doing things. In the meantime, Annie got two snack containers ready for the boys and a third for Ali.

"I hate to ask you to put your things on again, but can you take these out to Noah and Ryder?"

"Okay, Mummy. But you know what Noah will say. Boys only!" Ali pulled on her coat, shoved her feet into her boots and flew off like a shot down the porch steps, calling out to Noah as she went.

"Dad cleared half of the toolshed for Noah to use as a little hideout. He likes to go out there when he wants to be away from us girls," she told Joe.

Joe sympathized. "I had a tree house when I was his age. My sister wasn't allowed up there. I said so." He grinned and dumped the last of Noah's leftovers into the compost bin.

Annie nodded. "My hideout was my closet. It was huge."

"Bet you had a dollhouse in it."

"How did you know?"

He shrugged. "Isn't that every girl's dream?"

"Maybe. I suppose."

When Joe came to lean against the counter, Annie needed to do something to fend off the nervous energy she felt when he was so close to her.

"Coffee or tea?" she asked.

"Tea. If it's not too much trouble."

"Of course not." She set the kettle to boil, then pulled a clear teapot out of the cupboard and stood back to let Joe choose from one of the many mason jars on the shelf. "Pick whatever kind you like," she said.

"Green, white, jasmine, ginger, rooibos. Hmm, what to choose?" Joe selected a mint and ginger blend and set it on the counter.

"I worked in a bookstore and tea shop and learned how to blend teas from the lady who owned it. I still order from her, but I've had to scale down my supply to a few favourites."

"Books and Tea, what a novel idea."

Annie laughed. "That's why she called her store Novel-teas. Smart right?"

"That is clever."

Annie got her cookie recipes out of her file box and set them on the table. "One of these days I'll have to put these on my tablet. They're getting so dirty and faded I can hardly read them anymore. Most of these were my mother's, or my grandmother's."

"May I look?" Joe asked, reaching for the cards.

"Of course."

He thumbed through them while she brewed their tea. "How many of these cookies and squares do you intend to make today?"

"All of them. When they are done, we put an assortment in each box. It's an actual production line." She grinned. "Ali has been helping me do this since she was three, although then, she ate more than she put in the boxes."

"Who are the lucky recipients?"

"It's a long list," Annie said, then put her finger to her chin and gazed at the ceiling. "Let's see. The kids' teachers, the lady at the library who absolutely adores them, the couple who own Yummies in a Jar, the man who brings our mail, Noah's hockey coach, Turtle Ted, the bus driver, Wally at the garage in town and Felicity and Ben Pierce."

"Wow, that *is* quite a list." He turned to Ali, who was just coming back inside. "Do you do this every year?"

She nodded, her curls bouncing around her head, and cheeks flushed red from the cold outside. "I like cracking eggs," she said with a wide smile as she pulled a bowl closer to herself.

Annie handed her a carton of eggs. "Four to get us started," she said. "Joe, you're on dry goods duty and I'll cream the butter."

Joe pulled out his phone and leaned it against the toaster. "We need some music. What's your favourite Christmas song, Ali?"

"Rudolph!" she cried.

"Rudolph it is."

While they stirred and scooped and cracked and measured, Christmas music filled the kitchen. When the boys came in from outside, frozen from being in the shed, they stopped long enough to eat pizzas and sip hot chocolate. Then, while Joe and Ali continued to drop hermits onto a cookie sheet, Annie took the already cooled cookies into the dining room to set them on the table. Once there, she paused for a moment to hear Ali giving Joe instructions in the kitchen.

"That one is too big," she heard Ali say.

"I thought maybe I could sneak that one for myself," Joe said with a little chuckle. Annie pictured the grin on his face and the way his cheeks dimpled when he smiled.

"Silly. You'll have your own box," Ali told him. "Yours will be the nicest one."

There was silence except for the odd clink of a spoon against a mixing bowl. Then Ali said, "Okay. We're done. These go in the oven and then you can take the shortbreads to Mummy."

From the dining room, Annie heard the sound of the oven door creaking open, and some trays sliding across the racks. A moment later, she looked up to see Joe in the doorway balancing four trays of shortbread.

"Where do you want these?" he asked, looking for space on the already crowded table.

Annie made room for them, then reached up to give his cheek a wipe with her apron. "Saving that cookie dough for later, were you?" she teased.

"Ah, you caught me." He made three trips back to the kitchen for more, then stood back, hands on hips, and smiled. "This is really something. I'm so glad you shared this tradition with me, ladies. I've had fun."

"Me too!" Ali cried, sidling up to Joe and taking hold of his hand. "Isn't Mummy pretty when she's got flour on her face?"

Annie spun around to look in the buffet mirror. "Oh gosh. Do I?"

When she turned back, Joe was smiling at her, but he looked down at Ali when he said, "She looks very beautiful indeed."

His eyes found Annie's across the table, and she felt a flush soaring up her neck and into her cheeks. "Stop it. Both of you, you're making me blush."

Ali tipped her nose to the ceiling and scrunched up her face. "What's that smell?"

"Oh no! The hermits."

Annie raced back to the kitchen, but she was too late to save the last two trays. She dumped them into the sink and leaned back against the counter to look at the clock.

"Wow! It's nearly nine and time for my assistant to be in bed." She tapped Ali on the nose.

"Can't I help you put the boxes together?"

Annie shook her head. "Sorry Pumpkin. It's late." She nudged Ali's shoulder. "Come on, say goodnight."

Ali threw her arms around Joe's legs and squeezed. "G'night Joe." He bent down to her level with a wide smile and she wrapped her arms around his neck and held on tight.

Joe seemed surprised that Ali would hug him so freely. He looked up at Annie and mouthed, "What's this?"

"She likes you, don't you Ali?" Annie said.

"Uh huh, and I like Ryder too and Max. Max is a super dog." Ali released her hold on Joe and raced out of the room shouting, "Super dog, super dog," at the top of her lungs.

"Where does she get all that energy?" Joe asked, as Ali raced past the door for the third time.

"I wish I knew. I'd could use some of that myself some days." Pushing off the counter, Annie waved her hand toward the hallway. "Now I've got to wrestle that energy into bed. If you aren't in a hurry, there's a bottle of wine in the fridge, left behind by a guest the other day. I could use some help to put those boxes to-gether."

"I'd be happy to."

As she went past the living room, Annie called out to Noah. "Half an hour more and then it's upstairs for you."

"Ah Mum. Ryder and I are watching a movie."

"You can watch the rest another day. Half an hour, young man. No arguments." He would be a bear in the morning if he didn't get a good night's sleep.

She refused Ali's usual bedtime story and knew that despite her daughter's protests, she would be asleep before Annie got back downstairs. She checked the nightlight, made sure Ali's goldfish had food, and then closed the door behind her on the way out.

When Annie returned to the kitchen, she found Joe with a tea towel over his shoulder, closing the dishwasher. The kitchen was spotless. He'd even swept the floor.

"Thank you," she said. "You didn't have to do that."

"It's the least I could do after such an entertaining evening." He handed her a glass of wine. "Ready to tackle those boxes?"

"Are you sure? I wasn't thinking about this. Shouldn't Ryder be getting to bed, too?"

"Are you kidding? What kid doesn't want to stay up a little later than usual? Besides, he doesn't have school in the morning like your kids do."

"Okay then. It will go pretty quickly."

They stood in the dining room archway, ready to do battle. Joe took a step inside and set his glass on the buffet. "Okay. Show me how the magic happens."

Annie handed him a tray of shortbread. "Just go around the table and put two in each box and I'll come behind with something else. I leave the chocolate ones to last so they don't melt into everything else."

"Okay, let's do this." Joe started off as instructed, putting two shortbread cookies into the boxes as he made his way around the table. When he got to the end, he picked up a plate of hermits and followed Annie, who had lemon drops. When they had finished filling all the boxes, Annie combined the last few strays onto one plate.

"You should start a business and sell these," Joe said, brushing cookie crumbs from his hands to an empty plate.

Annie smiled and handed him a leftover snickerdoodle. "No one would pay what I'd need to charge to make a living at it. Besides, the fun is in giving them away. It's a little part of Ali and I, and now you, in every box."

Their eyes met and lingered for a moment, his filled with something she could not pin. Curiosity? Intrigue? There was something definitely there. Annie felt a stirring inside, in response to whatever look he was giving her. Don't kiss me, she thought as he took a step closer. It will only confuse me more. But he *did* kiss her and when he did, Annie felt herself melting against his body, a yearning long buried inside her, urging its way to the surface. When the kiss ended, and they looked at each other, there was a question in his eyes.

She couldn't deny she was tempted to find out where this might lead, but she had the kids to think about, and Joe had Ryder. She needed to be careful with her emotions and chances were that Joe was just passing through. No matter how handsome he was, or how willing he'd been to help out, Annie needed something stable in her life, despite what her body was trying to tell her at that moment. She pressed lightly on his chest to stop a second kiss.

"I should…" She held her breath as she watched him pull away. The space between them cooled, and all too quickly, so did Joe.

"I'm sorry," he said, raking his hand through his hair. "I got caught up in the moment. That was…"

"Nice?" she whispered. His eyes widened in surprise. "Joe, I won't deny that I'm attracted to you." She took a step closer to him.

"But I overstepped. I'm sorry." He moved toward the door. "I really should go. Ryder needs his sleep, and I think we've over-stayed our welcome. I'm sorry. Truly. It was insensitive of me."

Suddenly, he was leaving. Leaving her, leaving the room, leaving the house, gathering his things, and Ryder, as if she was contagious with something and he couldn't get away fast enough.

"Wait. Joe. Can we talk about this?" She followed him to the door, but he was already pulling his coat over one arm and reaching for the door with the other. He looked back at her, a painful expression on his face.

"We'll be gone most of the day tomorrow, so we won't be troubling you again."

"You're not troubling me, Joe. Please, I don't understand the rush." She was desperate to know what had gone so terribly wrong in just a few seconds. What had she said?

"Where are we going tomorrow?" Ryder asked, sliding his feet into his boots.

"A surprise," Joe said, avoiding Annie's questioning look. "Let's go, kiddo. Time for bed."

Then they were gone, out the door, down the porch steps and into the shadows of the night.

She stood in the doorway, arms clutched about her, watching them walk side by side toward Moose Cottage, with Max bounding off ahead. The spotlights from the house and the peaks of the lodge silhouetted them against the snow. Ryder quickened his step to keep up with Joe's and nearly stumbled. Annie's hand stretched out to catch him, though they were far beyond her reach. Ryder caught his stride again and took his uncle's hand, which slowed them to a better pace.

Why the hurry, Joe? Annie wanted to ask. These arrangements for tomorrow were something he'd fabricated to deflect what had just happened between them. A couple of hours earlier, he'd offered to help her deliver the cookies tomorrow. There were no plans. He simply didn't want to be with her. What had she said, or done to push him away?

When she saw the flashlight on Joe's phone light up the steps of their cottage, she turned out the porch light and closed the door.

Chapter 8

"It will take a week for me to get the bathroom sorted out," Annie told the nurse, who was insisting it was time she took her father home. "We have a small bathroom on the main floor, but it isn't big enough for a wheelchair. It's a little complicated, but I have someone working on it."

"Tomorrow then?"

Annie raised her eyebrows. "You're kidding right? We have to rip out a closet, install a shower unit and rebuild the walls. I'm working on it but it won't be finished until next week at the earliest."

"A week is too long. It really should be tomorrow, if you can't take him today." The nurse pursed her lips. "We could arrange for him to go to one of the senior's homes in the interim if that would be better."

"Better for who?" Annie asked, irritation twitching at her lips. "Better for you, I suppose, so you don't have to deal with him. This is a hospital. It's for sick people. My father is sick."

"Technically, he's not. He's had a stroke, but he's much better. The help he needs he can get at home, or in a nursing home. That's not the same as being sick."

"I don't want to move him to a nursing home now, then move him again in a week's time. It will be confusing for him, unsettling. Wouldn't you say?" Annie tilted her head to one side, almost challenging the nurse to disagree.

Determination set in the woman's jaw. "But we don't keep patients once they are at his level of mobility. He could function just fine if he had a little help with certain things."

"Yes, things like bathing and using the toilet. Both of which he can't do in our home just yet. A week is all I'm asking. Less, if it can be done any faster."

The nurse's widening stance had Annie wondering if the woman was going to lose it, but she took a deep breath and seemed to soften, just a bit.

"It's most irregular. You've had time to organize this, Ms. Taylor. You should have seen to it."

"Time? His stroke was four days ago and I'm just learning now that you want to release him. How am I supposed to accommodate a wheelchair and everything he needs?"

"But as I suggested, there are alternatives. Oakwood Meadows, for instance, has an entire floor for respite care."

Annie was doing her best to keep her cool. Through a clenched jaw, she said, "I've already told you he's not going there. Maybe it's time you did what you're supposed to do, and that's take care of people who need it. What are our tax dollars going to, if not that?" She put the box of cookies Ali had marked for the nurses onto the counter, feeling she'd like to hurl them across the room. Then she stormed down the hall toward her father's room, gritting her teeth to keep from saying anything she might regret.

As she walked, she dialed Luke's number to ask how things were going. She'd spent the morning taking down most of the closet wall while Luke took Chelsea to a doctor's appointment. When she had left to visit her father, one half of the closet wall was down to the studs, though she'd done nothing to clear up the debris. She knew Luke would take care of that when he arrived, which should have been an hour ago.

Now, she was so angry she needed to talk to someone who would sympathize with her and have her back on this. Annie could not keep the frustration from her voice as she explained the situation to Luke.

"How can they possibly expect me to take him home any sooner?" There was a quiver in her voice as she did her best to keep back the tears. She didn't want her father knowing any of this. He couldn't see how upset she was when she got to his room.

"I'm on it," was all Luke shouted over the sounds of sirens passing.

"Where are you? I thought you were at the house by now."

"Chelsea's appointment took longer than I'd planned. I'm on my way now. I'm guessing the back door is still unlocked."

"Isn't it always?"

"Annie, you've got to stop doing that. One of these days, someone is going to walk in and steal everything out from under you."

"If they want my ten-year-old TV and my rickety kitchen set, they can have them. You know I have nothing anyone would want."

"It doesn't matter. Just lock your doors, please. It will make me feel better."

"Fine. From now on, I'll lock my doors. But right now, Dad is my priority."

Luke heaved an audible sigh that made her wince. He wasn't to blame for this. She shouldn't take it out on him.

"I get that," he said. "I'm ten minutes from Baysville, another fifteen to your place."

"Okay. I'm sorry. I'll see you later." Annie disconnected the call and brushed the tears she hadn't been able to stop before turning down the hall to her father's room. When she arrived, the physiotherapist was just bringing him back from his session.

Nancy was about a decade older than Annie, and a sturdy foot taller, with she had a heart the size of a mountain. She saw the worry on Annie's face and asked her what was wrong. While they waited for a nurse to help her father in the bathroom, Annie whispered her concerns, not wanting her father to overhear.

"I just don't understand the rush and I certainly don't want to move him twice," she told Nancy.

"It's the lack of beds. Always a shortage. You know, I could request more time to work with him here. It might delay his release by a few days."

"Could you?"

"No harm in trying. Let me put that request in. I can call you at home, if that's okay."

"Or my cell." Annie pulled out a business card from the lodge and handed it to Nancy. "I only need a few days, a week at the most, and we'll be ready for him to come home."

"Leave it with me." Nancy turned to pat Sam on the shoulder as the nurse helped him into bed. "Good session today, Sam. See you tomorrow. No chasing the nurses down the hall tonight." She laughed out loud as Sam grinned at her, one side of his mouth shaping into a smile, the other staying impossibly still.

"Hey Dad." Annie settled on the side of the bed and kissed his cheek once Nancy and the nurse had left the room. "How's it going?"

"Gooz," he replied. "I heed ree laps, today."

"Three laps. Good for you. I think your speech is clearer." Or I'm just learning to understand, Slur, she thought.

He smiled at her and stroked her hand. She looked down at it in surprise. "Dad. That was your bad hand. You just moved it on your own."

He grinned at her, eyes full of fun. "Shurprise!"

"Oh Dad, that's fantastic. You'll be zipping around our place in the golf cart by spring. I just know it."

One half of her father's face beamed with joy.

They had a nice visit, getting the small talk out of the way. Then, when the conversation ran dry, Annie pulled out the deck of cards and the cribbage board she'd tucked into her bag. They were easy company for each other, Annie moving both their pegs around the board and Sam doing his best to keep the cards in his hands.

Eventually, he grew tired and drifted off to sleep. She scrawled him a note and tucked it into his good hand, saying she'd be back the next day.

An afternoon without kids in tow meant she had time to accomplish a few errands, the last of which was to visit the bank and plead with the manager to accept one month's payment toward her debt. Reluctantly, he agreed.

"Only because it's Christmas," he warned. "You'll be getting a revised notice right after the holidays. This doesn't stop the foreclosure proceedings," he said. "All this has done is delay it a month." She would take that for now and after Christmas, she'd worry about the rest.

He leaned across the desk and gave her the stern school principal look she'd come to expect from him.

"I could put you in touch with a good realtor, Annie. Someone who could get you a good price for your place."

Annie bit the inside of her cheek to keep from arguing with him, but she couldn't help it. "The snowmobilers have started coming. That will help," she said, gathering her purse and pushing out of her chair.

"But will it be enough?" He slid a business card across the desk to her. "Call this number. They'll give you an estimate. You might be surprised."

When she got to the truck, Annie shoved the card into the console along with the three others he'd given her on previous visits. Each time she said she would not sell. She meant it then, and she meant it now. She scrolled through her emails, willing the bookings to come in for the ice fishing and snowmobilers. But there were none. Only advertisements for things she didn't want and spam email she deleted without opening. There was not even a quote request for the new rates she'd put up to entice retreat packages. The site had plenty of hits, but no one seemed interested in committing to a reservation. She dropped her phone into her purse and started the engine.

She arrived home, just in time to see the kids climbing down from the bus. Chelsea was close behind Noah, hurrying to keep up. She hadn't realized Luke had arranged with the school to have Chelsea ride the bus, but it made sense. She should have thought of it or offered to pick her up. Where was her head lately?

Inside, as she helped them out of their boots and coats, Luke came down the hallway, scooped up Chelsea and planted a kiss on her forehead.

"How was school?" he asked, spinning her around.

"Awesome!"

"Awesome? Well, that's wonderful." Luke tickled her until Chelsea begged him to stop. Then she held up a candy cane.

"Turtle Ted gave us all one. Can I eat it now?"

"I guess one little candy cane won't ruin your appetite." Luke set her down and looked up at Annie as the kids headed for the living room to watch TV.

Annie watched Chelsea hurry away and couldn't help looking at up at Luke. She'd seen how good he was with his daughter before, but something in the way he spoke to Chelsea today, the way her face lit up when she saw him, the way the two of them were together, left her wondering. Luke was a good father and a good man. Why couldn't she love him?

"Have a moment?" he asked, slicing into her thoughts.

She couldn't help noticing the icy tone in his voice or how much his attitude had gone from Mr. Fun Guy to Mr. I've Got a Job To Do in the blink of an eye. She preferred the first version, but it was her own doing that brought on his abrupt change. She nodded and followed him down the hall.

"How's it going? Do you think taking out that closet is going to be enough space?" The front entranceway was now a wide open space where the closet had been. "It looks so strange," she said, pacing the openness of it.

Luke extended his tape measure and laid it across the floor to show where the new wall of the bathroom would come. "I think we might have to lose a bit of the foyer, but it shouldn't be a problem. The bathroom will come out to here, but there's still room to get in and out of the front door and for Sam to turn his chair around." He moved around the entranceway as if he were pushing a wheelchair.

"Whatever we have to do. Do I need to hire a plumber?"

Luke scratched his chin stubble with the eraser end of a pencil. "I hired someone already. I can reframe it all, drywall it, paint and paper, but I can't do the plumbing."

"Thank you, but can we keep the cost as low as possible? I don't want to skimp on what Dad needs, but you know my situation." When Luke let out an exhaustive sigh, she knew what he was thinking, but she had no wish for a repeat of their previous discussions. "Luke…"

"Yeah. I know." He waved a dismissive hand and turned back to his work. Annie went to the kitchen to make supper.

During their meal of chili with a bowl of nachos for dipping, Annie suggested she take Chelsea and Ali to deliver Felicity and Ben's cookies. Noah was set on helping Luke and Annie had no wish to drag him away. He would only be bored if he went with them, so when they finished eating, she bundled Chelsea and Ali up and drove over to what had once been the Bailey Cottage but now prominently displayed a wooden sign which said, *Ben and Felicity's Castle.*

"Annie! What a lovely surprise!" Felicity said when she answered the door. "You've brought Ali and Chelsea too. Come inside out of the cold." She called out to Ben to come and see the visitors.

"I'd better put the kettle on," he said, when he came through from the living room. "Will you have tea, my dear Miss Ali and Miss Chelsea?" Ali giggled, and Chelsea put her hands over her face to hide her embarrassment.

"We brought you cookies," Ali said, reaching to give Ben the box.

"Oh, I've heard about these famous cookies. Let's put them on a plate and have them with our tea."

Ben filled the kettle while everyone took their coats off and found a place at the kitchen table.

"It's so roomy in here now," Annie said, watching Felicity prepare a tray of cups and plates and napkins, moving about her newly extended kitchen with ease. "I'll bet you love the changes."

"We do. Especially when we have all the kids here. Now there's room for everyone to stretch out and we aren't on top of each other anymore." She set flowery napkins in front of the girls. "We don't often get to see you these days, Chelsea. How's your Dad?"

"He's helping Annie fix the bathroom."

Annie explained. "We have to refit the downstairs bathroom for when Dad comes home. The hospital is hounding me about releasing him."

Ben settled into a chair beside Felicity. "You've got Joe there. With his experience, I'm sure he could help,".

"How is it you know Joe, anyway?" Annie asked, recalling the day Ryder had got his foot stuck and Joe had gone through the woods to get help.

Felicity and Ben exchanged an indiscernible look that had Annie wondering what they were holding back. Felicity nudged Ben's elbow.

"Why don't you take the girls out to the Muskoka room where they can play that new game you bought? What's it called?"

Ben winked at Ali. "She means Snakes and Ladders. Want to play?"

"Can I be the red guy?" Chelsea asked, climbing down from her chair. "It's my favourite colour."

"As long as I get to be black. It always reminds me of black licorice, my favourite." Ben poured three cups of tea, sweetened the girls' and added milk to all of them. Then he put the cups on a tray with some of the cookies. "Okay, lead the way, Miss Ali."

When they were alone, Felicity poured Annie's tea and her own. Then she reached out and took Annie's hand.

"How are you doing, Annie? It can't be easy, coping with everything on your own over there. Especially with your dad in the hospital."

"We're managing." Annie squirmed a little under Felicity's gaze. "The kids are a big help and Luke will come out if I need him." Annie sipped her tea, then set down the cup. "You're avoiding my question. I asked you how you know Joe?"

Felicity rimmed her cup with her thumb. "Well, let's see. He owns Melville's now, so he came out to do an inspection on the work here and to follow up with us."

"There's a *but* in there somewhere. I can hear it."

"But I've known him a little longer than that." Felicity picked at her napkin nervously, not looking up.

"What is it you're not telling me, Felicity? Should I be worried? He's booked with us for ten days and I have to think about the kids."

"Oh, no! Nothing like that. You and the kids are perfectly fine with Joe around."

"But there is something."

"Nothing like what you're thinking. Joe's a good man, Annie. A very good man."

"It sounds as if you know him, really know him."

Felicity nodded. "I've known him for about eight or maybe it's nine years."

"Is he a friend of Tom's or Olivia's?"

"I'm sure they've met him at some point in time. Why are you asking? You have this schoolgirl look about you, as if you were sixteen again and curious about a boy in your class. Is there something going on between the two of you?"

"He's a guest, Felicity. Really!"

"A very nice one. I wouldn't be surprised if you felt something for him."

"I hardly know the man," Annie gasped, her eyes now averting Felicity's gaze and dashing to the blackness outside the window. Had Joe said something to them about the kiss the other night? Had he told them he was interested in her? Or that she might be interested in him? Who else knew?

"Alright. Alright. He kissed me. Gosh, you're worse than my mother was at getting things out of me."

Felicity's eyes lit up. "Oh! How was that?"

Annie grinned, sheepishly. "It was nice. But then he just left, as if I had the plague or something." She threw up her hands and sighed. "I don't get it. What did I do wrong?"

"I'm sure you didn't do anything wrong. Maybe he felt he was rushing things. Even you said you just met him. Are you saying you'd like something more?"

"Maybe. Well, yes, if I'm honest. I think I would like there to be something more."

A satisfied smile picked at the corners of Felicity's mouth as she lifted her teacup and nodded her approval.

Chapter 9

It was an hour later when Annie pulled into the driveway, and found a delivery truck by the front door, and two men hauling a gigantic box into the house. Joe was there, directing them through the door. She sent the girls up the back steps into the house while she went to the front to see what was going on.

"I'm not sure it's going to go through," one of the delivery men said, wedging himself between the box and the open door-frame.

"Sure it will," the other called out. "If we take the cardboard off and remove the wooden slats."

Once they'd done that, the new shower unit went easily through the door and into the new bathroom. Annie followed them inside and gasped at the amount of work Luke had done while she'd been at Ben and Felicity's. The framework of the new wall was finished and half the drywall was up, but wisely, he'd left enough room to bring in the shower unit before closing up the wall.

"You did all this in a couple of hours?" She stepped back, out of the way, while the men set the new shower in place.

"I had help," Luke confessed. He flashed a hesitant look in Joe's direction, giving him nonverbal credit for his part in the work. Joe hadn't noticed because he who was shaking hands with the delivery men.

"Anytime man," one man was saying as he clapped Joe on the back.

"Where's my invoice?" Joe asked in mocking laughter, as they headed toward the door.

The man laughed, too. "Come off it. You know it's been taken care of, so why are you asking?"

Annie pushed past Luke and hurried toward them. "No. You can't…" she protested, but the men ignored her and closed the door on their way out.

Joe turned and set his hand on her arm to prevent her from going after them. "It's fine, Annie. Honestly, just let them go."

"But they need to be paid."

"You heard the man. It's taken care of," he repeated.

Annie frowned at him. Still irritated by his abrupt departure the night before and now frustrated by this sudden act of charity, she wanted answers. But for now, she let the matter drop.

Instead, she made no attempt to hide the smirk in her voice when she asked what he was doing there. "I thought you had other plans all day today."

"Luke called Melville's looking for a plumber and when he told me it was for you, I decided to do the work myself."

Fists on her hips, Annie protested. "I won't take charity. I'll pay you and I'll pay for the unit."

"There's no charge, so don't worry about it. I just called in a favour."

"But…"

"No buts," he said, placing a hand on her shoulder. "Can't you just let someone take care of you for a change?"

Her eyes flitted up at him. "What did you just say?"

He held her gaze. "Come on, Annie. You do a lot for everyone else. Why can't someone do something for you, for once?"

A couple of days ago, she'd said those exact words to herself. She was exhausted from the constant battles in her life; lack of money, solving customers' problems, fighting with nurses. Wasn't taking care of children enough for one person? Joe wanted to do something nice for her, but what was the catch? Nobody did things like this for no reason.

Her gaze flitted to Luke, who was bent over the base of the new shower. She knew what Luke's price was if she wanted him to take care of her. Funny how she always had to ask for things from him, though. He never seemed to be aware of her needs, but Joe seemed to know what she needed almost before she did. His eyes were fixed on her, waiting for her to say something.

"Okay. But next year they're getting a box of cookies. An enormous one."

Joe laughed. "They'll love it." He turned her attention to the new shower. "I wish you'd said something about this last night. I could have started first thing this morning."

"When last night?" She leaned closer to whisper. "You mean when you were running out the door?" She flitted a glance toward Luke, who, thankfully, had his attention on a sheet of drywall.

Joe waved Annie into her father's room. "Come and see what we've done in here."

She trailed after him, wondering if she really wanted to have this conversation or not. Joe closed the door behind them.

"I'm sorry about that. I should have explained. But I was worried Annie. Worried that we were taking things too fast. I mean, you don't know me very well and…"

"It was a kiss, Joe. A nice one, I'll admit, but still just a kiss."

"Are you saying you didn't like it?"

"No. That's not what I'm saying at all. I did, and I'd like to spend some time getting to know you, if you don't go running off whenever we get a little too close."

He grinned. "Okay. But you'll let me know if things are going too fast."

She nodded. "I definitely will." She stepped closer to him and kissed him on the cheek. "Was that okay?"

He smiled. "Yeah, I guess I can live with that, if you can." He turned her around to see what they'd done in her father's room earlier. Annie was surprised.

"How did you get all this and the work on the bathroom done in such a short time?"

Sam's dresser now stood between the two windows, leaving the bed closer to the door. An easy chair she did not recognize replaced the straight back one and a new reading lamp stood behind it. New throw pillows were added to the freshly made bed and a blanket that might have come from the upstairs linen closet lay over the bottom of it.

"This looks great," she said, inspecting the hospital corners on the bed. "Did you do this?"

"I had a good teacher," he grinned. "The chair was hanging around the office. I think George used to nap in it sometimes. It's not new, but it's in good shape. It reclines, so Sam can relax. I also brought a TV from the office, but it's still in the hallway. I wasn't sure where to put it." He crossed the room to stand beside the chair. "If he's watching from here, maybe it should go on the dresser. But if he's lying in bed, maybe it should go on the wall."

"How about one of those retractable wall mounts that swivel?" Annie suggested.

Joe slapped his forehead. "Why didn't I think of that?"

"You would have. Thank you for doing all this." She circled the room, then came back to stand beside him.

"Ryder and Noah helped too. They have been our apprentices." Joe rolled forward on the balls of his feet, his chest swelling a little with pride.

"Well, it's wonderful and I can't thank you enough."

Luke knocked and opened the door then. "Can I see you a minute, Annie?"

Joe backed out of the room. "I'll let the two of you talk."

When Joe left, it felt as if all the warmth in the room had gone with him. Annie looked up at Luke, who stood, hands at his sides, an impatient look on his face, as he closed the door.

"What do you want to talk about, Luke? I can pay you for this work, but it will have to wait until after Christmas when the ice fishing bookings start coming in."

"I'm not worried about being paid. You know that. It's about the letters that were on your desk."

"*In* my desk, you mean."

"No. I mean on your desk, Annie. Sitting out for anyone to see."

"No. They were in their envelopes in the middle drawer of my desk. It's where I keep all my correspondence until I've dealt with it."

"Not when I went into your office. I needed a pencil and paper. The letters were on the desk, out of the envelopes, for anyone to see."

He put a hand on each of her shoulders, drawing her gaze to his. "Is it possible that someone was looking through them?"

"Like whom?"

"Like Joe, maybe? I went out to the toolshed to get a few things and when I came back, he was in there. I told you, Annie. You can't trust this guy."

"You hired him."

"I called Melville's because they're the best and because I knew I could defer the bill for sixty days. I didn't know Joe would be the one to come out." He cocked his head to one side. "But that's not the point. I think he was taking pictures of your letters."

Annie frowned. "To what end, Luke? What could Joe possibly want with copies of my foreclosure letters?"

"I don't know, but I don't trust him. I told you there's something off about him."

"Maybe I forgot to put those letters away after I showed them to you the other day."

Luke grunted. "Doubtful. I know how meticulous you are with things like that."

"Well, then, there's another explanation, and I'm sure it will come out eventually."

Luke rolled his eyes and stalked out of the room, not quite slamming the door on his way out.

Chapter 10

The next morning, when the kids had left for school, Annie started the laundry, made the beds and then took a few moments over her morning coffee to rethink the letter incident from last night. Then, she'd been too angry to deal with the issue, but she had looked and just as Luke said, the letters were spread out on her desk, three of them side by side. She found it odd that Joe would come into the house without letting Luke know he was there; odder still that he would have taken these letters out of her desk. It would have meant he was snooping and Joe didn't seem the type who would do that. Yet there they were, and Luke had seen Joe in her office. Could he have been taking pictures of her letters and, if so, why?

Who was Joe Hewitt, anyway? Her fingers flew over the keyboard of her computer as she typed in *Joe Hewitt*, then added *plumber* to the search bar. A phone directory page popped up with six listings. Joe's Plumbing and Pipe Fitting, Joe and Son's plumbers, Joseph Plumber on twenty-fourth street, two Joe Simpsons on Plumber Lane and one J. Hewitt in Dorset. She checked the phone number against the one Joe had used to confirm his booking. It wasn't the same.

A Google search produced a newspaper article about the sale of Melville's in Huntsville two months ago. She clicked on it and saw a photograph of Joe Hewitt and George Melville standing behind a desk, shaking hands. The article gave only a little background on Joe and said that he was making no preliminary changes and Melville's would run much as it had done for the past thirty years. He hadn't been lying about that.

Her cell phone chirped, and she pulled it from her pocket to see an unfamiliar number on the screen. "Annie's Lodge. How can I help you?"

"Hello. Is this Annie Taylor?"

"It is. Who's calling?"

"My name is Gayle Sutherland, and I'm a real estate agent. I understand you might sell your property, and I wondered if you would consider giving me the opportunity to do an evaluation for you."

"Selling? No, I'm not… Gayle? It's Gayle, right?"

"That's right. Gayle Sutherland. You've probably seen my picture on the billboards just outside of town by the new subdivision near Deerhurst."

"I can't say that I have. Who did you say mentioned I might consider selling?"

"I don't think I said." She heard Gayle's fingernails tapping on a hard surface and knew the woman wasn't about to reveal anything.

"It doesn't matter. I think I have a good idea who's behind this charade."

"Does that mean you're not selling?"

"That's exactly what it means, Miss Sutherland. Good day!" Annie swiped to disconnect the call and threw her phone down on the desk. In a fit of frustration, she kicked the garbage can and sent it hurling across the room.

Luke!

His words, encouraging her to sell, whirled around in her mind and suddenly, the letters splayed out on her desk made sense. It wasn't Joe who'd been in there. It was Luke. He'd gathered all the information he needed, then contacted a real estate agent saying she wanted to sell before the bank could foreclose. Then there was this instant dislike of Joe, which he'd already a couple of times? Was he trying to set Joe up to be the bad guy here?

Out of the corner of her eye, Annie caught the movement of someone coming down the hallway. Joe came to lean on the doorframe. It was Luke she really wanted to talk to, but he wouldn't arrive until he'd dropped Chelsea off at school.

"Everything okay? I heard a crash." Joe leaned on the doorframe. When she didn't respond right away, he jerked a thumb over his shoulder. "It's coming along nicely in there. You want to look?"

"I'm a bit busy at the moment, and yes, everything is fine. Just me and the garbage pail having a disagreement."

Joe picked up the can and put it back beside her desk. "Looks like the can got the better end of the deal. You look like you're ready to kill someone, in the verbal sense, I'm guessing."

"I am," she snapped. "So, when I ask you what I'm going to ask you, don't mess with me, alright?" She pushed out of her chair and stood up to face him.

Joe put his hands in the air and backed away. "Alright. Ask away. I've got nothing to hide. But don't mind me if I put some distance between your anger and my body. I'm out of practice at the boxing ring." He leaned against the wall, a slow smirk spreading across his face that told her he was enjoying this. But it made her twice as angry.

"Why were you in my office yesterday?"

Joe frowned. "What makes you think I was in here?" He paused. "Oh, I get it. Luke said something, didn't he?"

This would get her nowhere. They would both deny it. "Forget I asked. Next question." She locked eyes with his. "What favours did you call in to get that shower?"

"It was nothing."

"Nothing?" She widened her stance and stared at him. "I want to know who owed you a two-thousand-dollar favour. I know what those things cost."

Joe lowered his gaze. Then calmly, slowly, he said, "Don't do this, Annie. It's not who you are."

"You don't know anything about me," she hissed, then turned back to her desk. He followed, matching step for angry step.

"You're wrong. I know plenty. You're a wonderful mother. You are well-loved and respected by everyone in the community, you are kind to people you don't even know, people like Mr. Gibson, who has a job now, thanks to you. Ryder and I had breakfast there yesterday morning, and he was in the kitchen. He sends his regards, by the way. And here's another thing I know about you, Annie Taylor. You would give someone the shirt off your back and your last loaf of bread, even if it meant you went without."

She knew he was right, and she didn't much like this miserable, angry person she'd become. She caught him staring at her, and his gaze softened as tears welled in her eyes. She thought of yesterday morning when she'd had it out with the nurse at the hospital, and later when she was short with the bank manager and just now, when she'd been rude to Gayle, what's-her-name from the real estate company.

"I'm sorry. I'm letting everything get to me."

Joe pulled her into his arms and ran his hands down her back. "You're under a lot of stress. It's okay. People understand."

She nodded, and he lifted her chin. Was he going to kiss her again? She hoped he would. She relaxed deeper into his arms, waiting, anticipating, but he pulled away.

"I'm sorry. I shouldn't."

"I thought we talked about this. It wasn't a one-sided kiss, Joe. I wanted it and if I'm being honest, I wanted more than just a kiss, but... I can't help thinking I did or said something wrong."

"No. No. It wasn't you, Annie. It could never be your fault."

"I don't know why, Joe, but I feel completely comfortable with you. It's as if I've known you all my life. It seems strange, I know, but I can't help how I feel."

She stumbled over her words, fighting to get a grip on this feeling he instilled in her. Her eyes found his, and in that moment, they seemed to be lost in time. Joe reached out and cupped her face between his hands, then kissed her hard, passionately, with hunger in every provocative move of his lips. When he let her go, he took a breath and sighed. "My sweet, sweet, Annie. I love you."

Breathless after the kiss, but stunned by what he said, Annie had to stop herself from laughing out loud. "I'm sorry. I don't understand. I'll admit that was a great kiss, but how could you possibly say that? We just met."

He shrugged. "Don't discount what you said a moment ago about feeling like you've known me all your life. I know how that feels because I love you, Annie. I want to spend every waking minute with you and when I'm sleeping, I want to feel you next to me and know that when I wake up, you'll be there. When you touch a plant, or a bowl, or a chair, I want to be that plant or bowl or chair. When you kiss your children goodnight, I want to watch you mother them and love them, and hold them. If you cry, I want to kiss away your tears and hold you until you aren't sad anymore. And when you're angry, I want to crush whatever is upsetting you, because it has no business bringing you pain or worry or putting wrinkles on that beautiful face."

She relaxed against him. "I don't know how you can know all that, when we hardly know each other, but I have to admit, I like the way it sounds." He held her a long while, a comforting silence filling the room until at last he drew her away from him. "What has upset you? Please tell me. Maybe I can help. At the very least, I can listen."

They sat in chairs near the window, facing each other, with the sun glistening off the lake, bouncing beams of light against the trees in the distance. Annie picked thoughtfully at her fingernails for a moment. Then, without hesitation, she told him.

"Luke is determined that I should sell this place and move in with him. It's his answer to my financial woes. He loves me too." She laughed. "So, you see why I had to ask how you could know you love me after just meeting."

"Do you love him?"

"Not the way he'd like me to. He's a good man. And he's kind to the kids, but the love you just described is not what I feel for Luke. I suspect that what he feels for me isn't that kind of love, either. It's an obligation or some false sense of duty or something. But it's not love. If you love someone, you wouldn't sick Gayle Sutherland on them."

"I have no idea who she is, but I'm sure you'll tell me." His thumb caressed the back of her hand as his eyes searched hers.

"A real estate agent. She wanted to come out and do an evaluation on the place."

"Ah. What do you want to do?"

Annie looked out the window where the lake dazzled in the sunlight, and stared at a set of rabbit tracks leading from the house down toward the dock. They disappeared over the side of a mound in the snow. Lucky rabbit, she thought. No bills to pay. No one making demands on you, you can't keep.

"I want to stay here," she said, at last. "This was our dream, and just because my husband isn't here to see it through doesn't mean the kids and I can't, or shouldn't. My father gave up his home to come here to help. How could I ask him to move again? Especially now, in his condition."

"Then we must find a way to make this place pay for itself. Try something new. Something you're not already doing."

Her lip curled into a smile when he said, we. She liked the enthusiasm that lit up his face. "Like what? Because if you've got ideas, Joe, I'm all ears."

"Well, why don't you sell off some of your evergreens? If you cleared an acre this year, then replant more just to Christmas trees, maybe it could be an annual event. At Hallowe'en you could grow pumpkins and at Easter time have an egg hunt."

"I hadn't thought of anything like that."

"I wasn't kidding when I said you should start a baking business. Package up the cookies, create a great label and get them out in the community. Maybe John and Lynn over at Yummies will take a few."

"But I'd need a lot more than that to pay off my debts."

"You have to start somewhere. What about the lodge? It's empty most of the time. Is there something you could do there? Maybe it could be a daycare."

"I don't have time to run a daycare."

"No, someone else could run it. You'd just rent it to them."

"I hadn't thought of that. I think it's too far away from town, but I had been thinking about yoga retreats or writer's getaways, things like that."

"That's the idea. Family reunions, maybe."

The more they talked, the more Annie began to imagine the possibilities. "I could make up fliers with a few future events on it so people would know what was coming."

"Sure, and why not have your Christmas Eve party again, only this time charge an admission? People know how hard everyone was hit during the pandemic. If you tell your story, they will understand."

Annie twisted her hands together. "I don't know. I'm not keen on taking money from people without something in return. It seems wrong."

"What if you charged a twenty-five-dollar fee for the Christmas Eve bash and everyone got a free box of your home-made cookies?"

"Those are pretty expensive cookies."

"They're not buying the cookies. They're buying their dinner and the good feeling they get from donating to a worthy cause. That way, you feel like you're giving something back. You don't have to decide today, but you have to do something soon, right?"

"Yes. I do."

"Then why not start with a tree sale? Luke and I can help with that. We can sell pre-cut trees or people can go into the woods and cut their own".

"Is there enough time to organize it all?"

"There would be, if we started soon."

Would there, though? She had knitting projects to do, the kids to take care of, guests coming and going and her father was coming home.

"I just don't know, Joe. I mean, it's a good idea, but I can't see how there would be time."

"How much would you charge per tree? Twenty, twenty-five dollars. You could sell your cookies and hot chocolate and play Christmas Carols over a loudspeaker."

"Twenty-five dollars a tree, times fifty trees is…" Her eyes rolled back while she did the math in her head. "…one month's mortgage payment! Okay. That's possible."

"You can start the sale on Thursday or Friday maybe, then have the Christmas Eve party on Sunday night to wind things up."

Annie felt herself pulled along by his enthusiasm. "I could make up flyers and give some out to the mums at school."

"Now you're talking." He pulled her gaze to meet his. "Look Annie. I know you think I don't know you very well, but I know you don't want to sell this place, and I think Luke is wrong for suggesting you should. You have a gold mine here. You just haven't tapped all the resources yet."

She nodded as his ideas percolated in her mind. Maybe Joe was right. Maybe there were other things she could do too that she hadn't thought of yet. But why did he care? What difference did it make to him whether she sold the place, or went bankrupt, or actually made a go of it? Oh right. He loved her. Well, maybe he did and maybe he didn't. Either way, he was right. She had to give it at least one more try.

"Okay. One last flailing attempt to save the ship from sinking," she said. "But there's something I want to know first. I asked you a while ago how you got a free shower unit for my father?"

Joe smiled. "Alright, if you really must know, I'll tell you. I did some work for a very wealthy man who was renovating a cottage. Well, no, it was more like a mansion, just north of Parry Sound, along the French River. He put me up in the gatehouse, fed me, gave me wine and I renovated his six bathrooms, put in a chef's dream of a kitchen, installed an outdoor shower, a hot tub, and built a sauna. It was about a year's worth of work."

"This led to a free shower because?"

"Because when it was all done, he said, if there was anything he could ever do for me, just ask. So, I did. One of the many companies he owns manufactures these things. Trust me, he can afford to donate a shower or two, or six."

"Who is this man?"

"He'd rather be anonymous, but it's all on the up and up. No shady deals. I promise. I wouldn't do that."

A ripple of curiosity ran through her. Who are you, Joe Hewitt, she thought to herself? You walk into my life and make everything better. "I don't know what I would have done if you hadn't come along."

"I'm just helping. No big deal."

"But it is a big deal to me. Thank you."

There was a moment when their eyes met, that Annie was sure Joe was going to kiss her again. She shifted slightly in her chair, anticipating, wanting him to kiss her, longing to be in his arms, where she felt safe, warm and cherished. That was exactly what she felt when he'd kissed her before. She wasn't as sure of her feelings as he was, but she knew this was not what she'd felt for Luke. This was more like the excitement she remembered from years ago. The first touch, the first kiss, the first caress of a cupped hand on her cheek. Oh, how she missed that intimacy with a man, with her husband.

Joe leaned forward in his seat, their knees touching, as he reached out to take her hand in his. "Annie, there's something I've been meaning to tell you."

"What is it?"

Just then, they heard a rumbling in the distance, and Annie's heart sank. She knew the sound of Luke's truck from half a mile away and that meant this quiet, intimate moment with Joe had to end.

"Ah, maybe we can talk later," he said.

"Sure."

Chapter 11

Annie hadn't even got her coat on before Ali, Noah and Chelsea got off the bus and tore down the driveway. Noah sped up the back steps, pushing his sister roughly aside, and nearly knocking Annie over in the process.

"Slow down!" She called out. "Why are you so early?"

"Ted is sick. We had another driver." Noah threw his backpack onto the floor and left a trail of mittens, hat, and boots all the way to the kitchen. "What's t'eat? I'm starved."

"Starving," Annie corrected as she pulled Ali's boots off and hung up her coat and hat. Making her way out of the mudroom, she gathered Noah's trail of mislaid items and flopped down on the chair next to him. Mother's intuition told Annie that Noah was keeping something from her, but she would leave it until he was ready to talk.

"Do you want a flatbread with salami and stuff on it?"

"Sure. Sounds good. Whatever."

Noah was already heading for the living room and she didn't have the heart to insist he change his tone or to explain his attitude. She turned to Chelsea and Ali, who were hovering over the apple bowl.

"I can't decide," Ali said. "They all look so red and juicy."

"Close your eyes and go eenny, meeny, miny, moe." Annie demonstrated for her.

Ali took her mother's advice, said the verse as she tapped each apple, then opened her eyes to reveal her choice. "Oh, I wanted that one." She pointed to a different apple.

Annie reached over and handed it to her. "Then have that one. What about you, Chelsea? An apple, or would you rather have something else?"

"An apple. But can you cut it please? I have that wiggly tooth in front." Chelsea stuck her finger in her mouth and pushed on her loose tooth.

"That is certainly getting wiggly. Won't be long now."

Ali held up her apple. "Can you cut mine too, and peel it, please?"

"Okay, then. Apples it is."

Chelsea headed to the living room, while Ali sat in her chair watching Annie.

"Did Mrs. Vickers tell you to listen more?" Annie asked.

"Nope. Now I'm too quiet."

"That's a shocker."

"Yeah. She said it's okay for me to talk when I'm answering a question, but not when she's trying to talk to the class. I'm just supposed to listen then."

"Anything interesting happen in Miss Wight's class?"

"You mean about Noah?"

"Maybe."

"Noah said I shouldn't tell you."

"He did? Okay then. You should keep his confidence."

"Coffin dance?"

"Con-fi-dance. It's when someone wants you to keep their secret. They trust you not to tell anyone else. Unless it's something dangerous or hurtful, we should never tell, right?"

"Right, Mummy."

Annie handed her two bowls of apples, peeled and sliced. "Now go watch TV with your brother and Chelsea while I get supper organized, okay?"

Ali nearly collided with Joe, who was standing in the doorway. "Hi Joe!" she said with a wide grin. "Is Ryder here too?"

"He's watching TV with Noah."

Joe laughed out loud when Ali barreled past Max, whose new permanent sleeping place seemed to be just outside the kitchen door.

As she went, she shouted, "Superdog!" which made Max perk up his ears. He gave her a grunt, then returned to his former sleeping position.

Annie started slicing salami for Noah's flatbread. "Does Ryder like these?"

"I'm sure he'd love one, but don't go to any trouble. I can take him home and get him something."

"Seems a little silly when he's already here and it takes next to nothing to make one more. Or two, if you want one, too?"

Joe shook his head. "I'm good. But I am in a kind of limbo with the bathroom. I could keep going, but I don't want to step on Luke's toes. He's got a plan, and I just agreed to do the plumbing work and help out with the rest."

"Where is he?"

Joe shrugged. "He said he had errands and left. About an hour ago."

"Let me call him. I still want to speak to him about that real estate agent."

"Maybe it wasn't him. Maybe…"

Annie raised her hand. "Don't defend him, Joe. It wouldn't be the first time he's overstepped, and I'm a little fed up with him pushing me all the time." She lifted the kettle. "Want tea?"

"I'd love some. But why don't I make it while you make that call?"

Luke answered on the third ring—unusual for him.

"Hey Annie," he sighed into the phone. "What's up? I'm just going to pick up supper, then go and get Chels. Sorry I left in such a rush."

"Chelsea is here, Luke. She got off the bus with my kids. Where are you?"

"She did? Shit. I forgot. Guess I've got too much on my mind. What did you want to talk about?"

"Joe was wondering if he should keep going or wait for you to come back. Shall I tell him to wait?"

"Yeah. That's good. Was that all? I'm just heading into the drive-through and I'm about to order."

"I've got supper going here. Why don't you and Chelsea eat with us?" Luke let out a grunt and Annie knew he was thinking what it would cost her to feed them. "It's not a big deal, Luke. What are a couple of meals while you work on the bathroom?"

"Asks the woman who can't pay her bills…" Luke sniffed. "I gotta go, Annie. Really. The line is moving up."

"One more thing, Luke. Really quick. Do you know a Gayle Sutherland?"

"The real estate agent? Her picture is on every billboard from here to Dorset."

"That's what she told me, although I can't say as I've ever noticed."

"Why? Have you decided to sell?" Was that a hopeful lilt in his voice?

"She called me. Someone told her I was selling."

"Oh, I see. I suppose you think *I* did that?"

"It crossed my mind. You've been pushing me pretty hard about selling."

"Annie, I gotta go. I'm at the order window. I'll be out there in half an hour. Can we talk about this, then?"

"Nothing to talk about if you didn't put her on to me. See you later."

Annie hung up the phone before Luke could defend himself further. She didn't want to hear platitudes or excuses. If he hadn't told Gayle directly, he might have mentioned it to someone else, someone who knew her. Still, he seemed genuinely surprised, so if it wasn't Luke, then it must have been the bank manager and that would be no surprise at all.

When she was about to go back to the kitchen for her tea, she saw Noah at the door to her office, a solemn look on his face.

"What's up, bud? Did something happen at school?" Noah pressed harder against the doorframe and let his head droop. "Am I going to hear from Miss Wight or Mr. Sawyer?"

Noah shrugged. "Probably, but I didn't start it."

"Maybe you'd better sit down and tell me what happened. I'd rather hear your side of it before anyone else's."

Noah shuffled to a chair and slumped into it. Annie knew exactly how he felt because she felt the same way, obviously for different reasons. Defeated, angry, and completely disillusioned. Before Noah could speak, the office phone rang. Annie looked down at the number and heaved a sigh.

"It's the school." When Noah winced, she let it go to voice mail. "I'll call them back. Tell me what happened."

Slowly, with much prompting, the story unfolded. Noah overheard a conversation in the washroom between two older boys who were talking about the new kids at school. Alfie Gibson and his two sisters, Delia and Emma. These boys suggested that the Gibson children were poor and maybe even homeless because they wore the same clothes every day and didn't have much in their lunches or for snacks. Noah had gone to bat, defending them, having remembered them staying in one of the fishing cabins the week before. The result was a toss-up in the boys' washroom, which Mr. Sawyer put a stop to.

"What did Mr. Sawyer say about all this?" Annie asked, when Noah seemed to be finished giving his version of the events.

"I have detention at lunchtime in his office for the rest of the week."

"And the other boys?"

Noah shrugged. "I don't know. He talked to us on our own. I told him they were wrong. I told him the Gibsons had stayed here, and that they weren't homeless. They were just visiting."

"That's true. But I'm also not sure they had a home to go back to. I think they were in a bad way when they came here. But I've heard that Mr. Gibson has a job now, so that's good news. You know, Noah, sometimes people can be cruel when they don't understand. Those boys have probably never been in a situation like the Gibsons were, so they make fun of them because they don't really know what it means to be homeless or poor. But then other kids, like you, seem to have a natural ability to see things from all points of view and to be empathetic. Do you know what that means?" Noah shook his head. "It means you can imagine yourself in someone else's situation and understand how it would feel. If someone is in pain, for instance, or super happy about something."

"Or poor and hungry and ashamed?"

"That's right. These boys were wrong to poke fun at someone else, but it's only because they don't get it. I'm betting if they actually had to go without food for a couple of days and live in their parent's car for a week, they wouldn't be laughing at someone else."

"What are you going to say to Mr. Sawyer?"

"What do you think I should say?"

"I think those boys should have to apologize."

"You think they owe you an apology?"

"Not me. To the Gibson kids."

"But do the Gibsons know those boys were making fun of them?"

"Alfie was in the washroom when it happened. That's why they did it."

"Ah. Well, that puts a different light on it, doesn't it?" Annie saw Noah shifting in his seat and knew he'd had enough of this discussion for now. Right or wrong, his attention span only went so far.

"I'll call Mr. Sawyer back and see what he has to say about it. I'm sure you have nothing to worry about. Fighting isn't good, at school or anytime, but letting someone be the brunt of other people's jokes isn't good either, so buddy, I'm proud of you."

Noah's face brightened. "You mean you're not mad?"

"Mad? No way. I'm proud of you for sticking up for the Gibson children." Annie stretched out her arms to give Noah a hug and sent him off to the living room. When he was gone, she dialed the number for the school.

"Mr. Sawyer, it's Annie Taylor," she said when the principal picked up the phone. "I understand Noah was in a bit of a scrape today."

There was a pause at the other end and then a small laugh. "Well, yes. I suppose you could call it that. Your son packs a mean punch, Ms. Taylor. Not even my grade fives will be messing with him in the future."

"A punch… I don't understand. He said they were arguing, but he didn't say anything about punches being thrown."

"Let me fill you in."

Annie sat quietly while Mr. Sawyer told her the part of the story Noah had left out. The part that included Noah punching both the other boys and neither of them getting in so much as a swing.

When he finished, she said, "I see. Noah tells me he has detention with you after school for the rest of the week. Can I ask what the punishment is for the two boys that started all this?"

"A suspension for the rest of this week and an in-person apology to Alfie when school starts again after the holidays. I have to tell you, that boy of yours has some moxie standing up to older and much bigger boys. Even though he was defending someone else,

I can't let this go. One boy has a black eye and his mother is scream-ing blue murder."

"Just one of them?" Annie asked, trying to keep the smile out of her voice.

She could hear the grin on his face when he said, "I hear you. Boys will be boys and all that. But there are rules for a reason, so Noah will spend his lunch hours with me for the rest of the week. To be honest, I quite enjoy having him around. He's a good boy. You should be proud."

"I am, Mr. Sawyer. Very proud. I promise you, Noah and I will talk more about how he can handle himself without using his fists."

When she finished her conversation with Mr. Sawyer, Annie found Ali and Chelsea in the living room colouring, and the boys en-grossed in a game of Battleships. Luke had arrived and he and Joe were at the kitchen table, discussing the next steps for the bathroom. Something told Annie they'd been talking about more than the work that needed to be done, by their sudden silence, when she walked into the room.

Luke looked up. "Hello Annie," he said almost curtly, then went back to his drawings.

The air was thick with tension. She noticed a frown crease Joe's forehead, as he lifted a hand to scrub at the stubble on his chin. Whatever this was, it was between them and she was not about to make it any of her business. She'd had enough for one day. The snacks she'd made a while ago weren't going to hold the kids much longer and she felt a rumbling in her own stomach as she pulled out her largest pot and filled it with water for pasta.

"Hey." Luke got up from the table and came to stand next to her. He still wants Joe to think I'm his, Annie thought, as Luke rubbed her arm. Her gaze flitted to Joe, who kept his head bent over their diagram. They'd definitely had words about something, she thought.

"We'll get the rest of the outside wall framed up tonight. Then Joe is going to finish the plumbing tomorrow morning. I'll come back when he's done to finish the drywall work and then we'll paint and paper. Should be done in a couple of days."

She nodded. "I'm sure the hospital will be relieved when I tell them Dad will be out of their hair by the end of the week." She looked toward the table where Luke had been sitting. "No burgers. Did you get something or are you joining us for supper? I'm making spaghetti?"

"With your famous garlic bread?" Luke asked, a grin pulling at the corner of his mouth.

"Is there any other way?"

"Yeah. If it's not too much trouble. I had an issue at the drive-through window. And before you ask, it's not worth rehashing. Just a bad day, that's all. Which is also why I was a little short-tempered on the phone. I'm sorry."

He and Joe headed down the hallway, and Annie got supper started. Later, when her sauce was simmering, and the water for the pasta had just begun to boil, her phone rang.

"Annie's Lodge," she answered, then put the phone on speaker so she could continue making supper.

"Hi Annie. It's Felicity. There was something I meant to ask you the other night, but forgot. You know we cleared out that big patch of land last year to put on the extension."

"I remember."

"Well, we weren't thinking about Christmas when we did it and this is the first year, we won't have a tree from our woods. I was wondering if you'd mind us cutting one down at your place. I'll provide you with a seedling to replace it. I'd pay you, of course. I think the going rate in town for pre-cut ones is about $40."

"Oh Felicity. You don't have to…"

A hand reached out to touch her arm and she looked up to see Joe nodding toward the phone. Understanding that he wanted to talk to her before she made this arrangement, she ended the call with Felicity saying, "I'm sure we can work out something, but can I call you back? I've got something on the stove."

"Of course. Thanks Annie. Talk soon."

"See?" Joe said, when she turned to him. "You didn't even have to put up a flyer."

Luke was standing in the doorway. "Joe mentioned this earlier. This tree sale is a good idea, Annie. I'm in. Chelsea and I will help. I can put up some signs in town for you, too."

Was this what they'd talked about earlier, she wondered? Had they argued? Had Luke been upset that it wasn't his idea? Or was it about the letters and who had been in her office the other day?

"Alright, let's do this. But I've been thinking about people going in and out of the woods. Is my insurance going to cover someone tripping or getting a foot caught or something, or heaven forbid, chopping their finger off?"

Luke scratched the stubble on his chin with a pencil. "After supper, get out your policy and let's find out. If you need something extra to cover you for the event, I've still got that pay envelope."

"Luke, you don't have to…"

"It's fine."

"Wait." She glanced up at him. "Was that the problem at the drive-through? You didn't have the money?"

He raised his hands. "No. I already told you it wasn't. Geez Annie! Just drop that. If you need to up your insurance, I'll cover it. You can pay me back out of the proceeds so consider it a loan. Heaven help us if you should actually break down and accept a little help." He shook his head and left the room, calling over his shoulder. "Come on, Joe. Those two-by-fours are waiting."

Dinner was chaotic as the kids ate in front of the TV and the adults sorted through insurance policies at the kitchen table. Foresight when they'd first taken out their insurance meant she had more than enough coverage, so there would be no loan from Luke or anyone else. Annie drafted a poster and made a list of errands for each of them. When they were finished, it was late and well beyond the kids' bedtimes. The new wall was not as far along as they'd hoped. Luke promised to come as soon as Chelsea was on the bus in the morning, and Joe agreed he could start early.

Annie went to bed that night feeling better than she had in a long while. Things were looking up. A Christmas tree sale might not be the answer to her long-term prayers, but if it paid for another week or two of her bills, she'd be grateful.

Chapter 12

Annie closed the last box of cookies and sealed it with the label Joe had helped her design. She and Ali had been baking every night after school, doubling the batches. Now they had fifty boxes of cookies ready to sell. She tilted her head at the lingering aroma of gingerbread from the last tray of cookies, still in the oven. These she would save for the kids.

It was Thursday night, and with only a few things that needed to be done before the sale, she was finally slowing down to take a breath. The last couple of days of preparations, both for her father coming home and for the Christmas Tree sale, had provided some challenges, but they were ready.

The bathroom was complete, and her father would have everything he needed on the main floor of the house. A team of Personal Support Workers would come on rotating shifts to help with meals, bathing, and dressing and Nancy would come out every day for his physio work. Tomorrow morning, Annie would bring him home, where he could continue his recovery with his family around him.

He'd seemed excited when she told him of their plans for the tree sale and that she was resurrecting the old Christmas Eve party tradition. There was something unusually bright about him when she mentioned it was all Joe's idea.

"He's a good man," Sam had said, with only the slightest of slurs.

Annie had frowned. "How could you possibly know that? You've never met him."

He'd smiled and tipped his shoulder in a half shrug. "I just know."

Luke had spent the day on the riding lawnmower with the snowplow scoop in front, clearing paths and parking lots to give easy access around the property, and Joe had gone into town to put up the posters.

Earlier they had set up long tables for hot drinks and cookie sales, which Noah and Ryder decorated with pine boughs and Christmas baubles. Everything had a festive look. Luke rigged up a sound system to play Christmas music, and Joe had rented an inflatable Santa to put at the top of the driveway to welcome people into the lot. They were ready. Almost.

Annie felt a twinge of nervous energy stirring in her stomach as she thought of how much they'd put into this sale. What if no one came? What if this was all for nothing? She ran her hand over the labels Joe had helped her make for her cookie boxes. She hadn't known it was possible to produce something so professional looking from her home computer. They were great. This idea was great. The sale would be great. It had to be.

As Annie went to the kitchen, she heard the soft voices of Joe and Ali upstairs. He was reading her a bedtime story, because only Joe could do the voices right, according to Ali. Annie pulled the last tray of cookies out of the oven and hung up the oven mitts just as Joe came downstairs.

"She's finally let you get away?" she asked when he came to lean against the counter. The space between them seemed to ignite with nervous energy. Had he sensed that, too? Annie moved away to stop her body from trembling.

"If Ryder's fine bunked in with Noah, you could leave him here. There's still a bit of the wine you brought in the fridge. Would you like a glass?"

"Why not?"

She handed him the bottle while she got the glasses down. "I downloaded a movie a while ago. Would you like to watch it with me?"

"I'd love to."

She lifted a brow. "Don't you want to know what it is?"

He handed her a half-filled glass of Chardonnay. "Doesn't matter. I'm just happy to spend time with you."

She led the way to the living room, kicked away the throw pillows and blankets the kids had used to make a fort earlier, and settled onto the couch. "I really appreciate all the help, Joe, and Ryder's too. I feel as if we've taken you away from your holiday. I'm sure you didn't come here to work."

"It's been fun and, honestly, it's nice to be around people. I wasn't looking forward to Christmas with just Ryder and me. It's going to be hard on him."

She nodded, thinking how difficult it must be for a child to lose their mother. She felt the sting every year, now that her mother was gone, and she wasn't a kid.

"Have you decided where you'll go when you leave here? Huntsville would be closer to your office."

"Maybe. Or maybe an even smaller town."

"Well, you can't get much smaller than Baysville." She sighed and sipped her wine. "That's why we bought this place. We didn't have kids then, but we knew we wanted to raise them away from the city." She gave a little sigh. "Now I just have to keep it from going under."

When Joe's arm naturally migrated to the back of the couch behind Annie, she unconsciously snuggled a little closer to him and let her body relax against his.

"This is nice," she said, letting her head fall to his shoulder.

"You said something about a movie?" He said after a moment.

"I did, but we can talk if you'd like. I feel as if I hardly know you."

"Are you sure you want to?" A flicker of hope lay in his question.

"I do. I'd like to know everything about you." At that moment, though, what she really wanted was for him to kiss her. She shifted so that they were facing each other. Would he? She wondered. He raised his hand to cup her chin, his thumb circling her jaw, his eyes full of desire, and hers giving him permission. But he did not make a move to kiss her. When she could stand it no longer, Annie pulled his face to hers, and kissed him; a long, sensuous kiss that left her wanting more and marveling at the curious way he seemed to know exactly what she wanted and how she would respond.

There was kissing and more kissing until Annie's head swam and her stomach twitched with desire and anticipation. When he cupped her breast, and his fingers worked at the buttons on her blouse, a shiver went through her and she pressed closer. She hadn't wanted this with Luke, hadn't felt this kind of longing, this yearning to be held and caressed and loved. Joe was different. This passion she felt with him was almost like... like it had been when her husband was alive. Could she love two men with that same intensity in one lifetime?

As quickly as things had begun, they stopped. Joe rested his forehead on hers and gently pulled his body away as he took a deep breath. "We can't do this, Annie. It's wrong."

She looked up at him in surprise, her fingers rushing to her swollen and bruised lips. "It feels perfectly right to me. It feels as if this was supposed to happen, as if you were meant to come here and for us to meet."

"I know. I know that's how it feels, but I..."

"Is there someone else?" Annie felt a shiver of shame running through her. She would never cheat on anyone and she wouldn't want to be with someone who did.

"God no. Never. I wouldn't… I haven't…." He pulled his arm from behind her and pushed to the edge of the couch. "I should go, Annie. We can't do this again, at least not until things are settled. I just can't. It isn't fair." He stood up and headed for the door.

"What things? You mean Luke?" She trailed after him, following him to the mudroom, watching him pull on his coat and wrap a scarf around his neck. "I've told him at least three times that I won't marry him. I don't love him, Joe. I never have."

"It's not Luke, Annie." His hand was on the doorknob. "I can't explain it all now. But until I can, I think we should take a breath." A blast of cold air wafted in when he yanked open the door. "I do love you, Annie. Nothing will ever change that."

She stood in the doorway, confused and disappointed, hovering on the fringes of anger, as he hurried down the lane toward his cottage. Her hands reached for her stomach, feeling like she'd just been kicked hard, square in the gut, and she didn't know how to make the pain go away. When he disappeared into the shadows, she closed the door and leaned against it. What did I do wrong? What is it he can't talk about? There must be someone else, some unfinished business. A separation, a divorce, something holding him back.

As she reluctantly climbed the stairs to bed, she heard Ali shouting from her bedroom and flew the rest of the way to Ali's room.

"Mummy. Help me!" Ali shouted, as Annie pushed open the door.

"I'm here Pumpkin. I'm here." Ali's sweaty body fell against her as Annie pulled her daughter into her arms and brushed the hair from her forehead. "Did you have a bad dream?" Ali nodded. "Want to tell me about it?"

Ali looked toward her door. "Is Joe here?"

"No darling. Why?"

"I want to tell him about my dream."

"You can't tell me?"

Ali shook her head and hugged her teddy bear.

"I'm sorry, honey. He's gone to Moose Cottage. Can you wait till tomorrow?"

Ali went limp in her arms, her eyes fluttered closed, salty tear tracks had already dried on her cheeks. "Good night, Pumpkin." Annie laid her back on her pillow and pulled the covers up, then kissed Ali's forehead and reached to turn out the light.

On the night table was a new picture that hadn't been there yesterday. It was Ali taken when she was just hours old, and in the arms of her father. The shot cropped out her father's face, so that the focus was on Ali and the tiny smile just edging its way into the corner of her mouth as she looked up at him.

How had she found this picture? It was in the photo album under the coffee table, had been for years. Annie hadn't given any thought to her children going through them and it had been ages since they'd last asked questions about their father. Ali had made that odd comment that she should marry Joe and she had taken quite a shine to him. She must be wondering about her father. Maybe she wanted to know, but didn't know how to ask. One day soon, she would have to explain everything to her children. But how could she do that, when she wasn't entirely sure what everything was, herself?

The appointments with her psychiatrist, Dr. Jim Sullivan, were supposed to be helping, but Annie wasn't sure they were making much progress. Admittedly, she wasn't grieving the loss of her husband anymore, at least not the way she had in the early days. In fact, at her last appointment, she'd told him about Joe and he agreed she might be ready for another relationship. But there were still things that worried her, like why there was little she remembered about her late husband. Why, when she tried to conjure his face, did she only see a blurred outline behind those steel-grey eyes and why couldn't she get rid of that closet full of his clothes?

It was because of the accident, Dr. Sullivan had told her. She'd been in a coma for six months, he reminded her. These things take time and one day, he promised, she would remember. One day, she thought as she replaced the picture and slipped out of the room. One day, she would be able to tell her kids everything about their father.

The door to Noah's room was open just enough so that when she peeked in, a beam of light from the hallway shone over the sleeping boys. They looked like two angelic little peas in a pod. She bent closer to kiss Noah on the forehead and instinctively did the same to Ryder. He twitched in his sleep and a smile formed on his lips.

"Night Mum," he whispered.

Annie stood, a whisper on her lips to Ryder's mother. "He misses you, but he's okay."

As she closed the door behind her, she was sure she heard a voice say, "I know. I'm here."

Chapter 13

As Annie pulled into the driveway, with Sam riding shotgun, she glanced at him to see his reaction to the changes. The open access to the front door of the house alone was enough to make a regular visitor wonder if they had come to the right place. But all the preparations for their weekend sale were surely a surprise to him, even though she had already told him what they'd planned. He looked confused, lost, and a little out of sorts instead of the smile she'd expected.

"I told you about the tree sale, Dad. Remember?" She unbuckled both their seatbelts and reached for the door, still watching her father. "Are you okay?"

He nodded slowly, then turned to face her. She gasped, doing her best to hold back the tears. It seemed he had aged a decade in the last week. His hair was no longer the salt and pepper gray it had been, but had gone snow white. But when she looked into his face, his smile was still the same, and the luster in his eyes was coming back. He was going to recover from this. She was sure of it.

"I'm okay," he said with a nod. Then he waved his hand toward the lodge and the tables they'd set up. "This is good, Annie. Good for you."

"Thanks, Dad." She patted his hand. "I'll get your chair out of the back." He nodded and adjusted himself in the seat, ready for her to open the door. Meanwhile, Annie hoisted the wheelchair the Red Cross had generously provided out and rolled it through the snow to his side of the truck to the plywood Luke and Jake had set out leading up the slope to the porch.

"Here we are." She reached up to take his hand, hoping she was strong enough to get him out of the truck and into the chair. His face worked itself into a ball of worry as they both stared down at the distance from the seat of the truck to the seat of the chair. He shook his head and grabbed the door and her shoulder at the same time.

"Can't, Annie. S'too far," he said, his hand trembling as he leaned back into the seat.

At the hospital, an attendant had picked him up out of the chair and put him into the truck as if he were little more than a grocery sack. She hadn't thought out what she would do when they got home, and no one had bothered to ask if they'd have help.

"It's okay, Dad. I'll get someone. Just stay put. Luke and Joe should be somewhere close by."

As she rounded the corner of the house, she saw both of them by the toolshed. Even from a distance, it was obvious they were arguing about something. Luke's face was on fire with anger, his fists clenched and raised as if he was about to throw a punch. Joe's hands were open and up in defensive mode, as if trying to calm Luke down. When Luke raised his arm to swing, Joe ducked, easily avoiding the blow. Luke slid on a patch of ice and pitched sideways. His feet went out from under him and he landed on his backside. Joe reached down to lend a hand up.

"Hey!" Annie made her way across the yard, arms flailing. "What gives? Have you been into the adult cider or something?" She stepped over the boxwood hedge that separated her from the men. On seeing her, they turned away from each other and from her. When she stood between them, neither could look her in the eye. "Well, are one of you going to tell me what the hell is going on here?"

Luke turned to her, a surprised look on his face, as if he didn't recognize who she was. He flashed a look between her and Joe, then back again. "It's nothing, Annie. Just a difference of opinion, that's all."

"Joe?"

But Joe simply cast a wary eye toward Luke and kept silent, an unspoken secret, a *boys only* thing going on between them.

"Fine, don't tell me what's going on, but my father is waiting in the truck for someone to get him inside and I can't manage him on my own. Do you think you two could get over yourselves long enough to lend a hand?"

"Of course," Joe said, stepping forward. "Glad to."

"Sure, you are," Luke sneered. He took two steps backwards, then added, "I've got something to do in the lodge, anyway." Before he left them, he shot a dagger at Joe, that made Annie wince, then shook his head and walked away.

Suddenly, she felt like the referee at a hockey game. But whatever this was—and she guessed it had something to do with her—they'd have to figure it out for themselves because she had other things to worry about.

"Coming Joe?" She called out, as Joe seemed to linger a moment, watching Luke's back as he made his way to the lodge.

"Right behind you," Joe called out, when Luke disappeared inside.

They walked in silence to the truck, Annie determined to stay out of this argument and Joe apparently fine with that. When she opened the truck door, her father looked past her to Joe and his face instantly brightened and his mouth curled into a half smile.

"Joe," he said, as plainly as if he'd never had a stroke.

"Hi Sam," Joe said, returning the smile. "How are you feeling?"

"Good. Good to see you."

"Wait. How do you know my dad?" Annie asked, as Joe reached out to help Sam down from the truck and into the chair.

But Joe didn't answer her and Sam mumbled something she couldn't hear.

"I don't understand, Dad. What are you trying to say?"

"I think he's trying to say mortgage," Joe offered when he had Sam settled into the wheelchair.

Sam nodded and tugged Joe's sleeve.

"Dad. We aren't going to worry about that right now. We'll talk about all of this when you're better." She strapped him into his chair and tucked a blanket around his legs. "Let's get you inside. It's freezing out here."

Sam's good hand reached out to pat Joe's arm, and they shared a smile. Annie decided that he probably thought Joe was the orderly at the hospital. Wasn't his name Joe too?

Getting into the house was a relatively simple task. As Luke had predicted, the threshold was only a small hurdle, and Joe easily swung the chair around and backed over it. That's a relief, Annie thought as they wheeled Sam into the new foyer. His eyes widened at the changes, and he smiled at Annie. She'd told him what they were doing, but she wasn't sure how much was sinking in or if he could imagine what it would look like. Joe wheeled Sam toward the bathroom to show him the new setup, and where to find his personal things, and then over to his bedroom, where Sam reached his good hand toward the bed and looked up at Joe.

"You want to lie down?" Joe asked. Sam nodded. "Sure, we can do that." He wheeled the chair closer and set the brake. With Annie on one side and Joe on the other, they lifted Sam onto the bed, took off his shoes and the winter coat he was wearing, then settled him under the blankets. Annie pulled up the duvet and tucked it around his arms.

"I'll get you some water, Dad. Anything else? You want something hot? A cup of tea?"

He shook his head, but reached out his good hand to her. "Thank you."

Tears welled in her eyes. "Oh Dad. It's good to have you home. You don't have to thank me." She flashed a look toward Joe, who was adjusting Sam's pillows and caught a look pass between him and her father.

In that instant, she realized that Sam hadn't mistaken Joe for the orderly at all. Somehow, these two knew each other. They were just too familiar with their looks, the way Joe was taking care of Sam and the way Sam patted Joe's arm in appreciation. She went to fetch the water, wondering where they could have met and how they knew each other.

When she returned, Joe had pulled a chair next to Sam's bed and the two of them were laughing like they had been old friends forever. He got up when she came into the room.

"I'll see you later, Sam."

When he was gone, Annie set a water bottle with a sipping straw in it on the nightstand, then drew the curtains to darken the room.

"I put a bell by your bed. If you need anything, just ring it, okay, Dad?" She lifted the bell to show him and set it back down again.

He blinked a few times, then closed his eyes. Beneath the blankets, he looked so small that Annie had to take a step back and suck in a breath to keep from crying. He was frail and helpless, not the same man at all who'd gone out to cut down a Christmas tree a few days ago. She leaned down and kissed his forehead, then left the room, closing the door softly behind her.

Joe was waiting in the hall. "Is he okay?"

"He will be. Now that he's home and we can take care of him."

"He's where he belongs." With a hesitant nod, he turned and headed down the hall toward the back door.

"Just a minute," she called out, following him. "What is going on with you?"

At the door to the mudroom, he turned and let out an exhaustive sigh. "What is it you want to know, Annie?"

"This fight with Luke. And what's up with my father? It's like the two of you are best friends or something." She fixed her stance, waiting for his answer. "I want some explanations, Joe. I'm fed up with the games."

"Oh Annie. This is no game. I told you I love you, but…" His eyes flicked toward Sam's bedroom and then he took a beat to draw a deep breath. "I really think it's best if I leave as soon as the sale is over." He put his hands up to stop her from protesting. "You don't have to refund me any money."

"Leave? I thought… No. You can't leave. What about Ali and Noah? What would they do without you? What would *I* do without you? I love you, Joe. I haven't told you that yet, but I do."

"I know you do, Annie. I've always known it. But that isn't the point right now, is it?"

"Always known? How could you possibly? You couldn't…Why isn't it the point?" Annie shook her head as tears welled in her eyes and Joe moved toward the door. "No! Don't do this. Don't leave me. Not again. Not like…"

Her hand flew to her mouth as she gasped. Something dark flooded her memory and suddenly the room began to spin. Annie felt weak at the knees. Her body went limp, and she slid down the wall toward the floor.

Joe rushed to her side and pulled her into his arms. "It's okay. I've got you. Come to the kitchen and sit down." He helped her to a chair, then hurried to fill a glass of water.

"Where are your pills?"

"My pills?"

"For your migraines."

"How do you know…?" Her hands went to her temples as an old and all too familiar pain throbbed in her head. "I haven't had one in weeks… I…"

The migraine that had begun in the hallway was going to be a bad one. Already bursts of light were pricking the darkness when she closed her eyes. She sipped the water and reached up to wipe the sweat from her brow as Joe sat down next to her and took her hand in his. When she tried to look at him, her vision blurred, and she swayed, feeling as if she might pass out again. Then she leaned against him and put her head on his shoulder, a soft moan escaping her lips.

"I'm going to call Luke to come inside," he said. "I don't want to leave you like this, but I have an appointment in town that I can't change."

"I don't want Luke. I want…" But he was already on his phone, his voice muffled by the pounding in her head.

"Yeah. Can you come inside? It's Annie." A pause while Luke said something. "A couple of hours at most."

Seconds later, Luke was standing in the kitchen, snow melting off his boots and onto the floor. Annie's first thought was to get a mop, but her head argued fiercely.

"I need to lie down," Annie finally said, pushing herself up from the chair, then sinking back into it.

Luke scooped her out of it. "I got ya." As they headed for the door, he turned to Joe. "Go do what you need to do. I'll hang around till you get back."

"What about Chelsea?"

"I'll call the school and have them put her on the bus."

Joe nodded. "I don't want to leave her like this, but it can't be helped. I won't be long."

Annie felt the strength of Luke's arms under her legs and around her waist as he carried her up the stairs. The familiar scent of his cologne filled her nostrils and pushed into her throbbing head. She'd never liked Old Spice, though it hadn't occurred to her to tell him that. Instead, she found another reason to complain to him. She hadn't wanted Luke to help her. She'd wanted Joe, but now he was gone.

"Boots," she said, letting her arm drop, her fingers pointing downward to the melting snow that Luke was tracking up the stairs.

"Hush. I'll clean it up."

"You'd better." She was half teasing, half serious. "Oh god my head," she sobbed. "It's killing me."

"Do you have any of those pills left?"

"In my night table drawer."

Luke got her a glass of water, then gave her a pill. "Lie back and rest and don't worry about anything."

"Thank you. I…" Her brow creased as she looked up at him. "I'm sorry Luke."

"Don't try to talk. We'll do that when you're feeling better."

"Okay. Maybe that's a good idea."

Luke was a blur, but she made out his half-hearted smile, looking back at her across the room. Then he closed the door and was gone and Annie was left alone. Sleep enveloped her in a warm and welcome blanket of blissful and heavenly silence.

Much later, when Annie opened her eyes, it was dark outside. In the quiet of her room, she listened to the sounds of the house. The creak of a tree branch scraping her window, the click of the furnace turning on, followed by the soft whirr as it pushed hot air into the vents. From downstairs came the faint sound of the TV and spurts of hushed laughter from her children. Ali's familiar giggle made her smile, despite the pain still throbbing behind her eyes. She lifted her head from the pillow and was instantly dizzy again. This was a bad one, she thought.

The headaches had started shortly after Ali was born. Something to do with the changing hormones and the surgery she'd had after the birth. Her labour had been difficult, not at all what it had been like with Noah. She'd been in agony and in the end, they'd done a C-section and then the hysterectomy. A few days later, the migraines started. After that, she had them off and on for a few years. Usually, they were the worst when she came out of her psychiatrist's office. She'd learned to make her appointments early enough that she had time to lie down before the kids got off the bus from school. When was the last one, she wondered? Dr. Sullivan had told her to keep a record, but they had been few and far between the last year or so, so she hadn't bothered.

A slow movement to turn her head to the clock on her nightstand seemed possible without pain. It was already time for the kids to be in bed. What time had she come upstairs? How long had she been sleeping? How had she gotten up here? The last thing she remembered was talking to Joe in the hallway. He'd been about to leave, but then Luke had come in, hadn't he? This was just like before. She'd have a horrendous headache and not be able to remember things afterwards.

She lifted her hands to her temples and attempted to massage away the pain, knowing that if the kids didn't get to bed soon, they would never get up in the morning. Tomorrow was the first day of the tree sale and they would all have to be up early.

Sitting up slowly, so as not to aggravate the tempest inside her head, she shifted to the edge of the bed. If she didn't need to relieve herself, she could have been content to stay right where she was. She reached the bathroom without falling, though she felt weak and dizzy and had to hold on to the wall and every doorknob along the way. Once there, she flipped on the light and winced as pain shot through her eyes. No light, she thought. I can do this in the dark. With the light off again, she felt her way to the toilet, lifted the lid and sat down. Pull your pants down, silly, she thought as she realized she'd forgotten to do that. When she was finished and flushed the toilet, she heard someone bounding up the stairs. Be quiet, she whispered, but in her head, she was shouting. Quiet. Quiet. Quiet!!!

Even the water rushing through the taps was too loud. Drips trickled down her wrists as she rested her head in her hands and her elbows on the counter. She stood a moment, swaying to and fro with pain. No matter how much she willed it, the pain would not go away. It was there, throbbing, pounding, threatening to crack open her skull and spill her brains out onto the counter. If only it would, and then she could rest. She dried her hands, then slowly opened the door, wanting only to return to the peacefulness of her bed, and the soft, soft pillow beneath her head. As she opened the door, she wavered and nearly lost her balance, but someone was there to guide her across the hall.

"Thank you, Luke. Are the kids okay?" Her vision blurred as she squinted to look up at him. Then her knees buckled, and she fell against him.

"Let me carry you," he said, scooping her into his arms. That wasn't Luke's voice.

"Joe?" She asked, looping her arms around his neck and resting her head on his shoulder.

"Yes. It's me. I'm here. Just rest." He laid her on the bed and let her head slide onto the pillow, then pulled the blankets up over her. "Don't worry about a thing. The kids are fine. Your dad is fine. I'm here Annie. I'll take care of you. I'll take care of everything."

Part Two

Joe

Chapter 14

In the kitchen, Joe filled the kettle and got out the tea he and Annie had shared the other night. Dessert tea, she had called it and that's what she had written on the jar. It tasted like a chocolate mint melting on your tongue. When it had steeped he took his cup to the living room, set it on one of Annie's sunflower coasters on the coffee table, then settled on the couch. The remote lay next to Noah's binder of Pokémon cards and he thought, for a brief moment, he would watch something on TV. Getting lost in someone else's drama might not be a bad idea. He'd certainly like to forget his own for a while, but now that everyone else was asleep and the house was quiet, he found it impossible to shut out the noise inside his own head.

Annie's migraine was his fault, and for that, he was angry with himself and with his stupid ideas. All he'd done was cause her more work and more stress. What was he thinking? A Christmas tree sale, hayrides, people milling around the place. He couldn't deny, though, that when she was in the thick of the planning, that was Annie at her best. The busyness of it, the anticipation, the excitement of what the weekend could bring, made her light up like a proverbial Christmas tree.

But in a few days, the weekend would be over, and Christmas would be too, and then they would have to talk. He had to explain things, and that wasn't possible if her head felt like it was going to explode. So, no more big surprises and no sudden moves. He'd been foolish, and he knew it. He wouldn't do that again.

He reached for the photo album that sat under the coffee table. He'd seen it the other night and wanted to look at it, ask her about the photos inside, but she'd had other things on her mind, and at the time, he hadn't objected. It felt amazing to hold her in his arms, to feel her soft and warm against him, and so completely willing. But it was too soon and there were things she had to understand before they went down that road. It had taken all his resolve to resist the urges that her kisses aroused in him.

When he opened the album, Annie stared back at him from the first page. Her green eyes squinting in laughter, auburn curls framing her angelic face. "So beautiful," he whispered as he turned the page.

Next were photos of Noah. Noah in Annie's arms at the hospital. Noah in Sam's arms sitting in the rocking chair, by the living room window. Noah's first birthday and a cake almost as big as he was, set out on the dining room table. There were four or five pictures of his first birthday party, with Annie in some, Sam in others, and people of all ages in the background, blowing bubbles, and wearing party hats. The next set was Noah's second birthday, and that's when Ali came in. Her hospital pictures were almost identical to Noah's. He paused at the blank space, knowing it was where the one on Ali's nightstand had come from. Joe sighed and turned the page. More of Noah and Ali growing up, birthdays, Christmases, picnics, boating, swimming lessons, friends and neighbours, all clearly marked with names and dates, a perfect keepsake journal of their childhood. Of course, Annie would have done this. She would want them to remember the happy times. It wasn't hard to realize why there was no husband in these photos. Obviously, explaining a father they didn't know was too painful for her. But in all the photos, there was not a single one of her husband. Not one. It did seem very odd.

He closed the album and slid it back under the table, swiping at a tear that threatened to spill down his cheek. Everything around him seemed to pull memories out of his past and lately, all he felt like doing was crying. He reminded himself that Christmas was always a sentimental time of year, but this year, being here with Annie and the kids, it was especially hard. Joe glanced around the room at the knickknacks on the shelf, the haphazardly piled colouring books on the coffee table and the couch cushions, scattered on the floor after their earlier pillow fight. These were the heartwarming things that meant a family lived here, and that was what Joe was missing most.

He made one last round of bed checks to make sure everyone was sleeping. In Sam's room, he switched off the light by his bed in favour of one on the other side of the room. Its glow cast golden shadows on the wall while Sam snored softly.

In Noah's room, he and Ryder lay crossways on the bed, their heads half buried under their pillows, feet dangling out the other side. "Sleep tight, you two," he whispered, adjusting the blankets to make sure they were both covered up. If he'd had any reservations about these boys getting along, he'd lost them almost instantly. They liked all the same things, and they were boys. Snips and snails and all that, he thought, as he closed the door to Noah's room.

Next, he looked in on Ali in her pink princess bedroom with the canopy bed and eyelet dust ruffles. Sugar and spice, that's exactly what Ali was. Her favourite bear, Frank, was tucked into the crook of her arm. Where had she gotten that name, he wondered? When he'd put her to bed earlier, she'd been frantic about him. "*I have to have him, Joe. You have to help me find him.*" After an exhaustive search of nearly the entire house, there he was, under the duvet, way down at the bottom of the bed. Only then did she settle onto her pillow. But then she'd wanted a story and a glass of water and her nightlight turned on. When he'd done all that, she'd looked up at him and smiled in a half dreaming state.

"I love you, Daddy," she whispered.

"I love you, too," Joe had said, not bothering to address her use of *Daddy*.

Annie's room was next, and peering in, he'd had to resist the urge to crawl in next to her and hold her through her pain. She seemed to sleep peacefully, and he was sure that in the morning she would be right as rain. She would be the life of the party when everyone came to buy their trees and her baked goods. If only she realized how talented she was, and how special, or how much everyone loved her. He couldn't believe the calls he'd fielded already about the weekend event. He was glad he'd suggested she put his phone number on the flyers and signs so she could focus on other things. She had enough to do.

On his way down the stairs, he remembered to avoid the step that creaked loud enough to wake the dead. In the living room, Max was curled up by the fire. He shifted and snuffed when Joe patted him goodnight, but flopped his head down again, too tired for anything else.

Joe stuffed a throw pillow under his head, pulled a homespun knitted blanket over himself, and shifted onto his side. Sleep would come now, he thought, and eventually, so would the morning, and it would be a busy one.

Chapter 15

Annie was up before dawn. Joe knew this because he heard her footfall overhead, moving between her bedroom and the bathroom. He was up, had folded the blanket and set the throw pillows at each end of the couch, just the way Annie always did, by the time the toilet flushed upstairs. The sound of the shower followed. Good, he thought. She's feeling better or she would have gone right back to bed.

"Come on, Max, old boy. You must need to go out by now."

It was still dark outside, though the sun was trying hard to squeeze its way over the tree line. A wintery blast welcomed them when Joe opened the door, but Max gave him no argument about the cold, bounding down the back porch stairs. Max's business outside would give Joe enough time to put on a pot of coffee, set the table for breakfast, and check on Sam. He set out cereal and bowls and spoons, and the peanut butter and jam. He would have made them all a bacon and egg breakfast. They might want something substantial in their stomachs on this day of all days. But he didn't want to use the last of her eggs and there was no bacon to be found.

Sam was still sleeping, so while the coffee brewed, Joe ducked into the main floor bathroom to clean up and change into the clothes he'd brought with him yesterday after his appointment in town.

The bank manager had given him grief, at first, until he produced the required documents.

"There will be a penalty." The man stiffened and lengthened his neck, decidedly to show off his importance.

"I've calculated for that. See here." Joe pointed to the breakdown of figures on the sheet he'd prepared.

Then, with a scratch of his chin and a grimace of disdain, the man had reached out to take the certified cheque Joe held out to him and marked everything paid in full.

It crossed Joe's mind that he might have been the one who'd put Gayle Sutherland onto Annie the other day, since there was a look of disappointment in his eye. Maybe he wanted to purchase Annie's Lodge himself or knew someone else who did. A foreclosure sale would have meant getting it for a steal, but Joe wasn't about to let that happen. He knew that when Annie learned what he had done, she would be angry. She never wanted charity because it made her feel as if she was powerless to manage on her own and that she was less than capable. Annie was anything but that. She just needed a little nudge and as far as Joe was concerned, this wasn't charity. This was an investment in her future and the kids, and he hoped she would see it that way.

From somewhere overhead, he heard her humming, another sign she was feeling better. He had no doubt that even if she weren't she would have dragged herself out of bed, make breakfast for the kids and put a cheerful smile on her pretty face. But coming down the stairs with a song on her lips—even an off key one—meant everything was okay.

She wore jeans that hugged her curves and sent his head spinning despite the hideous Christmas sweatshirt with crisscrossed candy canes she was also wearing. He laughed out loud when she came into the room and it startled her.

"Oh. I didn't expect to see you here this early." Her hair was still damp from the shower, spiraling around her face in a natural curl. She grabbed an elastic band off the fridge and whisked it into a sloppy bun out of the way.

"Did Noah let you in?" she asked, pouring herself a cup of coffee, then reaching for the milk in the fridge.

"The kids are still asleep. So is your father," Joe told her.

"But you're here. In my kitchen."

"I stayed. You…"

She frowned at first, then shock spread over her face as the colour drained from it. "We didn't… You weren't… I …."

"No. No. Nothing like that." He was quick to reassure her. "I slept on the couch." She tilted her head and squinted at him, an unspoken question hovering between them. "You had a migraine. Epic on the scale I'd imagine."

Instinctively, her hand went to her temple. "Ah. I haven't had one of those in a while. They used to be brutal. Sometimes they were so bad, I'd forget what happened. Whole blocks of time just vanished. My doctor says it's common. Sometimes I get the memories back, but when I don't Dad reminds me about things I've forgotten."

"How are you feeling this morning?"

"Right as rain."

The words seemed to catch in her breath and Joe waited for her to say something more, but she didn't. Right as rain had been something his mother had said, and somehow it had become something Joe said all the time too. It didn't surprise him to hear her say it, but it seemed to surprise her. Her eyes held a vacant look as she went through the motions of stirring her coffee, setting her spoon on the table and taking her first sip.

He sipped his coffee, too, watching her sip hers, looking for signs of a relapse, but except for the blank stare, she seemed completely recovered. Another day, another time, he would like to talk to her about what had set off this migraine. But for now, if she'd forgotten the tension between them, he'd accept that and be grateful.

He gulped down the last of his coffee and went to put his cup in the sink. "People will be coming soon. I should probably get outside and start setting up. When your dad wakes up, text me and I'll get him to the bathroom and whatever else he needs to do."

"There's a PSW coming at nine."

Joe nodded. "Well, he'll be up before then, so just message me." He held up his cell phone, then tucked it into his jeans pocket.

In the mudroom, he put on his boots and coat, but went back to the kitchen to remind her of something. When he found her still gazing into her cup, a deep frown creasing her brow, it was all he could do not to tell her she didn't have to worry about anything anymore. That he'd taken care of things. That this Christmas Tree sale wasn't going to make or break the lodge. But now was not the time. She looked up at him and smiled, until the phone rang, taking him out of his rather somber mood and sending her into action mode.

"Annie's Lodge," he heard her say as he headed out the door.

The tingle of the icy air nipped at his cheeks when Joe closed the door behind him and stepped into the morning. The sky was clinging desperately to the last shades of night, the stars reluctant to give up their last twinkle before fading into the coming morning. But by the time he rounded the house and headed toward the lodge, the first beams of sunlight were filtering through the trees. The weather network's promise of a perfect day seemed to be right for once. Not a cloud floated in the sky as Max came bounding from somewhere, nearly knocking Joe onto his backside with his enthusiasm. As he righted himself and rubbed Max behind the ears, Luke's truck pulled in and came to a stop just next to the lodge.

"Morning," Luke called out. There was nothing left of yesterday's argument in his voice and Joe couldn't help thinking Luke was doing well to keep his cool. Luke lifted a sleepy Chelsea out of the truck and set her down. She raised a weary hand to wave in his direction.

"Hi Chelsea," Joe said, making his way toward them. "Morning Luke"

"Is Annie up?" Luke asked. "There are a few customers are not far behind me."

"She is." Joe nodded toward the house. "Annie's in the kitchen, Chelsea, if you want to go inside." He looked at Luke then. "Coffee's on, if you want some."

Luke lifted a metal thermos out of his truck. "I got mine," he said, giving Chelsea a consenting nod that sent her to the house to find Annie.

"Maybe you can wake Ali and Noah up," Joe called after her.

They watched as she flew across the driveway and up the back stairs, squealing with delight. She's awake now, Joe thought.

"Look Luke. Maybe we should talk before Annie comes out here, or the kids are around," Joe began. But Luke stopped him.

"I spent a lot of time thinking last night. I wish things were different, but they're not. So, as soon as this sale is done, I'll clear out of here and I won't bother Annie again. I just hope this is the best thing for her and for the kids. And I hope you know what you're doing." He held Joe's gaze for a long moment before nodding. "Yeah. Well. I guess you do, and it wouldn't make much difference what I say anyway, would it? Are you going to tell her everything?"

"When the time is right, yes. That migraine! It must have been a doozy. She doesn't remember anything that happened last night."

"It was bad alright. Let's hope that's the last of them." Luke set his gaze on the lake, not meeting Joe's eye for a moment. Then, with a hesitant cough, he cleared his throat. "Did you, ah… Did you take care of things in town, Joe?"

Joe shifted his stance and nodded. "It's done."

"Good. I must admit, I could have helped some, but I couldn't have done what you did."

"You've been a huge help, Luke. More than you know." Joe looked up toward the road at the sound of tires crunching over the snow. "Guess this will have to wait. Here comes the first customer. We better look alive."

The day flew by with a steady stream of people coming right into the early evening. The apple cider and hot chocolate were a hit, and all of Annie's cookies sold within the first three hours. The hayrides ran almost non-stop out to the woods and back with either Luke or Joe at the wheel of the tractor, and only a handful of pre-cut trees now leaned against the lodge.

By the time they closed for the day, they were all exhausted but extremely pleased with the results. The fliers they'd put up in town brought most of the locals from Baysville, and an article in the Huntsville newspaper brought others from further away. Over two hundred people had come to their sale. Joe saw the smile on her face as she tucked the cash into an envelope and slid it behind the plates in a cupboard.

"See Mummy?" Ali said, when they sat down to a supper of soup and grilled cheese sandwiches. "Lots of people will come to our party on Christmas Eve."

"But everyone came today. There's no one left to come." Annie dunked her sandwich into her soup.

"We could still have our own party in the lodge," Luke suggested. He looked across the table at Joe. "As long as Joe's still willing to do the cooking."

"You bet," Joe said. "I've got lots of helpers, right Ali?" He caught her smile and grinned back at her.

"But we'd have to get Dad over there. Can we manage that?" Annie asked.

Luke nodded and nudged Joe's elbow. "Piece of cake with Joe and I on the job."

When Annie's face morphed from concern to happiness, it was obvious she was pleased that he and Luke were getting along. One thing they had in common, Joe thought, is that they would both do anything to make Annie happy, even keep the peace when that wasn't what either of them felt.

But it was the kids who seemed the happiest at Luke's idea. Ryder and Noah smiled at each other across the table, and Ali shouted for joy and threw her arms around Chelsea.

"Yay. Christmas Eve with my bestest friend of all."

On Sunday morning, Joe put a stack of flyers on the table next to the cash box to give out to everyone who came. They settled on a price of $15 per person or $50 for a family as an admission price for the Christmas Eve event. Annie hadn't wanted to charge anything, and in truth she didn't need to, but Joe didn't want to spoil this for her. She had to believe she was raising the funds she needed to keep this place afloat. And it would give her guests that warm feeling of goodwill everyone needed, especially at this time of year.

Joe was already thinking of ways to give the money back to everyone who might come. Something for the community, he thought, that everyone could enjoy. A donation to the school, or new books for the library, a plaque on the new school commemorating the history of the building that was once the old town hall and Baysville's first church. He would let Annie decide when the time was right.

The second day of the sale proved to be quieter than the first, but they were not without customers. By mid-afternoon, things had slowed to less than a trickle, as they expected. It was Christmas Eve and most people had their trees up and decorated by then. It was family time now and time for wrapping presents and stuffing turkeys and sipping rum-laced eggnog.

The girls helped Annie in the lodge, get dishes and silverware out of storage, and decorate and set the table. Meanwhile, the boys, delegated as assistants to Joe and Luke, helped with the cleanup outside. When they were finished, Joe suggested the kids should pick out a tree from the last of the pre-cut ones by the lodge. He would put it in the living room and they could decorate it while he and Annie finished getting the dinner organized.

Once the tree was up, Sam told him where to find the decorations. "You'll have to go up in the attic," Sam said, lifting his eyes toward the ceiling. "Annie has everything organized up there."

"I don't doubt that for a minute," Joe said with a grin, knowing he would find boxes or tubs clearly marked in Annie's careful printing.

There was a pull-down staircase that led to the attic, and once Joe was up there, just as Sam had told him, he found the boxes easily. He piled them by the trapdoor and was about to go down when something under the window caught his eye. A wooden trunk with bold bands around it and a shiny clasp. But no lock, he noticed. He could almost smell the cedar, even though he was at least fifteen feet away.

He knew before he opened the chest that this was an intrusion on Annie's privacy and he scolded himself for even standing next to it. But the urge to see the contents was too great. He lifted the lid and smiled as the familiar cedar scent exploded and wafted up to greet him. It was like being in the middle of a forest.

He peered inside, stopped short of reaching in at first, until curiosity could hold him back no longer. On top was a high school yearbook with a pressed gardenia bulging out of the middle pages. Annie's name was written on the inside cover, in her neat and delicate handwriting, and below it autographs from friends and teachers filled the page. He found her in pictures of the senior volleyball team, the drama club, and the track team. On her homeroom page, her headshot was next to Andrew Travers, a nerdy-looking boy with Buddy Holly spectacles and a mouthful of metal. Joe wondered what Andrew looked like now and if the braces had paid off. He was probably head of some huge global IT company making six figures and living in a high-rise condo in New York.

Joe set the yearbook aside and picked up a photo album filled with pictures of Annie. Her life from birth to graduation splayed out on the pages, beginning with baby pictures, then school age and all the clubs she'd gone to, Brownies, Girl Guides and Rangers. The last picture, her university graduation photograph, had another dried and pressed gardenia taped beside it. He set that album aside and dug further, past a bundle of letters tied with pink ribbon, a pair of baby shoes, a folder of short stories, journals dating from 2005 to 2007. He did the math in his head. University days, he thought, setting them aside.

Down deep, beneath a hand knitted baby blanket, he found two more photo albums. The first was filled with photos of Annie on her wedding day. In some she was laughing, in others a sensuous smile curled at the corners of her mouth. There were serious ones, too, but no matter how she posed, there was always that magical sparkle in her eyes. There were pictures in the living room where she stood between her parents, Sam looking proud and ready to give her away in marriage. There were photographs at the church, the stained-glass windows in the background, while the couple stood with their backs to the camera, facing the altar. The last photo in that album showed the back of a blue Corolla decorated with bows and ribbon, tins cans and a huge sign attached to the back. *Just Married.*

The other album was an account of the early days of Annie's married life—the years before children. There were pictures of friends and relatives, the usual Christmas and holiday shots, with the last part of the album devoted to this place, and the transition from Paradise Cove to Annie's Lodge. Joe flipped to the last few pages and found them blank, which made him think it was rather like her memory after a migraine—blank and without a single clue to remind her of what had brought it on.

The most interesting thing, he thought, was that in all these albums and this collection of Annie's past, there was not a single photograph or keepsake of her husband. Why, he wondered, had she erased him from her past?

A moment of self-loathing came over him for snooping through her things, and Joe slammed the book shut. He was ashamed of what he'd done, but he also knew exactly why he'd done it and why that trunk beneath the window had invoked such curiosity in him. He closed the lid and with a resigned sigh, took the boxes of Christmas decorations down to the second level, then lifted the attic stairs back into place and slipped the latch hook back where it belonged, closing the door and his thoughts to Annie's past.

Chapter 16

She stood in the corner of the main room of the lodge, next to the fireplace, a glass of eggnog in one hand, the other resting on Ali's head, caressing her curls. Joe watched from the kitchen side of the pass-through as Annie threw back her head in laughter at something Felicity Pierce was saying. It was good to see her laugh, as if her troubles were behind her and she was finally able to relax. She caught him staring at her, and tilted her head to one side, in a *'come out of the kitchen and mingle'* kind of look. But he was content right where he was, in a place where he could watch her, unnoticed, from a distance as she mingled with her guests.

Joe had cooked for thirty-five, having gotten responses earlier from several people. It had been a scramble after the sale, but now everything inside the lodge was perfect. The tables were set with green and red festive tablecloths and bright paper napkins alongside Christmas crackers. It was to be a buffet dinner, with everything set out on chafing dishes to keep the food warm. Joe relished the busyness of the kitchen, recalling the nights his father had done the same for private family dinners at the restaurant. He would be proud, Joe knew, that his son was carrying on an old family tradition.

He looked up from basting the turkeys when a shadow hung in the doorway. "Anything I can do to help?" Ben Pierce asked, stepping into the kitchen.

"Yes, as a matter of fact there is, Ben." Joe spun around and looked at the pot of potatoes he'd just drained. "Any good with a potato masher?"

"Sure. Just point me in the direction of one."

Joe pulled the utensil out of a drawer and handed it to Ben. Then he gave him an apron. "Felicity will have your head if you get stuff all over that Christmas Sweater. Where did you get that, anyway? It's hideous."

They both laughed as Ben pulled the apron over Rudolph's ginormous nose.

"My sister and Felicity cooked this one up," he said. "I think they rescued it from the secondhand shop in town."

Joe laughed. "It looks like something my grandmother would have made." He went back to basting the turkeys. "I noticed you're not using the cane anymore?"

"When we're out for a walk on uneven ground, I do, but for the most part, I don't need it. Listen, thank you for that last inspection on the renovations. It's nice to know Melville's is in good hands without George at the helm. That young fellow Ryan seems a good lad."

Joe nodded. "Agreed. I think he'll do fine. I have to admit, though, I haven't spent much time at the office or at any of the sites yet. After the holidays, I'll get more involved. It's been a bit hectic here, what with Annie's father and all."

"I'm glad to see Sam looking so well. It was scary for a while, I guess. I'm sure Annie would have her hands full without all the help she's been getting." Ben nodded to Luke, who was just coming to the door.

"Hey Joe. Ben." Luke stood at the door with his thumbs tucked in his belt loops. "Everything under control, or do you need a hand in here?"

"Can you carve a turkey?" Joe asked.

"Pfft. Can I carve a turkey? Which one?" Luke picked up the knife and sharpener that were set out on the counter as Joe moved one of the turkeys off the resting board.

"That's the first one," Joe said, returning to the oven to put the second one out to rest.

"What's going on in here?" Annie stood in the doorway.

"Just taking orders from the chef, my dear." Ben lifted a spoonful of potatoes. "Do you like your potatoes lumpy or smooth?"

"Oh smooth, Ben. Definitely smooth." She giggled and went to sample the gravy Joe was stirring. "Joe, this is fantastic! There's something in here that most people don't put in their gravy. What is it?"

"It's…"

She put her hand up. "No, don't tell me. I'll think of it." She made smacking sounds, patting her lips together as she tried to come up with the ingredients. "I know someone who used to make gravy like this."

"It's roasted bone marrow," Joe told her, as he took the sample spoon away and tossed it into the sink. "It's my father's recipe."

"That's it!" Annie cried. "Wait. This is your father's recipe?"

"It's not a big secret, Annie. Lots of chefs make gravy with bone marrow."

"Oh. Well, it's delicious." She waved her arm around the kitchen. "Thank you for doing all of this. You are a wonder."

It was when Annie teetered on her heels and nearly fell into his arms that Joe realized what he'd already suspected. Annie had been drinking too much eggnog.

"Why don't you try some of the stuffing," he suggested, hoping that a little food in her stomach might help to sober her up.

"If it's as good as the gravy, I'm in." She went to where Luke had scooped out the turkey's cavity and put the stuffing into a bowl. He dug a spoon in for her and grinned as she pushed it all into her mouth at once, cupping her chin to catch what didn't fit.

"Someone's having a good time," Luke said with a smile.

"I am," she mumbled. Her mouth still full, she nodded her approval of the stuffing, then swallowed it down. "It's been a long couple of weeks and now that Christmas is here, I'm ready to let my hair down and have a bit of fun."

"Good for you," Joe said. "But how about if you do it in the other room, while we get supper finished? You can tell your guests that dinner will be served in fifteen minutes."

As she left the kitchen, Joe took her glass from her and replaced it with a cup of coffee from the carafe he kept brewing. She frowned into it after the first sip and set it on a table near the door.

"Nice try," Luke said with a laugh. "She'll be fine after she's got a meal into her."

Joe grimaced. "I just hope it doesn't bring on another migraine."

But Annie was in top form that night. During dinner, she made a speech to thank everyone for coming, her helpers for making it a wonderful party and Joe for cooking all the food. They ate, shared stories of other Christmases, especially the ones that had been sparse through the worst of the pandemic. After they'd eaten, they gathered around the piano to sing Christmas Carols.

"Can anyone coax some music out of this thing?" Annie called out.

"I can."

Wally from the garage was the last person any of them expected to sit down at the piano and play with such skill, but after running his fingers up and down the keyboard a couple of times, he turned out to be a capable pianist. Felicity and Ben danced with the kids when he played *Jingle Bell Rock*, and Ali led a conga line through the hall, when he gave them a jazzed up rendition of *All I want for Christmas*, which didn't really have a conga beat, but they made a line, anyway.

By ten o'clock that night, Ben declared it was time to go home or Santa would skip their house if they weren't in bed sleeping. Noah scoffed at such nonsense and said he wasn't at all tired, but Ali yawned and held her arms up for Joe to carry her while Annie said goodbye to her guests.

At the door, Annie pulled him closer so he could join her in saying goodbye. "You're the man responsible for this evening," she said, when he tried to protest.

Truthfully, he was proud to stand next to her. He was warmed by the enthusiasm of the guests, and a familiar feeling grew inside him. With Ali in one arm, the other naturally fell around Annie's shoulders.

Ben and Felicity were the last to say goodbye. "Thank you for a wonderful evening, Annie and Joe. It feels just like old times." Felicity hugged Annie and kissed her cheek. "Thank you for getting us all together again. I've really missed this."

"It was Joe's idea," Annie said, passing the praise.

When Felicity pulled Joe into her embrace, she whispered in his ear. "It's been so good to see you. I hope this all works out. You know we love you, right?"

He nodded, then reached out to shake Ben's hand. "Merry Christmas to both of you, too. Thanks for celebrating with us."

Chapter 17

Ryder woke up early on Christmas morning, not that Joe hadn't expected him to. He would have preferred another hour of sleep, but when he heard the boy stumbling around in the bathroom, he switched on the light on his nightstand.

Last night, Ryder had wanted to sleep over with Noah, but Joe had insisted that they should sleep in their own beds. He thought Annie should have Christmas morning with her father and the kids, on their own, even though there was nothing he'd have liked more than to wake up next to her, any morning, every morning.

"Flush the toilet!" Joe called out, as Ryan's stream went from a trickle to a drip, and then everything went quiet.

He rolled to the side of the bed and squished his toes into the softness of the mat on the floor. He was as eager for this Christmas morning as Ryder was. Annie was only a few feet away, just down the path, and if he was a lucky man, he just might catch her under the mistletoe later. The thought made him blush and kick himself for thinking like a teenager. But he couldn't help it. It was all he could do these past couple of days, to keep himself from pulling her into his arms and holding her, kissing her, taking her upstairs and making love to her. They'd been so close the other night, he'd found it hard to resist. But he couldn't. Not until they cleared everything up. Not until she knew the truth.

He brewed a pot of coffee and made oatmeal for their breakfast, then sat down at the table with Ryder.

"Whad'ya get me for Christmas, Uncle Joe?"

"I'm not telling you. That would spoil the surprise."

Ryder grinned at him, then dove into his food. "Good," he said with a mouth so full some of it came back out again.

"Geez, Ry." Joe handed him a paper towel.

"Sorry."

But Joe wasn't angry. He was laughing because Ryder always had a good appetite for food and for talking.

Ryder swallowed, so there were no oatmeal mishaps when he said, "I know what Ali's giving Noah, and I know what Noah got for Ali."

"Do you? Well, you'd better keep all that to yourself. It won't be long now."

Ryder's face suddenly turned somber. "Are we leaving tomorrow? Chelsea said she heard her dad say we were. She said she was going to miss me. That's sweet. She's a cute kid." Ryder shoved another spoonful into his mouth and looked at Joe.

Joe didn't know what to tell him. "Maybe. I'm not sure."

"I like it here. Why can't we stay?"

"In a cottage? Forever?"

"It's nicer than that house we were living in before we came here."

"That was temporary. You know I had that work thing."

Ryder lowered his head. "I know."

"What if we lived in town? Then you could go to school with Noah and Ali and Chelsea. Would you like that?"

Ryder beamed. "I'd love it!"

"You might have to go to an after-school program if I'm working and can't get home until five. Are you up for that?"

"I could just hang out on my own. I'm almost eight," Ryder tried his luck.

"Sorry kid. The law is the law. Not yet. I know you could handle it, but what if I got stuck at work or who knows?"

"Okay, if I have to, I have to."

"Good boy. We'll talk about it more later, because right now, I've got a big ham to cook for our supper. Are you up for kitchen duty, sous chef Ryder?"

"Yup."

"Great, but first, let Max out. I think he's been crossing his legs long enough."

Max lifted his head off his paws and raised one eyebrow in Ryder's direction.

"Come on, boy. Let's see if we can find some rabbit tracks."

"For goodness' sake, don't let him catch one."

When Ryder returned, Joe put him on potato peeling duty and was surprised to see how quickly he worked. When he'd finished preparing the ham and the glaze, he looked at the empty bowl next to Ryder.

"You've finished?" he asked, surveying the peeled spuds waiting to be sliced up for potatoes au gratin. "Wow, I'm impressed, buddy. Great job."

Ryder smiled up at him. "It's for Annie's special Christmas. I'd do anything for her."

So would I, Joe thought to himself, getting out the mandolin to slice the potatoes. When they were finished, he glanced up at the clock. It was still only nine in the morning and while he was sure that Ali and Noah would have dragged Annie out of bed hours ago, he didn't want to disturb their family time. He set the lid on the potatoes and looked at Ryder.

"We're done for now. So, I think it's time you opened your present, don't you?" He nodded toward his bedroom. "It's in the closet."

Ryder frowned when he brought back a large box, brightly wrapped and sporting a huge red bow. His eyes lit up, and he threw his arms around Joe's neck. "Thanks Uncle Joe."

"You haven't opened it yet," Joe said with a laugh.

"Whatever it is, I'll love it."

Joe grinned and ruffled his hair. "I know you will too. Go on. Open it. Over here," Joe said, leading him to the sofa and patting the coffee table.

The fire he'd started earlier crackled and sputtered beside them and outside a light snow had begun to fall. It was a near perfect morning, and it brought to mind Christmas mornings when he and his sister Violet were young, Christmases before everyone in his life had gone away.

Ryder's eyes were as round as two moons when he tore off the paper and looked down at the box. His arms flew around Joe again. "A PS5! Oh, thank you, Uncle Joe. Thank you!"

"There are also a few games to get you started. There's a hockey one in there. I think we should set up a tournament, if you don't mind getting your butt kicked. I'm pretty good, you know."

Ryder's face fell, and he lowered his gaze. "I really wish Mum was here, too."

"Me too, kiddo. Me too." Joe held him for a few moments while Ryder cried out the tears that needed to fall. It was his first Christmas without his mother. Her death was still far too fresh for Ryder and for Joe, too. There hadn't been enough time to adjust yet, especially when they were *'two men bachin' it,'* as Joe called it, and no maternal influence in the boy's life. It had been good to have other people around them this year, especially Annie.

"Can we hook it up to the TV in here?" Ryder asked when the moment passed.

"I don't see why not. So you're ready for me to kick your butt, are you?"

"Ha. I doubt it."

"When we get settled, we'll get a big screen TV and do this every night."

"Now that's what I'm talking about," Ryder said with a wide grin.

Later, Ryder was flaunting his victory, having won three games to Joe's two, when they heard voices outside the cottage. He went to the door and Noah and Ali burst in, a blast of icy air and a flurry of fresh snow coming in with them.

"Wow, cool!" Noah cried when he saw what Ryder and Joe were doing. "Can I play?"

Joe relinquished his controller to Noah. "Watch out! He's good."

Noah took his place on the couch beside Ryder. "Yeah, but so am I."

Ali ran across the room, arms stretched out to Joe. "Merry Christmas, Joe! Merry Christmas!"

He scooped her up and let her hug him tight around the neck. "Did Santa bring you something nice?" he asked when she finally released him.

Ali frowned. "Yes, but it wasn't what I wanted."

"Oh? Want to tell me about it while I check on the ham?"

"Sure." Ali let her coat fall to the floor and trailed after Joe to the kitchen, where he lifted her onto the counter so she could watch him work.

"So, what did you get?"

"I got a bead set. I like it and I was hoping for one, but…"

"But?"

"But I really wanted a tracing pad."

Joe frowned. "I'm not sure I know what that is." He looked up when Annie coughed in the doorway to get Ali's attention. He hadn't heard her come in, but she stood there, coat and hat still on, snowflakes melting on her collar, her hat and her hair. No messy bun today, Joe thought, as she pulled off her hat and her hair tumbled down around her shoulders.

"It's kind of like an etch-a-sketch, but not really," Ali was saying, drawing Joe's attention back again. "There are a bunch of things you can trace and then you make pictures with them. Then colour them afterwards."

"Her best friend at school has one," Annie said softly, coming to stand beside her daughter. "That's why she wants one, too."

"Ah, I see. Well, you never know. The day isn't over yet, and I have it on good authority that there are more presents to come." Joe smiled at Ali, but caught the questioning look in Annie's eye. He shrugged and said, "I think Santa got mixed up a bit and left some things here, instead of at your place."

"Santa never gets mixed up," Ali said with absolute certainty.

"Well, how do you account for the things that Ryder and I found in my closet this morning?"

"What things?" Ali sent Joe a well-practiced frown.

"Well, let's just check this ham and then we can take a look."

Wonderful aromas were already wafting from the oven, but when Joe lifted the lid to baste the ham, it was heavenly.

"Mmm. Smell that, Ali. Doesn't that smell like a little bit of heaven, right there in that pan?"

"Huh! That's what Mummy always says. A little bit of heaven in a pan."

"Does she?" Joe looked up at Annie, who shrugged.

"I guess I do sometimes. I have no idea where I got it from. Must be something my mother used to say." She slid Ali down from the counter. "Run and play with Noah and Ryder, will you? I want to talk to Joe for a minute."

Ali looked up at him. "She's going to ask you to come to the house and have Christmas with us. Please say yes. Please. Because then we can open the rest of the presents."

"Will you?" Annie asked with pleading eyes.

They stood, looking at him. Annie was still wearing her coat and flakes of snow were melting on her shoulders and in her hair and Ali's big blue eyes were almost begging.

"How can I say no? You're both impossible to refuse." He clapped his hands. "Alright but I will need everyone's help to carry the presents and the food up to the house."

"And don't forget Superdog!" Ali cried, racing from the room to tell the others.

Joe found a box to put the food into and sent Ryder to pack up the presents from his closet.

"Can we bring the PS5 too?" Ryder asked.

"Sure, just don't drop it in the snow."

The kids were off in a hurry, Ali doing her best to keep up with Max, while Ryder took cautious steps, holding tightly to his new PS5. Annie and Joe carried the food and the presents and followed along behind.

Up ahead, Ali stopped to catch snowflakes on her tongue. She scooped up a handful of snow and tossed it at Ryder. It landed innocently at his feet as he pulled the box for his new PlayStation out of harm's way.

Joe set the box of food down on the ground. "Just got to tie my boot," he said, secretly gathering snow in his hands.

"You don't have laces in your…" Annie started to say but got a face full of snow before she could finish. She bent and filled her hands and tossed it back at him, sending a shower of snow down his collar and inside his coat. Then, in a fit of giggles, she chased him over the boxwood hedge and halfway to Raven's Nest Cottage. Suddenly he stopped and turned around to face her and she stopped too, a huge handful of snow poised to launch.

"Don't do that, Annie," he warned, panting heavily.

"Or what?" She gulped in a breath of air.

Joe laughed and staggered as he bent to pick up some snow. "Or I might just have to wash your face in snow."

"Bring it on," she grinned, then hurdled the snow at him.

It was too soft to do anything other than float around him, and Joe was too quick for Annie to get away. She screamed and giggled as the chase was reversed. He was sure she could have run faster, and could have dodged left when he caught up to her and pulled on her sleeve. She could have twisted and got away, but it was obvious she had no desire to. He knew the game. It was as familiar as the sun in the sky, the smile on her face and the snow in his hand.

He pulled her into his arms and let the snow fall to the ground. "I wouldn't really, you know."

"I know," she whispered, as he bent to kiss her.

Their lips were icy cold and snowflakes clinging to their eyelashes melted and trickled down their cheeks. He smiled when the kiss was over and looked into her eyes.

"Merry Christmas, Annie."

"Merry Christmas, Joe."

He kissed her again, a long passionate, hungry kiss, that left him wishing they were alone, and that no one was waiting at the house for them. It wasn't only her words that tugged at his heart, but the way she looked at him, the way her eyes said something more than just Merry Christmas. Her look told him she cared and that beneath the confusion that always seemed to lurk behind her eyes, there was something else. Dare he hope for recognition?

"Your ham and potatoes," she laughed when they broke apart with a sigh. "We left them in the snow."

"Better get it before some wild animal does." He pulled her close for one last kiss. "But just now, while we are alone." He glanced over his shoulder and saw the kids already climbing the steps to the house. "This is nice."

Chapter 18

In the house, Sam was sitting in his wheelchair, next to the fire in the living room. He called out when Joe and Ryder appeared at the door.

"Merry Christmas!"

"Hey there, Sam, Merry Christmas." Joe reached down to give the man a warm hug.

Sam grinned. "I'm glad you're here," he said, his words coming through so clearly now it was hard to tell he'd had a stroke.

A look passed between them as Sam's eyes searched Joe's. Joe nodded, then rubbed his hands together before the fire.

"I think we should get this party started. What do you think, Sam? Your grandchildren are dying to open their presents. I'll just put this food in the oven first." Joe scooped up the box and took it to the kitchen, followed by Annie, who leaned against the counter.

In that moment, she was impossibly sexy, wonderfully inviting, and innocently beautiful. He wanted to pull her into his arms, to caress the back of her neck, to feel the softness of her body resting against his.

"Annie…"

Then a little person rushed into the room.

"I'm hungry!" Ali ran straight to her mother and suddenly Noah and Ryder were there too, asking for something to eat.

"Alright. I get the hint."

They made sandwiches and Annie filled a bowl with chips, a rare treat for her kids, and for the next hour, they ate and played games until Ali was nearly bursting with the excitement.

"Can we open the presents now?"

"Aren't we waiting for Luke and Chelsea?" Joe asked.

"They're at his mother's house in Gravenhurst, so they aren't coming. "

Joe couldn't say he was disappointed. It was a pleasure not to have to play nice for once. He stuck a Santa hat on his head, then handed one to Sam.

"How about if we hand out the gifts?" He headed for the tree. "You know, we had a tradition in our house that the youngest person got to open all their gifts first."

"We do that too," Noah cried, jumping up, then plunked down again and lowered his head. "Sometimes being the oldest sucks."

Annie gave him a hug. "But waiting helps build character, and the anticipation.

When all the gifts were handed out, Sam turned to Ali. "You first Sweet pea. Which one first?"

Ali opened her gift from Joe first. "A Trace Pad!" She hurried to give him a hug. "Thanks. You picked the bestest present ever." Her other presents were a book from Sam and a doll from Noah. She hugged them both and said thank you, but it was the trace pad she hurried back to when it was Noah's turn to be centre stage.

Noah opened a new boxed set of Pokémon cards from Annie, the three latest books in the Dogman Series from Joe, and a new hockey stick from Sam.

For Ryder, there was a royal blue toque and scarf set from Annie, a game for his PS5 from Sam, and hockey cards from Noah and Ali.

"I can't wait till next year and I can sign up on a team." Ryder gave Joe a hopeful glance. Joe smiled back. That was what he hoped for Ryder, too.

Annie's gifts were all envelopes. From Sam, there was a gift card for her favourite restaurant in Huntsville, which brought a smile to her face and the reward of a kiss for Sam. Ali and Noah had made her a card and put coupons in it for Mummy Days, when they would help out more around the house.

"Thanks guys. That's very kind of you. These are going right on the fridge."

Joe's gift to Annie was a large manilla envelope with a red ribbon tied around it. "Maybe you should open that one later," he said, thinking now that it might embarrass her.

"Why?" Annie said, prodding the bulky envelope with her fingers. Then she tore off the ribbon, opened the seal and pulled out a framed photograph of herself, taken a few days ago. It was a candid shot Joe had taken with his phone that had caught her smile just right. She'd been talking to Felicity and had waved him away shyly. But Joe had waited just a few seconds longer, till she thought he was focused on something else. Then he snapped the picture and in that single frame had captured everything that was beautiful about Annie.

He watched her looking at the photo, as if she were seeing herself for the first time and sensing how others must see her. She never gave herself credit for her looks, always dressing in shapeless clothes, and pushing her hair into that sloppy bun. Yet, even then, to him, she was gorgeous. But in that photo, in that moment frozen in time, Annie was breathtakingly stunning.

She looked across at him and smiled. "Thank you. It's…" She met his gaze, and he held his breath, waiting.

"Lovely," Sam said, looking over her shoulder. "You sure got her good side, Joe."

Good side? Joe wanted to scream as he pinned her gaze with his. She was radiant. She was breathtaking. She was … perfect.

In an instant, the moment passed, and Annie broke away from Joe's gaze and looked at her father. "I don't have a good side," she said, passing the photo on to him. Sam set it on his lap and smiled approvingly at Joe.

"You're next," Annie said, tossing a nod toward Joe's gifts.

"Alright. Want to help me, Ali?"

Ali put down her markers and sat down next to Joe. Together they opened a navy-blue scarf and toque set from Annie, which Joe traded for the Santa hat he had been wearing. Ali wrapped the scarf around his neck three times before she came to the fringed end, which she tucked under his hat because she didn't know what else to do with it.

"This one next," she said, handing him a package from her and Noah that Joe was sure Ali had wrapped all by herself. Inside was a box of cookies, saved from the first batch they'd made together.

"Dessert!" Joe said, setting them on the coffee table.

One gift remained and when Ali handed it to him and Joe saw it was from Sam, he frowned. He'd been doing all of Sam's Christmas shopping and he knew he hadn't bought anything for himself.

"How did you manage this, Sam?" Joe asked, opening the wrapping to find a black velvet box inside. When Ali anxiously urged him to open it and Joe saw what was inside, he gasped. "I can't take this, Sam.".

"You don't have a choice," Annie told him. "When Dad sets his mind to something, there is no changing it."

"What is it?" Ryder asked, coming to stand next to Joe. "Wow. A pocket watch. Cool!"

"It was my grandfather's," Annie explained. "It's been in Dad's dresser ever since he died. He's always had trouble getting it to keep good time."

"Joe can fix it," Sam said, lifting his good hand toward Joe. "Can't you?"

Joe nodded. "I know someone who could look at it, but Sam… Are you sure?"

Sam nodded. "I'm sure."

Joe blinked back tears and lifted the watch out of the box. The back was plain gold, except for the initials WHT carved into it, and worn to a buffed shine from constant use. The front, slightly more ornate with a leafy pattern engraved into it, opened with a click to reveal black roman numerals set against a cream-coloured face. There was nothing fancy about it, no markings to say it had a value beyond the sentiment with which it was given.

"Thank you, Sam. I will always treasure this, and your kind-ness." He stood up to shake the man's hand and clamp a hand on his shoulder. Sam's nod told Joe everything he needed to know.

"It's Grandpa's turn," Noah cried, slicing through the senti-mental moment Sam and Joe were sharing. "Open ours first, Grandpa." He pushed a gift towards his grandfather.

Sam's gifts were all things to help him get better, a ball to squeeze, to strengthen his weak hand, a fancy hand-carved cane, for when he could give up his wheelchair, books to read to help pass the time and a grey toque and scarf set from Annie to keep him warm.

"I can't think of a better Christmas," Sam said. "Except when Violet was alive."

"I miss her too, Dad," Annie said. "But I feel like she's right here with us."

Joe and Annie slipped into the kitchen to get everything ready for dinner. Joe had clipped the pocket watch through a button-hole in his shirt and dropped it into his pocket.

"I'll make sure this goes to Noah one day," he told Annie, as they organized the hot food. "I'm surprised Sam didn't keep it for him."

"Honestly, I am too. I suggested it and we had a very heated argument over it." She stood next to him then, and put her hands on his chest, slipping the watch out of his pocket to look at it again.

"But he was insistent, and he told me that when the time came, you'd do the right thing with it, so I have to trust my father's instincts." She replaced the watch and looked up at him. There was a question in her eyes that begged to be answered.

"I have the greatest respect for your father and I would always honour his wishes. I don't know what possessed him to give this to me, but I will do right by him. Trust me."

She shrugged and stepped back. "I guess I have to, don't I?"

Joe reached out to pull her back and wrapped his arms around her. She was tense at first, resisting his touch when his hand went to her jawline and his eyes found hers. But when he kissed her and drew her tighter to him, he felt her relax and mold against his body. For a moment, the rest of the world drifted away, and it was just the two of them, and a wave of emotion rippled through Joe's body. When he released her and searched her face for some hint, some miniscule trace of what might be, of who they could be, he was overcome with emotion.

"Annie, I was wondering…"

"When do we eat?" Noah cried, bursting into the kitchen, and spoiling the moment.

Annie looked at Joe and smiled. "Guess that moment has passed."

"For now," he grinned, handing Noah a bowl of dinner rolls. "We're coming. We're coming."

They sat down to dinner with Christmas music playing in the background and everyone talking at once about their presents, about what they would do tomorrow, and sharing memories of the best Christmas they could remember.

Joe caught Annie's eye when he passed her a bowl of peas. "Just like old times?" he asked.

"Just like old times," she agreed.

Chapter 19

Joe woke on Boxing Day with a lump in his throat and what felt like a boulder sitting in the bottom of his gut. Today had to be the day he told Annie what he had done. If he didn't, she would wonder why the bank wasn't sending out the revised foreclosure notices. Eventually she would find out and it was better that it came from him than that stuff-shirt down at the bank. He braced himself for her reaction, worrying what this would mean for their future.

She'd been jubilant that the tree sale had generated enough money for the two months' back payments she still owed; or thought she did. Sam had put her off, saying it was Christmas and nobody did anything at any bank until at least the day after Boxing Day. But Annie had been sure that the moment the bank was open for business again, an email would come, followed by the customary hard copy a few days later, in the mail. But Joe knew there would be no email and nothing coming in the post.

He rolled over and sat up, then let his feet dangle over the side of the bed, waiting for the wine fog from last night to clear from his head. He only had one glass with dinner, but afterwards, when Ryder was tucked into bed and he'd sat alone, staring aimlessly at the TV through a long night of bad Christmas romances, he'd downed an entire bottle of Merlot on his own. Joe had never been much of a drinker, had never gone in for the hard stuff and didn't much like the taste of beer or cider. But he could be talked into a glass of wine from time to time. Something about the way things ended last night, Annie corralling the kids and heading them off to bed and he and Ryder, coming back, alone to this lifeless, Annie-less cottage, had put him in a solemn mood. So, he'd reached for the wine and drunk himself into a stupor, then dragged himself to bed for a night of fitful dreams.

He reached for the glass of water on his bedside table and gulped all of it, feeling as dry as a desert until it slid down his throat and the icy cold hit his belly. The stone remained unmoved, and he knew why.

Best to get this over with, he told himself, pushing off the bed and reaching for his jeans on the chair. He found the clean shirt he'd laid out last night, before he started drinking, on the seat of the chair and pulled his arms into it, goosebumps popping up and down his arm, from the icy morning air. He stumbled over the suitcase at the end of his bed, packed and ready for a swift getaway, one he regretted but knew was inevitable. That, too, he'd done before the wine took over his thoughts. Otherwise, he might not have been so prepared.

Ryder was awake, staring at his own suitcase, already packed for him, and the box containing his new PS5 at the foot of his bed.

"I thought we had one more day," he asked sadly, when he followed Joe into the kitchen in search of breakfast.

"I found us a house, buddy. It's right across the road from the school and we can move in today. Then later we can go into town and get you that TV I promised for your room." Joe lifted a box of fruity cereal. "Want this, or eggs and toast?"

Ryder chose the cereal and scraped the chair out so he could sit down. After the first couple of mouthfuls, he pushed his bowl away. "Can we get our stuff out of the storage place?"

"Some of it. I'll have to get a truck for the big stuff."

"Maybe Luke can help. He's got a truck."

Joe would rather not be obligated to Luke for anything, and he couldn't see Luke wanting to help him, but Ryder didn't need to know that. "Luke's a pretty busy guy. We'll figure something out."

Ryder shrugged. "K. But can I say goodbye to Noah?"

"Of course. I'll come to the house in a few minutes. I'm just going to clean up from breakfast and pack up the car." Ryder grabbed a towel and stood by, ready to help dry the dishes. "Nah, that's okay. You go see Noah and Ali. It won't take me long to tidy up here."

Ryder didn't need to be told twice. He pushed his arms into the sleeves of his coat, stepped easily into his boots, and called Max to the door. "Come on, buddy. Let's go find a squirrel."

Max didn't need any coaxing, either. He bounded out the door after Ryder, down the stairs, and up the path.

When Joe finished tidying the kitchen, he stripped the beds, putting the sheets into a black garbage bag, along with the towels they'd used. He set them by the door, ready to take them up to the house when he went. He ran the vacuum over the floors, and carpet runners, cleaned the bathroom and replaced the toilet roll that had next to nothing left on it. Then he stood back and surveyed his work, realizing in that moment that Annie would do it all again. He was as sure of that as he was that the sun would set tonight and rise again tomorrow. She was particular about everything, and nothing escaped her critical eye. Nothing except the obvious, he thought.

After he'd put their things into the car, he tossed the bag of linens into the backseat and drove up the back lane to the house. Ryder and Noah were building a snowman while Ali watched them from the living room window.

"Hey Joe," Noah called out when Joe got out of the car.

"Morning Noah. Looks like you guys are having fun. Good packing snow? What's up with Ali? Why didn't she come out too?"

"She's got a cold, so Mum said she should stay inside today." Noah tossed a snowball in Joe's direction that exploded at his feet.

"Phew," Joe said. "I dodged that one." He grinned at Noah, who was preparing another snowball, then hefted the bag out of the car. He got up the back steps just as both boys launched a flurry of snowballs at him. "Help me, I'm getting bombarded," he cried out, then knocked on the door, pretending to beg for shelter. Both boys went into a fit of giggles and scooped up more snow. Ali came to his rescue and opened the door.

"Hurry Joe. Come inside before they make more."

"Thank you. You're a lifesaver." Joe set the bag of laundry on the washing machine. "Is your mum around?"

"She's with Grandpa. The lady didn't come to help him this morning."

Joe knew Ali meant the PSW hadn't shown up for her shift, meaning Annie would have to see to Sam's needs. Sam would be embarrassed, Joe knew, to have his daughter helping him in the bathroom, so he slipped off his boots and went down the hall. At the bathroom door, he knocked. "It's Joe. Can I help?"

Annie came out of Sam's bedroom and nodded toward the bathroom. "He's okay for now. He's just… Well, you know." She dropped a pillow into a clean pillowcase and patted it. "Ryder and Noah went out to play in the snow."

"I know," Joe grinned. "I got pelted with snowballs just now."

She grinned back. "Boys will be boys."

Annie went back to Sam's room, and Joe followed, hoping he could help. Sam's dirty sheets lay in a pile by the door, along with his pyjamas and the clothes he'd been wearing yesterday. He took the fresh fitted sheet from the pile on the dresser and unfolded it over the bare mattress cover.

"You don't have to do that," Annie insisted, tugging a corner into place.

"I know, but I want to." He tugged the corners on his side of the bed.

She looked across at him and pursed her lips. "Why do you want to help so much, Joe? Fixing dinner for the Christmas party, then again last night. Baking cookies with us, helping with the tree sale." She put a hand on her hip and gave him a scrutinizing look. "I just don't get it."

"Annie. You must have figured out by now that I would do anything for you."

"Yeah. So you said." She got the flat sheet and flipped it out, letting it fly up, then float down to the surface of the bed. Simultaneously, they fitted tidy hospital corners at the bottom.

"My mother was a nurse," Annie said, smoothing the sheet with the palm of her hand.

"I know."

"You do?"

"Yes, you told me when you taught me how to make corners the first day I came. Remember?"

To Joe, she seemed strange this morning, her mind flipping from one thing to the next, without waiting for one subject to be closed before opening another. Something wasn't quite right, but he wasn't sure what.

"Right. I forgot. What did your mother do? Or did she work?" She asked.

"My mother was a nurse too, but she didn't teach me how to make corners. I think she thought I was a hopeless cause."

She nodded. "I was at first. I thought it was a ridiculous thing to do, but eventually, I hated my feet sticking out on cold nights, so I learned." She pulled a blanket over the bed, then went to get the duvet and handed one corner of it to him. "My mother worked on the children's ward, with the cancer patients." They lifted the duvet and let it float over Sam's bed until it settled into place. "I think Dad has some pictures in an old album somewhere. It's how they met. His best friend was seeing a nurse, who set him up on a blind date with her friend from the hospital. A couple of years later, they had weddings within a month of each other and they were friends ever since."

She was smiling; her face lost in the memory of happy times, and Joe thought he could never love her more than in that moment. That's why it was going to be so hard to tell her what he had to. She would be furious. She would not understand and she would push him away.

"Annie, there's something I need to tell you."

"Sure. Just let me get Dad out of the bathroom."

"No, let me do that, okay? He's too heavy for you and you shouldn't have to…" Joe thought of Sam needing his bum wiped or not getting his underwear in place and things sticking out that shouldn't. It was one thing for a nurse or a wife to do those things, but Sam wouldn't want his daughter to do them.

"Okay, if you don't mind." Annie gathered Sam's washing and headed toward the mudroom.

Joe went to the bathroom and knocked on the door. "Sam. It's Joe. Okay to come in?"

"Come in," Sam called from the other side.

Joe helped Sam get dressed in the clothes Annie had taken into the bathroom for him. When they were finished, Joe was amazed to see Sam walk down the hall to the kitchen. He was leaning heavily on his new cane and moving from one doorframe to the next, slowly, carefully, helping his bad leg when he needed to. Knowing it was a struggle, Joe stayed close by to steady him when he needed it and to provide words of encouragement.

"Did you see that?" he asked Annie when she came into the kitchen after putting in the first load of washing.

She beamed with pride and kissed her father's cheek. "He's amazing. Before long, he'll be right as rain again." She shook her head, seemingly confused about something, then looked at Joe. "Coffee?"

"I'd love some."

She got down three cups, filled them and brought them to the table, along with milk and spoons. When she finally sat down, she patted her father's hand.

"A good start to today, Dad. We'll manage without Kimmy, won't we?"

"Is that the PSW who couldn't make it today?" Joe asked.

Sam nodded. "Car trouble," he said, then added milk and sugar to his coffee.

Joe watched him guide his bad hand with his good one and marveled at the recovery he was making. It was good to see him doing so well. It would make leaving today a little easier.

He reached into his pocket and set an envelope in front of Annie. "This is for you," he said, taking a big gulp and doing his best not to hold his breath. He watched her pick up the envelope and cast a wary glance his way.

"What's this, another picture you took of me when I wasn't looking?" She didn't open it at first, but looked at him, obviously wondering what it could be, then set it back down on the table.

"It's a Christmas present." He pushed it a little closer. "Open it." Joe looked across the table at Sam, who shrugged and set his face with a serious, paternal expression.

"Look at it, Annie," Sam said. "It's important."

"You know what's in here?" she asked, fingering the envelope gingerly. Then she shrugged. "Okay." From inside, she pulled out a series of documents. "What's this?" she asked, laying the envelope to one side and putting the papers down on the table. A frown creased her forehead as she reached up to rub the scar that Joe knew lay just under the hairline. Her eyes widened as she looked at him. "This is the deed to the lodge, to this property. Where did you get this?"

"I gave it to him," Sam said.

She shot a glance in her father's direction. "Why?"

"Look at the rest of the papers, Annie," Joe said. Cautiously, he lifted the edge of the deed to reveal the paper below it.

Annie scanned the pages. "You bought my house? My lodge? But I didn't agree to sell it." Annie flipped through the rest of the papers, skimming the fine print and coming to the signatures.

"No. I didn't buy it. It's still yours."

She came to the last page and set the package down with a thump. "You paid off my mortgage? I don't get it. Why would you do that? I have the money to get caught up now. I can make those two outstanding payments."

"But now you don't have to." Joe flicked his gaze to Sam as they waited for a breathless moment.

"You're wrong." She shot an enraged look in his direction. "I just don't owe it to the bank anymore. Now I'm indebted to you."

Sam reached out to cover her hand with his. "No, Annie. Joe…"

"Stop Dad! I appreciate you trying to help, but this has nothing to do with you."

"Actually, it does," Joe said. "Sam put up some of the money."

"What?" Annie flashed a look at her father. "Where did you get that kind of money?"

"Savings." Sam shrugged. "It'll be yours one day, anyway." There was no slur in his words now. Sam was coming through loud and clear and it was obvious Annie didn't like what she heard.

Joe saw something click for her and knew that she realized what Sam had been trying to tell her for days. "Mor gee," he'd been saying. Trying to tell her he had the funds to help her.

"Okay, Dad. I get that you wanted to help but…" A tear spilled down Annie's cheek, and she swiped at it angrily and turned to Joe. "What's your interest in this now that you're part owner of my lodge? Should we tear down the cabins and clear the land for that pumpkin patch you talked about? Should I build a boathouse over the dock and…"

"Stop, Annie." Joe said softly, reaching for her hand. "It's not like that…"

She yanked her hand away and glared at him. "What's it like then? You tell me. Because from where I sit, you two have just bamboozled me into a deal I wouldn't have made. I have no idea how you got this by the bank without my signature." She shot out of her chair, grabbed her phone from the counter, and began scrolling on it.

"What are you doing, Annie?" her father asked.

"Getting my lawyer's phone number. Surely this is illegal." She glared at Joe. "You can't have this place. Do you hear me? I won't let you take it from me."

Joe sent Sam a reassuring look as he stood up and gently took the phone out of Annie's hands. "I assure you, I am not interested in taking away your lodge, Annie. I only want to help."

She began pacing the floor, pulling away from Joe each time he tried to catch her, rubbing at the scar, pushing her fingers into her temples. Joe knew the signs that a migraine was coming on. Finally, she stopped, reached into the back of a cupboard, and pulled out an envelope.

"There's four thousand dollars in there. It's from the sale. Take it. It's the first installment on what I owe. I'll pay you the first of every month, just like I would have paid the bank."

Joe pushed the envelope back toward her. "I don't want this, Annie. I did this to make it easier for you, not because I want you to feel obligated to me."

"But I *am*, aren't I?" She pushed the envelope back at him again and looked at him, hard. "What are you, Joe? Some self-proclaimed hero who goes around rescuing damsels in distress?" She pointed to the window and outside where the boys had been playing.

None of them had realized they'd come back inside, or that Ryder was standing in the hallway.

Annie ranted on. "Is that really your nephew out there or did you take him in for some down-on-her-luck single mother who couldn't afford to raise a son?"

Ryder came into the kitchen then, his cheeks rosy from the cold outside, or perhaps it was the anger that welled inside him. Noah wasn't far behind, dripping snow from his wet boots onto the kitchen floor. Ryder looked up at Annie, fists balled at his sides.

"Don't yell at him. Uncle Joe was my mother's brother. She got cancer and died. And all he's ever done is take care of me and look out for me. He took care of her too when she was sick. You don't know anything!" Ryder turned around and raced out the door and down the back steps.

Annie hurried to chase after him. "I'm sorry Ryder. Wait."

Joe was not far behind. He pushed past her, nudging her out of the way. "I'll go. He just needs a minute to cool off." He looked at Annie as he pulled his coat over his arms. "Maybe we all do."

Sam was waving a hand at him. "Tell her. Tell her," he repeated.

"Tell me what?" Annie asked.

Joe flicked his gaze between the two of them and shook his head. "I gotta find Ryder. Then we'll be out of here."

"Sure, just leave me to deal with it all, why don't you?" Annie burst out.

Then, when he paused, moved closer to her and went to take her in his arms, she slapped him hard across the face. Joe stopped then and watched her face go from anger to shock. She took a deep breath.

"Sure, go ahead and leave. Just like…"

"Just like who, Annie?" he asked softly.

She looked up at him, tears filling her eyes. "What?"

"You said I was leaving you to deal with it all, just like who?"

She shook her head as if trying to drag something out of the depths of her memory. "I don't know."

Joe took both her arms and turned her to face him. "Yes, you do, Annie. Yes, you do. Say it. Don't leave, just like, who?"

A film of confusion clouded her face as Annie looked up at him. She met his eyes for the briefest of seconds, then looked down at the floor between them.

"Yeah. That's what I thought. I've got to find Ryder." He released her and when he passed Sam on his way out the door, Joe laid a hand on his shoulder. "I'll see ya, Sam."

Joe found Max sitting by the car and knew Ryder was already inside.

"Can we go now?" Ryder asked when Joe opened the door.

"Don't you want to say goodbye to Noah and Ali?"

"I already did." Ryder crossed his arms over his chest and stared straight ahead.

Joe opened the door on the other side and let Max into the backseat, then climbed in behind the wheel and drove away, the lodge fading into the background of his review mirror.

Chapter 20

The bungalow across from the school, where Joe and Ryder now lived, belonged to Wally and Doris from the garage. In a conversation Joe and Wally had the day they'd come to pick out a Christmas tree, he'd learned that Doris had inherited it when her mother passed away, and neither of them knew quite what to do with it.

"I'd give you the going rate," Joe had said. The location was ideal, since Ryder could practically roll out of bed and into his classroom.

"It might need a little fixing up," Wally had said. "I haven't had a good look at the plumbing or anything. You'd be better at that sort of thing than me, anyway. We could work out a deal for your labour and I'd pay for anything you need, naturally."

"Consider it rented then," Joe said, offering his handshake as collateral.

Wally shook on the deal, but had a confused look on his face. "I thought since you were back…"

Joe held up a hand. He knew what Wally and anyone else who'd seen him thought. "We're not there yet," Joe had said. "For now, we've just got to keep things on an even keel."

"Well now. I don't expect there would be too many who'd even remember you, Joe. Felicity and Ben, of course, and we do, because you were always a customer. Most folks who had small businesses in town gave them up during the pandemic, except John and Lynn over at Yummies. The doc's new, of course, so no problem there. Just Millie at the library."

"I've never set foot in that place and I can't recall ever meeting her. Maybe I'm worrying about nothing."

"Probably so." Wally had opened up his phone. "Let me give you the code for the lockbox on the door of the house. Then you can go in whenever you're ready. I'll write up a lease agreement for the first of January, but if things work out and you want to break it, you'll get no argument from us."

So, on Boxing Day, after leaving Annie's, Joe and Ryder had moved in. All they had at the time were a couple of sleeping bags, a few clothes, and a bit of leftover food. It didn't matter because the next day they hired a truck to bring their stuff from the storage unit and it wasn't long before they were settled in.

On the first day back to school, they enrolled Ryder in Miss Wight's second grade class and visited Millie at the library to enquire about the after-school program. Ryder was thrilled to be in the same classroom as Noah and the boys seemed to have forgotten their abrupt departure on Boxing Day.

They were both settling in, but life as two bachelors was lonely, and Joe spent much of his time thinking about Annie and how they'd left things. He was trying to give her some space and let her work through things, but it was driving him crazy. It was Jim Sullivan, her psychiatrist, who'd advised that he take a small step back. Not a giant leap. Don't go too far away, Jim had said, but give her a chance to digest everything that has happened. Jim had been Annie's psychiatrist since she came out of the coma. Joe had seen him a few times too, to work through the trauma and the guilt he shouldered for letting everyone else take care of his family. Joe liked him and, most of all, he liked the way he was with Annie.

Joe called Sam every day, sometimes more than once, hoping for some crack in the ice that was Annie's attitude. He didn't blame her. She didn't understand, but once she knew everything, she would. For now, he had to go slowly and wait for the ice to melt.

A week went by before he sent Annie a text message. At first, she hadn't replied, but he persisted with a greeting every morning, until she'd finally responded, then slowly the communication had begun again. It was still not great; they hadn't made any giant leaps to narrow the gap or heal the frustration she felt over Joe stepping in to pay off her mortgage. In fact, he purposely kept clear of discussing it. He kept it simple. How are you? What a beautiful day! How are the kids? Simple things. Safe things. Now, finally, she was responding.

He and Ryder had fallen into an easy routine of school and work, supper and homework, a movie night now and again, then bed. Dull. Boring for many. But for them, it worked. Ryder was still adjusting to life without his mother, and Joe knew a routine would help.

Melville's was working out too. He liked running the crews and fielding concerns, putting together bids for contracts. Now he was looking at another venture he thought might pay off in time. There were several low-rise apartment buildings on the market, and he'd been thinking of renovating them into condo units for resale. But there was no rush for him to decide. The buildings he'd looked at were overpriced so no one was going after them anytime soon. If they did, then he would look at something else. It was all just a distraction, really.

If there was a drawback to Melville's it was that his take-home pay was less than it had been when he did private contract work. But there was really no need for him to worry. His grandfather had left him a substantial inheritance that would see him through the rest of his days, and his sister had provided for Ryder's future. That money was being held in trust until he was older. He'd put his own inheritance into Annie's mortgage, along with a little extra he'd saved up, and the money Sam had set aside. All in all, he had no financial worries and now neither did she. But there were other things Joe worried about. Things like what he would do if Annie never forgave him.

It was a month before he saw her again. On a Friday, near the end of January, Joe left work early to take Ryder to supper and the opening of a new Marvel Comic movie. He stood on the side-walk outside the school, an ever-growing line of parents filling in on either side of him, waiting for the dismissal bell. Joe spotted Luke to his right and nodded in his direction, but neither of them spoke or made a move to close the gap between them. Joe kicked his feet to-gether to keep them from freezing and jammed his hands deeper into his pockets.

A toddler, tearing away from his mother's grasp, stopped just short of Joe when he tripped over the curb and landed face first in the snow. He stood up and screamed, as surprised at the break in his stride as he was by the cold snow on his face. Joe reached out to help him up just as the mother caught up.

"Thanks," she huffed. "He's a fast one. I should put him on a leash." She caught Joe's confused expression. "It's a joke." She picked the boy up and wiped the snow from his face. "Don't get me wrong, there are days when I think it's the only way to make sure he doesn't escape, but I would never do that to a kid."

"Is he alright?" Joe pointed to a bruise already forming on his cheek.

"Oh Nate. Does it hurt?" The woman scooped up a handful of snow and put it on the bruise, which made Nate squeal even harder. When she took the snow away and stopped fussing, he calmed down, but he still squirmed to be set free. "Nope, don't think so, buddy. There are too many cars coming in and out of the parking lot."

She set the boy down, but kept a firm grip on the hood of his coat. Then she extended her hand to Joe. "Melody Anderson. Nate's older brother is in grade four with Rebecca Copeland."

Joe nodded and shook her hand. "Joe," he said, not offering anything more, though he noticed her glance at his left hand. Despite the gold band he still wore on his finger, he felt her gaze on him while he turned his attention back to the doors of the school.

She edged a little closer until their arms were touching, and he felt her intention despite the thickness of their coats. It seemed she was settling in next to him for a lengthy stay.

"Son or daughter?" she asked.

"I'm sorry?" He stepped aside, putting a more comfortable space between them.

She moved a little closer again. "I assume you're here to pick someone up."

"Oh. Yes, I am."

He offered nothing more. He wasn't there to make friends, and he certainly wasn't looking for what she was offering. She turned to look at him, her mouth open to ask something, but the ringing of the bell pierced through the air, drowning out her question. He shrugged and took a further step away from her as Nate made another attempt to escape her clutches. Saved by the bell, and a restless toddler, he thought with a little laugh.

Glancing through the waiting crowd, Joe spotted Annie a few feet away, talking to one of the other Mums. He didn't bother to excuse himself with Nate's mother, even though she was saying something about a café meetup on Fridays. He simply smiled, then headed in Annie's direction.

When the mother Annie had been talking to left and headed toward the Kindergarten doors, he moved in closer.

"Hello Annie."

Her smile faded when she heard his voice and turned to look at him. "No bus for your two today?" he asked.

"They have dentist appointments." She turned her gaze to the doors and tucked her hands into her pockets.

At least she was speaking.

"Ryder likes the school and his teacher," he said.

"Noah said Ryder goes to the library after school. Not today?"

"We made some plans."

Small talk. Like their text messages every morning. Stuff they already knew or could easily figure out. Things that didn't amount to a hill of beans. He looked at her and pulled her gaze to meet his.

"How's your dad?" he asked.

"Getting better every day. We gave back the wheelchair. He has a walker, but mostly he's just using his cane now. Staying inside so he doesn't slip in the snow."

"That's great news."

"Yes, it is. He doesn't enjoy sitting around the house, though, so he's pretty bored. He knows there's work to be done, but he also knows he can't do any of it."

"I could... If you need..."

Annie held her hand up. "Don't Joe. You've done enough. I really don't want you thinking I need rescuing."

Oh, but you do, Joe thought. He didn't say what he was thinking. "Sure. I get it. Sorry."

He took a step away when the doors opened, and kids began filing out of the school. They gathered in lines, fumbling with backpacks, pulling hats on at the last minute, when the cold air hit them. Ryder came out of the school walking next to his teacher, talking animatedly to her, no doubt about the movie they were going to later. He pointed at Joe and they headed in his direction, with Noah trailing close behind.

"Hello, Mr. Hewitt. Julie Wight," she said when they got closer.

"Yes. We met when I enrolled Ryder a few weeks ago."

She nodded toward the fence, away from the crowd of waiting parents. "If I could have a word?"

"Ryder, will you wait with Annie for a minute?"

"Sure!" Ryder elbowed Noah, and the two began kicking snow at each other's feet.

As Joe followed Ryder's teacher to a place away from the crowd, he cast a glance back at Annie, who was already gathering Ali into a hug and zipping up her jacket.

"Is everything okay with Ryder?" he asked when they could speak privately.

"Oh yes. He's a bright boy. I wondered if you were coming to the parent-teacher interviews. I didn't see your name on the list."

"Should I make an appointment at the office?"

"No, that's not necessary. I know my schedule. I have Tuesday evening wide open. Would six-thirty work for you?"

He hesitated and looked back at Ryder. "Yes, I think I can manage that. I'll have to bring Ryder along, though."

"Of course. It's important for the students to be there to talk about their progress. Sometimes they have questions too."

Joe nodded. "Okay. I'll put it in my calendar."

"Good. See you Tuesday evening then."

As she walked back to her students, Joe had the distinct impression he'd just been hit on a second time. Something in her tone and the way she hung around just a little, as if there was something else she'd wanted to say. He felt his cheeks flush a little and couldn't help feeling flattered, but there would never be anyone else for him but Annie.

"Hot date?" Annie said flatly when he went back to collect Ryder.

"Parent-teacher interviews," he said, puckering his cheek on one side. "I always hated those when I was a kid, waiting to hear the blast from my parents about my grades, or my attitude." He shuffled his feet and kicked at the snow. "When are yours?"

"Monday. After school." She edged closer to her pickup, beckoning Ali, who'd gone to play with Ryder and Noah. "Julie is single, you know. And she's very nice."

"No. I mean, maybe she is, but…" Didn't she know there could be no one else in his life? "Annie, could we have coffee sometime? Just to talk?"

"What would we talk about, Joe?"

He caught the tilt of her chin as she looked into the distance, again avoiding his gaze. "Please don't be angry with me. I thought we were past that, since you aren't ignoring my texts anymore."

She shrugged. "I'm not sure I have anything to say."

"But I do. And I need you to hear it. All of it. Look, I don't want to talk about this here, with other people around, especially the kids. I could come out to your place." He swung around and waved his hand toward his little blue-sided bungalow. "Or come to our place sometime."

She heaved an enormous sigh and kept her gaze on the schoolyard. "It's taken me a while to accept what I can't change. I appreciate what you thought you were doing for me. I will pay you back every single penny with interest. But beyond that, I'm not sure we have anything to talk about."

When she reached for the truck's door handle to open it for Ali, Joe moved closer. "So, the fact that we both said I love you means nothing now?"

"Did it ever?"

"It did to me."

"You knew me for two minutes and you were madly in love. How is that possible?"

"Don't do that."

"What?" She looked at him, this time meeting his gaze with anger in her eyes. "What am I doing?"

"That sarcastic, blowing me off kind of attitude. It's not you Annie."

"How would you know?" She fiddled with the straps on Ali's car seat.

He reached out to touch her arm, to draw her attention back to him. "I know you better than you realize." I've known you all my life, he wanted to say.

"You butted into my life without asking. Went behind my back and got my father involved and…"

"Got him involved! Annie, it was his idea," Joe exclaimed.

She frowned at him. "Oh really. So, this is my father's doing? I highly doubt it." She spun on her heel. "Where is my daughter? Ali. In the car now, please."

But Joe wasn't letting this go. Now that he'd started, he had to finish. "It's the truth, Annie. Whether you want to believe it or you don't. Sam is the one who asked me to do this. He couldn't see you going through the frustration and the worry, knowing he could help."

There. It was out in the open. But the moment it was, Joe wished he hadn't said it. From the look on her face, he knew Annie was angry at her father now, and that was the last thing Joe wanted to happen.

"It was a kind of mutual thing. We both wanted to help," he placated, hoping it would smooth things over.

"If Dad really wanted to do something, he could have done it without you."

"He tried, but you wouldn't listen." Joe shook his head. "Besides, when the bank is ready to foreclose like that, the payments will only settle what's owed. They want all their money, not just some of it. They still would have foreclosed, and you would have lost the place."

Ali came bounding up to them, full of smiles and laughter.

"Hi Joe," she said, slipping her backpack off her shoulders.

Annie grabbed her hand and pulled her just a little too hard as she lifted her into her seat.

Ali squirmed. "Ow! Mummy, you're hurting me. I want Joe to do it." Ali fixed a stubborn gaze on her mother.

"Ignoring the facts isn't going to change anything," Joe protested.

She ignored him and Ali too, when she struggled and reached out to Joe. "Don't do this, Ali. We'll be late."

"I want Joe to do it." Ali kicked her foot hard against the back of the front seat.

"Fine." Annie glared at Joe. "She's all yours." Then she went around to the other side of the truck. "Noah! Get in, please, or we'll be late."

Noah and Ryder came bounding up to the truck, stumbling and knocking into each other, thumping their fists and laughing.

"See ya," Noah said, brushing past his mother to climb into the truck.

"Yeah, see ya," Ryder called back, heading around the back of the truck toward Joe. He peered past him to wave at Ali. "See ya, cutie."

But Ali's eyes were fixed on Joe's. "She doesn't mean it. Don't give up," she whispered.

"Pardon?" Joe asked. "What do you mean, sweetheart?"

She put a finger to her lips and whispered. "Don't give up on Mummy. She won't be mad forever."

"Oh, she's not mad, honey. She's just a little worried."

"Shhh. She's getting in." Ali threw her arms around Joe's neck. "I love you, Joe," she said, then kissed him on the cheek. "Grandpa misses you, too."

Joe smiled. "I miss you too," he whispered. Then he closed the door as Annie started the engine.

Joe put his arm around Ryder's shoulders and as they stood together, watching Annie's truck drive away, he felt as if his heart were about to break. Again. They were so close now, closer than they'd ever been, but even still, the gap between them felt about the size of the Grand Canyon.

Chapter 21

Joe was looking forward to spending some time with Sam. Since Annie had parent-teacher interviews after school that day, and was taking the kids to Huntsville afterwards, he and Sam had decided Joe should come to the house for a visit. Joe cleared his schedule, eager to talk with Sam face to face rather than their secret, late-night conversations on the phone. He was also looking forward to seeing the man he loved as much as he had his own father. Sam had assured him he was doing much better, but Joe wanted to see that for himself.

When he pulled into the lodge driveway, he noticed a couple of snowmobiles parked by Raven's Nest. Good, he thought, the winter enthusiasts were booking in. Skimming his eyes over the lake, he paused for a moment when he saw two ice-fishing huts sitting twenty or more yards off the shore. Who had helped her get them out there, he wondered? Maybe Luke was around again, helping, hovering, putting pressure on her. But Luke had made him a promise, and he seemed to be a man of his word. Maybe someone else had come out to help her get them onto the frozen lake.

Sam called out to him when Joe knocked on the back door and opened it. "In my room, Joe. Come on in."

Joe slipped off his boots, and hung his coat and scarf on an empty hook in the mudroom, and went inside. He found Sam sitting at a table by the window, with photo albums spread out in front of him. A particular one Joe hadn't seen for years was on his lap.

"Taking a walk down memory lane, Sam?"

A mutual respect flickered between them, and Sam nodded. "Something like that." His speech was nearly perfect, with only the slightest little pucker of his lip when he smiled. Sam pointed to a chair. "Take a load off, son. I'm glad you came."

"Me too. It's good to see you doing so well."

"Coming along. Still can't get outside on my own, though."

"I noticed the ice-fishing huts. Who helped with those?" Please don't say Luke, Joe thought.

"Ben came with Cam Meyers and a couple of other neighbours. They're coming back next week to put two more out."

Joe stiffened. "I haven't forgotten how much work that is," he said. "I wish I'd been here."

"All in good time, son. All in good time." Sam took a deep breath. "Ali told me about seeing you at the school on Friday. That little girl loves you, you know."

"The feeling's mutual. Same with Noah. And you. You know that I hope."

The older man nodded. "Me too." He clapped a hand over Joe's and swung the photo album in his direction. "Take a look at these. Know who that is?" He tapped his finger on a photograph in the top corner of the page.

Joe peered closer at the picture of two women in nursing uniforms proudly holding up their diplomas.

"That's Mum," Joe said, pointing to the woman with the slighter frame. "And this is Violet, your wife. I always thought it was so cool that you named your daughters after each other's wives. True friends."

Sam laughed. "Well, your father and I had nothing to say about it. I think Annie and Vi agreed long before they met us." He sighed. "I miss them both. Annie was a good friend, and Vi was the love of my life."

"I know how that feels."

Sam looked across at him. "I know you do, son. And I'm sorry."

"It isn't your fault."

Sam flipped over the pages. "Look here. This is when you and Annie were little. See you're there, in the wading pool, and

Annie is in her mother's arms, squirming to get out and get into the water with you."

Joe smiled and flipped the page over. "I remember this one," he said when he came to a picture of the two families sitting under a Christmas tree. "This was at your house in London, wasn't it?"

"It was, and your father set up the timer on the camera. We all sat there grinning like idiots while he ran around and yelled, get ready, get ready!" Sam slapped his leg and laughed at the memory. "Someone always blinked or had a blurred head or something, but this one was perfect, so we made a few copies of it."

"I was six, I think. Annie was four. I always remember having Christmas together."

"And Easter, and Thanksgiving and summer vacations. Vi and Annie were more like sisters than friends."

Joe flipped through more family photos, pointing to one or another that he recalled. Until there were no more of his mother, or of Sam's wife, and no more that included him.

"That's when you moved away," Sam said. "When your mum died, your poor dad just had to get out of that house. Too many memories."

"He was never the same. Died a month after we moved. He never wanted to be without her."

"Then you went on to university alone. Must have been hard on you."

"I suspect you haven't had it easy either, Sam, since Vi died."

"But I have Annie and the kids. And you."

"That's true." Joe looked at his hands. "Ryder is all I've got left."

"No. Son. You're wrong." Sam's hand reached out to Joe. "We'll always be family. Always."

Joe's head fell into his hands and he moaned. "But what if she never remembers? What will we do then?"

Sam shook his head. "Something is about to happen. I can feel it in my bones. I was hoping the Christmas party would do it, but…"

"I thought so too, but that all backfired." Joe shook his head. "She's so angry with me, Sam. I don't know what to do."

Sam picked up one of his albums. "I've got an idea," he said, pushing out of his chair. "I tried this once before, but I think it was too soon after the accident. Maybe enough time has passed now."

Joe followed him to the living room, where Sam set the album on top of the others under the coffee table. "You think she'll notice it?"

Sam grunted. "Oh, she'll notice it alright. She notices everything that isn't where it's supposed to be. Now let's just hope she opens it up and has a good look."

They both turned sharply when they heard a vehicle in the driveway.

"One of the guests?" Joe asked, hurrying to look out the window. "Oh no. It's Annie with the kids. I thought we would have more time."

Sam stiffened and lifted his jaw. "It's my house too. I can have a guest if I like. Just come sit with me and everything will be fine."

Joe followed Sam back to his room and was perched on the edge of the chair when they heard the back door open and the usual thumping of boots and backpacks on the mudroom floor. Moments later, Ali flew into the room and raced over to him.

"Joe! You're here!" she climbed up on his lap. "I'm so glad to see you."

"I'm glad to see you, too. But what about Grandpa, doesn't he get a hug?"

"Of course." She slipped out of Joe's grasp and went to kiss Sam, then hurried back to Joe. "Noah hurt his hand so we can't go shopping."

"Is he alright? What happened?" Joe was about to set her down, ready to check on Noah.

Ali shook her head and whispered, "Don't go in there. Mummy's in a bad mood."

Joe and Sam exchanged a smile over Ali's head. "Why?" Sam asked.

Ali's head fell against Joe's chest and with a heavy sigh she said, "Cause Joe's car is in the driveway."

When they heard Annie's voice from down the hall, Ali scrambled from Joe's lap. "I'm going up to my room. See ya later."

She hurried out of Sam's room and up the stairs just as Annie came to the doorway, arms crossed, a stern look on her face.

"I know this is your house too, Dad, but could you let me know when you're having company?"

Fire couldn't have spewed hotter than Annie's words. Joe felt a little guilty that he and Sam had gone behind her back this way. He dropped his gaze to the floor and, in doing so, his eyes fell on her bunny slippers. Instantly, the remorse left him as the one eye out of four stared up at him, still floundering for life. He let out a little smirk and nodded toward Sam, who smirked too.

"What's so funny?" Annie shrieked. Then she followed their gaze. "Really!" She turned on her heel and stormed from the room.

"Wait, Annie." Joe jumped up and followed her. "I'm sorry, but it's really hard to take you seriously in those slippers."

"There's nothing wrong with my slippers."

"If you say so, but they are a bit silly now that the ears have fallen off and there's only one eye." He couldn't stop smiling as her features worked themselves into an angry mess of frustration and irritation.

She looked down at her feet and wiggled them, one at a time, and lifted them up to inspect them more closely.

"Damn you, Joe Hewitt. I like my bunny slippers." Then she turned and stomped down the hall toward the kitchen.

Joe followed. "I'm sorry. I really didn't mean anything by it. They're fine." A grin slipped across his face. "Maybe a little repair job might help." He knew why she refused to replace them with another pair, but did she?

She lifted her chin in defiance, as she pulled things out of the fridge to make the kids their snack. "You might think they're dorky, but I like them."

There was a little smirk at the corner of her mouth then, too, a sign of something other than anger wedging its way in. It grew as he leaned against the kitchen counter and smiled back at her. Eventually, he nudged her into a full-blown laugh, using only facial expressions. He used to do it all the time when she was in a snit about something. Usually, like this time, it worked to ease her mood. He sensed the shift and took a step closer.

"I don't think they're dorky. I think they're adorable. And so are you." Her eyes held his as he moved closer still until he was so close he could smell the peach shampoo she'd used this morning. He took a deep breath and held it, still holding her gaze.

"So beautiful," he whispered, reaching out to touch her cheek. She took a step toward him, closing the space between them, and something familiar about the look in her eye gave him hope. "Annie," he whispered and pulled her into his arms.

She was tense at first, her arms between them pushing lightly, fighting his hold. But when he caressed her back, whispered into her hair and closed his eyes, she relaxed until the tension in her body was gone and she let her arms drape over his neck.

"Oh, Joe."

Just two little words whispered with a soft sigh, but they gave him hope. Don't say anything, he told himself. Let her make the next move. She's like a deer in the wild, if you move, she'll bolt. He didn't want that to happen. He wanted to hold her as long as he could. For now, it was enough. It would have to be.

She looked up at him, her mouth opened just the slightest bit, for a kiss or to say something, he wasn't sure. For that tiny moment in time, he thought she just might reach up and kiss him. He would not kiss her first. Not this time. This time it had to be her.

But then...

"What's for supper, Mum?"

Noah came from the living room and brushed past them, as if seeing them in each other's arms was as natural a thing as breathing. Annie pulled away and turned to Noah, but something in her gaze, as she looked back at him, told Joe her anger was gone.

"I should start dinner," she said when she'd sent Noah off with an apple. She moved closer again, her hand on his arm, her eyes meeting his. "Will you have dinner with us?"

"Ryder is at the library. I have to go."

"Bring him back here, why don't you? He and Noah can do their homework together. I hear they have a project to do."

"What about Noah's hand? Ali said he'd hurt it."

She scoffed. "It's a scratch. Noah hates going shopping, so he makes up excuses not to go."

Joe didn't want to miss the opportunity of spending an evening with them, while Annie was feeling so generous. "Alright then. If you're sure. I'll be a few minutes. What can I bring?"

"You could pick up a dessert at the bakery."

"One cherry cheesecake coming up," Joe said, reaching for his coat.

She looked at him in surprise. "How did you know that's my favourite?"

Because I know everything about you, he thought.

"Lucky guess," he said, looking past her where Sam stood at the other end of the hallway, flashing him a knowing smile. "See you in an hour," Joe called out. Then, to his surprise, Annie reached up on her toes and kissed him, not a little peck on the cheek good-bye, but a full, open-mouthed, hungry kiss.

"I do love you, Joe," she said, when they broke apart. "But I'm not quite done being angry about this mortgage business."

He nodded. "Okay. We'll talk about it when you're ready."

Closing the door on his way out, Joe's heart swelled. His patience was finally being rewarded. Even though this was just a baby step, something about it felt like a giant leap across an enormous chasm.

Because this time, Annie had come to him.

Chapter 22

The last time Joe could recall buying a cherry cheesecake was the day before Ali was born. Amid what Annie had thought were Braxton Hicks contractions, she'd had a craving and, knowing it was the only thing that would satisfy her, Joe had gone out to find one.

The little bakery in town was closed, so he went to Bracebridge. He looked in every store he could think of, but the only kind he could find was blueberry. Annie would have hated it. So, he went on to Huntsville, calling her every few minutes to make sure she was alright and to update her on his findings. Finally, just as it was about to close, he came to an Ice Cream shop and went inside.

"This is a long shot," he said to the teenage nymph of a girl behind the counter. "But I need a cherry cheesecake. Any chance you might have one?"

The girl smiled, her pixie-like eyes sparkling with delight. "You're in luck. There's one left." She went to the display case and pulled it out for closer examination. "That's eighteen dollars," she said, when he nodded his approval.

"That's highway robbery, but I'll take it." The girl didn't offer a smile at his attempted humour. Reluctantly, he pulled out his credit card and paid, leaving the shop holding the box as if the cheesecake were precious crystalline glass.

By the time he got home, Annie was in full-blown labour. He shoved the cheesecake into the fridge, picked up Annie's already packed suitcase, and helped her to the car.

The cheesecake was the last thing on both their minds as Annie went through hours of difficult labour before her eventual C-section, and later the hysterectomy. She was in the hospital for more than two weeks, and by the time she got home, the cheesecake was skeptical at best.

"I know where I can get another one," Joe had offered when they tossed it into the compost bin.

"That's sweet of you, but the moment is gone. Thank you, though," she had said.

This time they would have cheesecake if he had to make one himself, he thought. Would it trigger a memory? Who knew? Anything might, Jim Sullivan had told them. Go with the flow, and that's what he'd been doing for the past five long years.

The bakery in Baysville was open, and, as luck would have it, they had one cherry cheesecake left, as if it were waiting just for her. Joe paid for it and put it in the car, then went to get Ryder, who was playing chess with one of the helpers, at the library.

"I didn't know you could play chess," Joe said as they headed to the car.

"I'm just learning." Ryder gave a little shrug and opened the car door.

"Maybe you can teach me sometime."

"I'm not very good." Ryder climbed into the back seat and buckled up. "Where are we going?"

"To Noah and Ali's house for supper. Hey, you know what? Sam plays chess. Maybe he could help you."

"Cool. Yeah, maybe he can." A sly grin formed on Ryder's lips. "Maybe he can teach both of us."

Making dinner with Annie felt like old times, and to Joe she was like the woman she'd been before all this had happened, before the accident, before the coma, before their lives were torn apart and his heart was yanked out of his chest. Except for the three children in the living room, waiting for their dinner, it might have been eight years ago, and they were making supper after a long day's work on the house, or the grounds. He couldn't believe that she'd been living in this catatonic state where he, and the life they'd had together, didn't even exist.

Sometimes it was like that, the doctors had said, when a person woke from a coma. Sometimes it takes a few weeks for their memories to come back. Sometimes months and sometimes a few years. Sometimes…He didn't want to entertain the thought…never.

Joe refused to believe that she would never remember how much in love they'd been, how good they'd been together, how happy they'd been when they bought this place and got out of London. It killed him now when she spoke about a late husband, because that's what he was to her. She hadn't a single memory of any aspect of their past together.

They sipped wine as they worked and talked about the kids, her father's stroke, and plans for the lodge. She chopped vegetables while he seasoned the meat, working around each other in perfect harmony, like a well-conducted orchestra. Joe didn't push her to say anything, or ask any of the million questions that slid to the tip of his tongue. He just let her talk and marveled at the wonderful woman she'd become. He watched her smiling at him the way she used to, with that sweet, sweet curve of her lips that made him want to take her in his arms and kiss her and never let her go.

Eventually, without probing, she came to her relationship with Luke. As if sensing his concern, Annie qualified the connection as a friendship, not much more than a brother-sister kind of thing. It was Luke, she said, who had read more into it, and she knew now it was time to settle it once and for all.

"Is this enough?" she was asking, as his thoughts dissolved and landed him back in the present. "Earth to Joe. Where are you?"

"Sorry. I was somewhere else for a minute."

"Yeah, no kidding. Are these enough carrots?"

He looked down at the pile she'd sliced. "Perfect." Everything she did was perfect. Together, they scooped up all the vegetables and put them around the meat.

"It doesn't look like a big enough roast for all of us," she said, when he put the lid on the pan.

"It's enough and we have plenty of vegetables which are better for us, anyway."

She looked up at him in surprise. "I always say that."

I know you do, he thought. "It's true. We eat way too much meat." He rubbed his hands together in anticipation of the meal to come. "What shall we do while that cooks?"

Annie lifted her wineglass and nodded toward the fridge. "How about a refill?"

Joe took the wine out of the fridge and refilled their glasses. When they sat down at the kitchen table, she said, "Enough about me. Why don't you tell me about Ryder and how you came to be taking care of him?"

"Well, let's see. Where do I begin this story? I suppose I'd have to go back to the accident. That was five years ago." It was daring to bring this up, but it was where the story started, so there really was no other place to begin.

"You were in an accident? Was it bad?"

"It was, yes. We were on a family vacation with Violet, that's my sister, and Ryder. We were coming through the mountains where they have those runaway ramps in case trucks can't slow down." She nodded, indicating she knew what he meant. "We'd had a truck behind us for a few miles and I kept saying he's going too fast. He needs to slow down. A couple of times we managed to get a little ahead of him, but he'd just catch up again. Anyway, on one especially long downward slope, he came at us fast and hard. There were cars on the left so we couldn't move over, cars in front, so we couldn't speed up. We were sandwiched in with nowhere to go. He was going so fast he missed the ramp and rammed us from behind. We hit the people in front of us and it became an instant chain reaction all down that stretch of highway. The truck jackknifed, and the trailer swerved out and scooped us up, shoving us into other cars and dumping us all in the median. Everyone was swerving and trying to get out of the way, but it was impossible. I still have nightmares sometimes. I hear the squealing tires, the screeching brakes, and metal twisting as we all piled up on top of one another." He paused to watch her face, wondering if any of this sounded familiar to her. She showed no signs of recognition, but a look of deep concern spread across her face.

"How awful."

"It was. A lot of people died. We probably should have, too. We were lucky, but we were not without problems." He paused again, searching for any sign that she remembered something. When she said nothing, he continued. "My wife had a nasty gash on her head and needed stitches. At some point during the ride to the hospital, she lost consciousness."

Annie absentmindedly rubbed the scar at her hairline but still said nothing. She simply stared at him, waiting for him to go on. So he did.

"Violet and Ryder were in the back, so…"

"She didn't make it?" Annie's voice was soft, curious, full of concern.

"She did. Ryder, like our two, was fine. Shaken up and crying, of course, but the kids weren't hurt. He has no recollection of the accident now, but if he hears brakes squealing, he starts shaking uncontrollably. Violet had some bumps and bruises, and a broken leg, but all of that would mend. However, what they discovered at the hospital was that she had cancer."

Annie gasped. "She didn't know?"

Joe shook his head. "Came at us all like a Tsunami. We had no idea. They tried chemo and did all kinds of experimental things with Violet, but in the end, there was nothing they could do except keep her comfortable." He sighed. "Ryder's father had never been in the picture. I'm not sure Violet ever told him he had a son. Come to think of it, I don't think she ever saw him again. She asked me to be his godfather and legal guardian. When things got really bad and she couldn't take care of herself or Ryder anymore, I moved in with them and took care of them both until she passed."

Annie had been folding and unfolding her hands while she listened to Joe, and now she looked up at him with tears in her eyes.

"How awful," she said. "But what about your wife and children? They aren't with you now. Did they…? Are they…"

"They are very much alive. They're fine. Actually, they're great."

"But you're not together." She was hesitating, and he knew she didn't want to pry too much, yet she was curious.

If only he could tell her the truth. If only he could hold her in his arms and say, '*yes they are very much alive and I'm looking at her right now.*' There was nothing he could have done to avoid the tears that welled in his eyes.

She covered his hand with hers and caressed the back of it with her thumb. "I'm sorry, Joe. You don't have to tell me everything. I'm truly sorry."

He swiped at the tears and nodded, but words escaped him.

Just then, a bevy of cries from the living room erupted.

"I better see about that." Annie got up from her chair.

"I'll check on our dinner," he said with as much of a smile as he could muster.

As she left the room, Joe felt a tightness in his chest, as if someone's fist had reached inside and squeezed his heart. It was an ache that hurt so much he thought he might burst. How could he be so close, touch her, kiss her even, without her knowing who he was? When he'd gone away, as the doctors had advised, it had been the hardest thing he'd ever done. She hadn't known who he was then, she'd and wanted nothing to do with the strange man who kept insisting he was her husband. She kept insisting that her husband was dead. In her mind, he was, and so she could not accept that Joe was him. She might not remember still who he was, but on some level, she loved him and accepted that he loved her. This was a chance to be a part of her life again. Even if that meant starting over, that's what he would do. He just had to make sure he didn't screw it up this time.

He set the roast on the counter to rest, then gave the vegetables one last basting and pushed them back into the oven to brown. Leaning against the counter, he smiled at the simple, familiar reminders. Being in this kitchen again, making dinner with her like they used to, talking about things that mattered brought him unimaginable comfort. Maybe she would remember and maybe she wouldn't, but this was what he had to hold on to.

His eyes watered, and he shrugged it off, hearing voices outside the kitchen. Somehow, he had to cope with the intensity of his feelings. Everything lately had brought him to tears, it seemed. But telling her about the accident, as if she weren't a part of everything that had happened to them, was always the hardest. The first time he'd told her that story was when she came out of the coma. Then, like now, she'd had no idea who he was, and in his need for her to remember he'd botched it up, tried to push everything onto her at once. He'd become frustrated to the point of anger that she couldn't remember any of it. Then, he didn't understand. Then, he didn't know that her mind had shut this out because she was so angry with him. Then, he wanted only to have their life back.

'*Talk to her,*' the doctors had said. '*Tell her about her children, about your life together. Hopefully, it will spark a memory.*'

But nothing had.

The last thing he had wanted to do was go away, but when Violet became so ill, Annie's doctor and Sam and Joe decided he should take care of his sister and Ryder while Sam took care of Annie. Having Joe around didn't make sense to Annie, and all he did was create confusion for her. Sam moved in with her, and Joe moved into Violet's townhouse in Gravenhurst. He took extra jobs, worked double shifts, tended bar at night, and did whatever he could to save money. He and Sam set up a joint savings account and once a month, Joe deposited money into it for Annie and the kids. As long as Annie could manage without it, Sam didn't have to mention the there was a nest egg waiting.

It was her doctor who first suggested Joe should come back, more prominently this time. Other times, which Annie clearly had no recollection of, he'd been the man in line behind her at the grocery store, or a diner at the café when she and Sam took the kids for breakfast. Once or twice, he'd gone to the lodge on the pretense that he was a business acquaintance of Sam's, but Annie had paid little attention to him, and nothing he or Sam did sparked a memory for her.

Lately something in her was changing, her doctor said. She was talking more about her late husband, and other details were surfacing. Christmas, Jim had said, might be the perfect time for Joe to become a permanent fixture in her life again. They'd thought that even if she didn't remember him from the past, maybe she could fall in love with him again. He was determined to make this work if it took the rest of their lives.

She came into the kitchen, her hair all fuzzy and disheveled, eyes laughing with fun.

"You've been having pillow fights," he said, recognizing the glow on her face.

"I lost. Can you tell?" she said with a laugh. "Hard not to when it's three against one." She punched him playfully on the arm. "You could have helped, you know." She filled their wineglasses and handed him his. He wouldn't drink it. He wanted to keep a clear head.

"Dinner's ready," he said, setting his glass down, and taking her into his arms. "But if it's okay…" He bent to kiss her, tasted the wine she'd just sipped on her lips and felt her respond passionately, desire growing in both of them. He wanted that kiss to last forever, in case something new came to light for her and she pushed him away again. Every touch, every kiss might be their last, or it might be the one that sparked a memory for her. Would this kiss, right here next to the sink, in their kitchen, remind her of a kiss long ago, just like this one, that began the night when Ali was conceived?

She broke away with a gasp and looked up at him, a startled expression on her face. Something had clicked. They both knew it. But only Joe knew what it was. Good, he thought. Baby steps. One thing at a time.

Dinner was fun with everyone talking at once, passing food, helping the kids cut their meat, and Sam too, because his hand was still a little awkward. Joe caught Sam's approving nod, more than once, as they shared a secret moment across the table. Then both would look at Annie and smile at the radiance that glowed from her. Annie was at her best, with her family all around her.

The evening was over far too quickly, but the kids had school the next day and Annie had a yoga retreat checking in, in the morning.

"That's good news," he said. "Your package deals are paying off."

"Yes, but I need to give the lodge a good cleaning," she said, when the last dish was in the dishwasher. "I haven't been in there since Christmas."

"I could give you a hand," Joe said, hanging a tea towel on the hook. He saw her pucker one cheek in thought and kicked himself for offering too quickly. Don't push, he told himself. No matter how much he wanted to be with her, he had to remember this was like courting her all over again. Because on some level, way down deep inside, she was angry with him, maybe even hated him. And he knew why.

Annie hadn't wanted to go to Florida that winter. She was worried about money and taking Ali when she was so little. But he and Violet had convinced her it would be fun. And it was. They'd had a great time. Three weeks of sunshine and sandy beaches, a mountain of shells and tans as dark as southerners. Everything was wonderful, perfect even, until the accident and then the world caved in on all of them.

As if she was thinking the same thing, Annie reached up and rubbed the scar just under her hairline, then looked at him.

"There is one thing you could do. If it's not asking too much."

"Name it."

"I have a carpet on order that's supposed to come tomorrow. Something to make the lodge look a little homier and warmer, I hope. But I have a doctor's appointment, so I won't be around when they deliver it. I hate to ask Dad to go over there. I don't want him to fall. But if you're working, I could change my appointment, I suppose."

"No, it's okay. I own the company, remember? I'll be here whenever you need me. What time do you expect the delivery?"

"They gave me a four-hour window between one and five. Sorry I can't be more specific than that. My appointment is for two-thirty. If it comes before I leave, I could let you know."

"It's fine. I'll come for one, regardless. I was hoping your dad might teach me to play chess. Ryder is learning at the library, and I'd like to at least be good enough to play with him."

"I'm sure he'd love to," she said, tilting her head to one side. "I haven't seen him play in years. In fact, his chess board is in the attic, along with a bunch of other things of his. How did you know he played?"

Joe shrugged for her benefit. Sam had tried to teach Joe how to play on numerous occasions in the past, but Joe's mind had been on other things. Annie mostly.

"I suppose he mentioned it."

"Huh. Well, I'm sure he'd love to teach you. I could never get the hang of it. All these pieces that move in different directions. Some jump and some don't. And what's up with that thing where you bring one piece up and another around it? Kind of weird if you ask me. I'm more of a scrabble or monopoly kind of person."

"Yeah, I remember." He bit his lip the moment he said it, then attempted to fix it. "I remember playing both of those, too."

Looking around at the tidy kitchen, he realized there was no excuse for him to stay longer. "I guess I should pack Ryder up and be on our way."

"I guess," she said, a little dreamily, as if she was also thinking of a reason he should stay.

He wanted to kiss her again, one more time before he left, in case something set her off tomorrow and they had to back pedal again. As if reading his mind, she stepped closer and put her hand on his shoulder, then the other one came up too and the next thing he knew, they were around his neck. His hands naturally went to her waist and pulled her closer to him. Oh Annie, he thought. Please,

please, come back to me. He bent to kiss her, clinging desperately to the moment and praying it would last. She responded, and their bodies melted together until there was nothing left but their breath and the beating of their hearts. They had a connection. It had always been there. She'd just forgotten about it.

When it became obvious that the kiss wasn't going to be enough for either of them if he stayed much longer, Joe broke away.

"I really should get Ryder home," he whispered, watching her face, hoping for some sign of recognition from her.

"Yes, I suppose you should."

He nodded, unable to say anything. What could he say? And so, he said the first thing that popped into his mind. "See you later, alligator." And then he laughed.

"On the morrow, Mr. Sorrow," she continued. And then she laughed, too. "Don't get me started. There's a list of those. My mother and her best friend used to do the whole thing all the time." She paused and thought for a moment. "She was a lovely woman. I'm named after her and she named her daughter after my mother. Violet and Annie." She looked up at him in surprise. "Oh, like your sister, Violet. What a coincidence."

"Maybe it isn't," he said, as they headed toward the living room to round up the kids. But Annie hadn't heard him, or if she had, she said nothing.

"Hey guys. Ryder and Joe are leaving, and it's time you two went upstairs. Baths and bedtime. School tomorrow."

Their moment was gone, but Joe would never forget it. He tucked it into his heart, along with all the others, and said goodbye to Sam and Annie and the kids.

When Ali reached up to put her arms around him, he bent low, so she whispered in his ear. "I love you, Daddy."

The words took him by surprise, and he glanced up to see if Annie had heard them, but she was busy helping Ryder find a missing glove. He smiled at Ali and kissed both her cheeks, '*like they do in France*,' he told her.

When Ali released her hold on him, Joe rested his hand on Noah's shoulder. Noah flashed him a grin that seemed odd, even for a seven-year-old, then wrapped his arms around Joe's waist.

Something was up, but Joe had no idea what it was.

On the drive home, Joe took care on the dark, snowy roads that wound around the lakes and brought them down into the village of Baysville. He had to keep forcing his attention back to the road. He'd been thinking about Ali calling him Daddy and Noah's strange look and the sudden need to hug him.

"What did you guys watch on TV?" Joe asked, glancing in his mirror at a yawning Ryder.

"Nothing. Well, I dunno. Ali was watching something. Noah and I were looking at pictures."

"Oh? What pictures?"

"In a book. Pictures when Ali and Noah were little." Ryder was quiet for a long moment, which gave Joe time to think. If they'd looked at the first album, the one Sam had put there for Annie to see, then things might have fallen into place. There was no mistaking who the groom was at Annie's wedding, in Sam's album, or who was holding Ali and Noah when they were born, or who was pushing Noah in his stroller. When Sam had put the album there, neither of them had thought of the kids looking at it.

"Are you Ali and Noah's dad?"

"Yes." Joe watched for Ryder's reaction, but there didn't seem to be one.

"If you're their dad, and my mum was your sister, does that mean I'm their cousin?"

"Yes, it does. That's clever of you to make that connection."

"So, Annie is my aunt?"

"That's right too."

"Why didn't you tell me?"

"It's a long story, and a little complicated." They pulled into the driveway of the bungalow, and Joe switched off the engine. "I will tell you all of it, but not tonight. It's late."

"Okay. But why does Annie act like she doesn't know who you are?"

"She has what they call amnesia, a mental block. Sometimes, when people have a traumatic experience, they block out things they don't want to remember."

"So, Annie doesn't want to remember you or that you're Ali and Noah's father?"

"Sort of. Like I said, it's complicated. Some of it even I don't understand. I know I've told you not to keep secrets, but this one is important. Annie's health depends on it. Does that make sense?"

"Not really, but I'm just a kid."

"You're becoming less of a kid every day, bud. Now let's get some sleep, okay?"

While Ryder got ready for bed, Joe made a quick call to Sam to warn him that the kids had seen the pictures. Sam assured him he would find time to talk to them before they said anything to Annie.

Chapter 23

Joe rose late the next morning, bleary-eyed and restless after a night of frightening reoccuring dreams he hadn't had in years. In them he was reliving the accident and the days that followed. They were so real he'd woken himself up shouting at one point. Not wanting to dream again, he'd gone to the living room and put the TV on softly so as not to disturb Ryder. At some point, he must have dozed off because he woke to the screeching of the first bell at the school across the road.

"Wake up!" he called out, kicking the blanket off himself. But Ryder was already up and dressed and, in the kitchen, having a bowl of cereal.

Ryder looked up when Joe walked into the room, rubbing the sleep from his eye. "I didn't want to wake you," he said.

Joe patted his shoulder. "Thanks, but were you just going to go off to school and leave me sleeping on the couch?"

Ryder grinned at him. "Not like I have far to go, Uncle Joe. I can see the playground from here."

"True enough." Joe put on a pot of coffee and pulled some things out for Ryder's lunch. "Hey, how would you like to take Ali and Noah's bus after school and come out to the lodge? I promised to help Annie with a delivery later this afternoon."

"Sure. But you have to tell the school, and they have to tell the bus driver."

"I'll have to alert the library too, so they aren't expecting you after school."

"I guess so."

"Come on, then." Joe stuffed Ryder's lunch into his backpack and handed it to him. "I'll walk over with you and get everything arranged."

"In your pyjamas?" Ryder looked down at Joe's legs.

"Nope, I guess not. Give me two minutes."

Inside the school, Joe followed Ryder through a throng of children running in and out of doorways, shouting, laughing and calling out to one another.

"You know where the office is, right?" Ryder asked him, when they reached the corridor to his classroom.

"I can find it. Have a good day, Ry."

"You too, Uncle Joe."

In a flash, Ryder was lost in the crowd and all Joe could see of him was his Toronto Maple Leafs toque bobbing between a bevy of other brightly coloured hats.

He found the office easily, remembering it from earlier visits. It too seemed to be a din of activity and noise. It wasn't how he remembered school, but then that was a long time ago and things had changed. AT the desk he found a middle-aged, auburn-haired secretary, with a pair of cheaters dangling from her neck. Her head popped up and she raised her eyebrows at him. "Can I help you?"

"Good morning," Joe said. "I'd like to arrange for Ryder to take the bus with Ali and Noah after school today."

"Of course. If you'll just fill in this form." She fished for a file in the cabinet behind her and brought out a piece of paper. "Once we have this in the system, you could email or call if you'd like to arrange this again. Now I just need the children's last name so I can look up which bus they're on."

"It's Hewitt." Miss Wight, who Joe hadn't noticed was in the room, came to stand next to him. "I have both Ryder and Noah Hewitt in my class."

"Oh, that's Turtle Ted's bus." The secretary grinned at Joe. "Everyone loves Turtle Ted."

"I've heard that about him," Joe said, shifting to one side while he filled out the form, which allowed for the next parent in line to move up.

While he was filling in the details a thought niggled at him. Why hadn't this business of surnames surfaced until now? Ali and Noah's birth certificates were registered with his last name, Hewitt and it made sense that that was the name they'd use at school. Annie had chosen, at some point, to go back to using her maiden name, and all that made sense. What hadn't Annie recognized his name and made the connection when he'd made his booking? And why hadn't any of them thought about this until now?

He handed the form back to the secretary, whose line had dispersed now, and left the building, still puzzling over this surname issue. His plan had been to get a couple hours of work done before going out to the lodge but there was something he needed to do first.

Caffeinated coffee at his elbow, he opened his laptop and found the government website he was looking for. He scanned and uploaded the necessary proof that allowed him to order Noah and Ali's birth certificates and his marriage certificate. Then he re-quested they be shipped by express post. The sooner he had them, the better. No doubt Annie had copies of these somewhere, or had she conveniently put them out of her life, like she had everything else about him?

When that was done, he put in a call to Annie's psychiatrist. Why hadn't this business of children's surnames ever come up be-fore? He knew Annie had reverted back to her maiden name some-time after he'd left—another attempt to disconnect a 'dead' husband from her life. But why hadn't she changed the kids' names too? And when he booked into the lodge with the surname Hewitt, why hadn't it registered to her, or to the kids? Noah, at least, should have seen the connection, and Ali was a pretty clever little girl. Why hadn't she said something? Did they even know what his last name was?

Jim was with a client, the receptionist, with the smooth and professional voice told him. If Joe wanted to speak with him, it might be best to book an appointment. Joe didn't want to wait. Maybe Sam knew something. A quick text to him and a reply came back almost instantly. It was one word.

'*Later*'.

He got busy then with office work, to distract himself from the answers he couldn't find. In the past, he'd taken on as much work as was humanly possible, hoping he wouldn't notice how long Annie's recovery was taking. But now he was getting restless and there wasn't enough work, or volunteer activity, or hobbies to make the time go fast enough.

He made a quick lunch out of leftovers in the fridge, then showered and shaved. As he reached for a bottle of aftershave on his dresser, one that he'd bought for himself, he passed over it and reached further, to the one at the back; the one Annie had given him, the one she loved. He opened the lid and sniffed. Was it possible for aftershave to go bad? He dabbed a little on the back of his hand. Surprised that it didn't burn or cause an instant rash, he splashed a little onto his hands and applied it to his face. They say (whoever *they* are) that sounds and smells are the things most likely to trigger memories. Maybe this scent would spark something for Annie.

The drive along the narrow windy roads certainly brought back memories for him. He recalled the first time he and Annie had come up to look at the lodge, hopeful, after viewing more than twenty properties, that this would be the one.

"I've got a good feeling about this one," Annie had said, practically bouncing out of the seat when they pulled into the drive-way. After three days of viewing, she hadn't lost her enthusiasm, though he was ready to go home and regroup, source out some new places, talk to other agents.

He'd thought Paradise Cove was a dumb name for a place in northern Ontario when he'd heard it. It made him think of somewhere in Florida, amid the palm trees, with a pelican perched on an oval sign and pink flamingos on either side of it. But he'd been wrong. It was paradise, and they had both felt it the instant they pulled off the main road and into the driveway.

They followed the wooden arrow shaped signs, directing them to a log cabin lodge and parked. Annie sucked in a huge gulp of pine-scented air and looked across at him. They both smiled, their eyes wandering to the lakefront cabins down one lane and the cottages down another. They got out of the truck, and waiting for their agent to catch up with them, wandered down to the shoreline. It was early autumn, and the leaves were just beginning to turn. Across the lake to the opposite shoreline, it was as if someone had laid a carpet of colour there, so high it was reaching up to the blue, blue sky.

"It's breathtaking," Annie said, taking Joe's hand in hers. "I love it here."

"Me too. I think we've found the one."

They'd turned then to look at the house, nestled against a grove of trees between the lodge, where they'd just park and the path that led to a group of fishing cabins. Windows across the back of the house looked out over the lake, and Joe had imagined the view from inside.

"The house looks like it has good bones. I like that we could put some deck chairs on the porch and watch the sunset."

"It might look okay from the outside, but it's an old house. What if it's falling apart in there? We can't move into a dump." Annie had leaned against him, her head on his shoulder, watching a flock of Canada geese swoop in and land on a stretch of beach not a hundred feet from where they stood.

"We could live in one of the cottages, if we had to, while we fixed things up inside."

She glanced in the direction of the row of cottages, turned back to him and stifled a giggle. "We could christen every one of them." Her face flushed at what she was suggesting. They'd been married nearly two years, and she was just coming out of her shell with the intimate side of their relationship, but it always embarrassed her to let him know it. It was one of the things he loved about her. One of the many things.

He blinked, fighting back tears as he pulled into the driveway and parked next to Annie's truck. It seemed he was always just one memory away from crying these days and sometimes that made him feel helpless, weak and overly emotional.

He opened the back door of the car to let Max out. He could have left him curled up on Ryder's bed, but, like Joe, Max enjoyed himself much more up here. Free of the confines of the car, Max bounded down the lane toward the fishing cabins, no doubt in pursuit of a furry creature.

Max wouldn't hurt a flea, but he couldn't take chances Annie's guests might feel uncomfortable with such a large dog wandering around. Joe's whistle brought Max to an instant halt. He turned and looked back, as if thinking about it for a moment. The woods, or Joe? Until a second whistle, sharper and longer than the first, sent him hurrying back. Max sat in the snow at Joe's feet, looking up at him, disappointment written all over his face until Joe fished a biscuit out of his pocket which Max sucked down his throat in one gulp.

"I'll take you for a walk in the woods later, okay, boy?"

The back door opened with a squeak, reminding him that he was going to oil the hinges. He'd thought of it yesterday, but they'd been busy with dinner, and time had gotten away from him. Rusty hinges and dog treats were lost to him when he saw Annie standing in the doorway, leaning against the frame.

"Thanks for coming," she said, then beckoned him inside.

Sam was at the kitchen table, the chessboard ready with the pieces laid out in their correct positions. Max made himself at home, under the table, out of the way, while Joe looked down at the chessboard.

"We're really going to do this, aren't we?" Joe said, clapping Sam on the shoulder good-naturedly.

"You wanted to learn," Sam reminded him.

"Yes, I guess I did."

Annie went to the coffeepot.

"If you're pouring one for me, I'll pass," Joe said. "I've drunk enough coffee this morning to fill a pond. But if you have some of that tea you call dessert in a cup, I'll take that."

"Sure," she said, filling the kettle and taking down a cup. "Tea is better for you, anyway. There's a quote I like, from C. S. Lewis." She looked at him in surprise when he joined her.

"You can never get a cup of tea large enough or a book long enough to suit me."

Her eyes met his, and he laughed.

"You like to read too?" she asked. He nodded. "Huh! Books and Tea, who would have thought?"

"I would," Sam interrupted. "Joe reads almost as much as you do."

"Oh, and how would you know that?" Annie teased. "You've known him all of two minutes."

Joe and Sam exchanged a knowing glance while Annie brewed the tea.

"Sit down, Joe," Sam insisted, pointing to the chair opposite him. "You need to focus if you're going to learn this game."

Joe went to the chair, but it wasn't where he wanted to be. He wanted to be near Annie, to stand behind her, pull her into his arms, kiss the back of her neck and feel her lean back onto his shoulder so he could cradle her head against his, just like they used to do.

They would look out the window at the view over the lake and count their blessings and be grateful that this place was theirs.

But that had been something they used to do, so maybe not today.

He pulled out the chair and sat down. "Any news from the delivery folks?" he asked, while Annie steeped his tea.

"Just an email this morning to remind me they are coming." She glanced up at the clock. "I have to leave in a few minutes so, I hope you two are okay here."

"We're fine," Sam insisted. "Stop hovering like an old mother hen." He smiled good-naturedly at her, while tossing an eye roll Joe's way.

Annie smiled at Joe, then kissed the top of her father's head on her way to the door. She called back as she opened the outer door. "Be good boys and don't get into any trouble." Then she laughed as she pulled the door closed behind her.

Sam and Joe laughed, too. "So much like her mother," Sam said. They both stood up to look out the window and watch her get into the truck. When they heard the engine spring to life and saw her drive away, they sat down again.

"Coast is clear," Sam said. "Thanks for the warning about the kids. I didn't give it a second thought when we put that album in the living room. I never dreamed they would touch it. They never do. But they were both full of questions that Annie couldn't answer. So, they came to me." Sam shook his head. "I couldn't lie to them, Joe."

"It's okay, Sam. You've been carrying a huge burden for a long time now. It isn't fair."

"I'd carry it to my dying day if I thought it was helping, but I don't think it is. Annie thought the kids were playing tricks on her, but I could see in her face she was trying to work things out. I'm hoping she's going to unload a bit of this at her appointment today."

"Jim was so sure that the time was right for me to come back. I hope he's right."

"We just have to be patient."

Joe nodded. "Tell me something. Did you know that the kids are registered at school in my name?"

Sam looked up in surprise. "No, it didn't even cross my mind."

"What is odd is if the kids go by Hewitt, wouldn't you think my name on the reservation would have triggered something?"

"I suppose, like everything else about you, she's disconnected." Sam shrugged.

Joe bit back a groan. He knew Sam was right, but it still hurt when he heard it. "I suppose we could second guess all this till forever. Help me take my mind off it and tell me about chess. I've forgotten everything I once knew, which wasn't much."

Sam grinned and picked up the tallest piece on the board. "This is the king. When he dies, the game is over."

Joe grinned. "Makes sense."

"Before that, he can only move one square in any direction at a time."

"If he's the king, shouldn't he be able to go anywhere?"

"He has people to move for him." Sam picked up another piece, followed by another, and another, demonstrating their moves.

Joe was completely confused by the time he got to the last one. "Let's just try a game and you can tell me along the way if I'm making a mistake or not."

They spent the better part of an hour bent over the chessboard, with Joe making bad moves and Sam correcting him, then explaining why. He was a good teacher and by the end of the third game, Joe was catching on and that was when they heard the delivery truck.

"I'd better get that," Joe said, heading for his coat. "Won't be long." Max stirred under the table. "Stay Max and keep Sam company." Max put his head down again and let out a resigned groan.

Outside, the air was so crisp it pinched Joe's nostrils together the moment he stepped onto the back porch. In the parking lot in front of the lodge, the driver was getting down from Garrison's delivery truck. When he turned around and saw Joe, both men were surprised.

"Luke!"

"Hi Joe." Luke said. "Didn't expect to see you here."

"Afternoon Luke. I could say the same," Joe said. "I didn't know you worked at Garrison's."

"Why would you?" Luke went around to the back of the truck and hefted a huge, plastic wrapped carpet out of it and balanced it over his shoulder. "The invoice says the lodge, so I'm assuming that's where you want me to put this."

"Ah, yeah. Let me open the door for you. Are you sure I can't help with that?" It looked awkward and Joe thought if they each took an end, it might go better. He reached out to take the front.

Luke shook his head. "I'm good. Just get the door, if you don't mind."

Joe hurried up the steps and opened the door for Luke, then followed him inside.

"I suppose you thought you'd see Annie today," Joe said, as Luke dropped the carpet in the middle of the floor. "You know, if you truly want what's best for her, you really should stay away. Like we agreed."

Luke's look was as icy as the air outside. "What if that's not you, huh? What if I'm what's best for her?" Luke shifted the carpet closer to the fireplace and stood up to stretch the kinks out of his back. "But I'm a man of my word. I told you I'd stay away, and I have. Until now." He fished a knife out of his back pocket, slit the ties that held the carpet in place, then made a slice into the plastic to find the end of the rug.

"How is she?" he asked, when Joe bent down to help him unroll the carpet.

"The same," Joe said.

"She still doesn't remember you?"

"Not yet. But we're hopeful."

"You don't think moving in here is a little drastic?"

"Moving in?" Joe shook his head. "I don't live here, Luke. I just came this afternoon because Sam isn't well enough to come outside yet, and she had an appointment."

"My mistake." Luke scratched the back of his neck and looked down at the floor. "I don't know what to say, Joe. I mean, I'm sure you're a good man and all, but where Annie's concerned, I get a little worried. It's hard staying away."

Don't I know it, Joe thought. Try staying away for five years. He took a step closer to Luke. "I know this is difficult for you, this waiting to see what she's going to do, but you have to be patient."

Luke threw up his hands and took a step back. "Don't do that. You don't know. You couldn't, possibly. I love her, Joe. I've loved her since the day I set eyes on her. And so does Chelsea. I thought we'd be together. I thought that if I just waited long enough, she'd come to realize that too, and we'd get married."

That tipped the scales for Joe. He did know. He knew exactly what Luke was going through, but to the nth degree.

"You think I don't know how you feel? Hell, Luke. Annie and I have been married for ten years. We had five amazing years and two kids together. Do you know what it feels like to have your gut wrenched out when your wife wakes up from a six-month long coma, and doesn't know who you are? She knows her parents, her children, but not you. The man she's loved and who has loved her from the time they were children. We were always in love, Luke. Always. Our families were best friends. It's always been Annie and Joe, Joe and Annie." Joe flopped down on the couch and put his head in his hands. "And then I ruined everything."

"*You* did? How?" Luke sat down in a chair next to him, his voice softening.

"I insisted we all go on that damned trip to Florida." He heaved a great sigh and leaned back. "It had been a rough year after Ali was born. Annie had to have a hysterectomy. Ali had colic for the first three months and never stopped crying. Noah fell off our bed and broke his arm. It was just one thing after another and finally that winter, I'd had enough. I said let's take a holiday and go somewhere warm, get out of this godforsaken cold for a while."

"So, you went to Florida?"

Joe nodded. "Not before we argued about it. A lot. I finally convinced her that if my sister and Ryder came too, she would have some female companionship and Noah would have someone to play with. Her parents offered to stay here and take care of things, so in the end, Annie agreed. We had a great time. It was sand and sun every day. Eventually, we headed back, and that's when the accident happened." Joe raked a hand through his hair. "I still have nightmares, people screaming, babies crying. Our babies. I see Annie's head smashed against the window, the glass shattering all around her, and the blood. That's when I wake up, sometimes screaming."

Luke shook his head. "I didn't know, man. I'm sorry. I just thought... Well, I don't know what I thought. She told me you were dead. But then when you showed up and told me to stay away, I guess I just figured the two of you had been separated or something and she hadn't wanted to tell me that before."

"Her doctor says that she's blocked me out, some form of amnesia. I guess on some deep level she's so angry with me for pushing that trip that the only way to deal with it is to pretend I don't exist."

"And you think that she'll just suddenly remember it all and forgive you?"

"Maybe not suddenly, not all in one day, but I live every day for the time when that forgiveness comes and we can be a family again. It's not like this is the first time I've come back. But it's the first time I stayed as a guest and then stuck around in town. The kids don't remember me. They were too young when the accident happened. Then later, we decided it would be better if they didn't see me, because eventually they would start asking questions. And that might set her off."

"Why now? What's changed?"

"For one, I have Ryder and since he and Noah are just weeks apart in age, I thought they should know each other, even if it's only as friends, for now. But mostly, because Annie's doctor saw a few signs that suggest she is remembering things."

"What things?"

"She remembers a trip to Florida. At least some of it. And then there's the tea."

"What tea?"

"The one she calls *dessert in a cup*. Annie worked in a tea shop before we were married. The woman called it Annie's Blend. Annie always said it tasted like dessert in a cup. We ran out of it, right before we went to Florida and Sam says there hasn't been any in the house since, until now. She ordered it after Ryder and I arrived."

"So, she ordered the tea, big deal. She probably just wanted it. She drinks tea all the time."

"We always drank it together. After the kids went to sleep, we'd sit in the chairs in the bay window of our bedroom, drink our tea and talk about the day. It was what we did every evening."

Luke nodded slowly, a look of understanding coming across his face, as if the truth were taking shape in his mind.

"I'm sorry, Luke," Joe said. "But we have to give her time."

"Which means I have to keep my distance." He ran his hands across his thighs and stood up. "I thought I might see her today. It's why I asked for this run. I usually just stay close to town, but when I saw her name on the schedule, I couldn't help it. I thought maybe we'd talk." At the door, Luke turned to shake Joe's hand. "Thanks, man. For your honesty and for looking out for her."

"It's me who should thank you, Luke. You've been here for her when I couldn't and for that I'm grateful."

Luke shook his head as he made his way to his truck and Joe couldn't help feeling a little sorry for the guy. He obviously cared for Annie, and Joe knew Luke was hurting right now. He waited while he climbed into the delivery truck and headed down the drive before returning to the house.

When Joe hung his coat up and went into the kitchen, Sam was on the phone.

"Let me put you on speaker, Jim. Joe just came in," Sam said as Joe sat down. "Okay, doc. Carry on."

"How was she today?" Joe was eager for some good news.

"Remember Joe, this is going to take some time," Jim began.

"You say that every time we talk, Jim. We know this, but is she beginning to open up? You thought there was hope, signs What's changed?"

There was a slight hesitation before Jim spoke. "A few things came up today. So, whatever you're doing, keep it up. She mentioned a couple of migraines again, but she can't remember what transpired just prior to them. I suspect they're triggered by a memory and once the headache is over, she can't recall that memory. Perhaps if you kept a journal, Sam, in the event she has any more."

"Will do, Jim. Anything else?"

"I'm guessing you put out a different photo album from the others?"

"I did," Sam admitted. "The kids found it before she did. She's convinced we've photoshopped the pictures and put Joe's face over their father's. As if I'd have a clue how to do that."

"Was there anything besides the pictures?" Joe asked.

"Yes actually. She mentioned a cherry cheesecake and then your aftershave, Joe. She said it was familiar, but she couldn't re-member why."

"There's another thing, Jim," Joe leaned closer to the phone. "The kids are registered at school under the name Hewitt. It's how we registered their births. Now, Annie knows my name is Hewitt, yet she's never put that connection together."

"Interesting." Jim mumbled a little into the phone. "Maybe a topic for next appointment." Another pause, followed by a deep sigh. "I wish I had more to tell you. I know this seems like it's miles away, but trust me, these little things aren't as little as they seem. Eventually, she's going to realize that the actual truth and hers are not the same. That's the crux of it all, getting to the truth."

"Okay, Jim. Thanks again."

"I suggested she come once a week, instead of every other. I'd like to strike while the iron's hot, so to speak. If she has too much time in between appointments, these triggers might fade into the background. I know it's costly but…"

"Whatever she needs," Joe said. "I'll take care of it, like al-ways."

"You're a good man, Joe, and a patient one. Let's keep a good thought, alright? You should make an appointment for yourself sometime soon. Let's talk about how you're doing through all of this."

"I'm okay, Jim," Joe said.

"Make that appointment." Jim said it with insistence so that Joe eventually agreed. They disconnected the call, and Sam looked across the table at Joe.

"It's a good sign, don't you think? Her recognizing your cologne, and the photo album."

Joe nodded. But his heart was breaking into tiny pieces, one more each time Annie didn't remember him and their life together. Less than a month to their tenth anniversary. Wouldn't it be wonderful if this Valentine's Day they could spend it together?

They heard Annie's truck pulling into the driveway not long after they hung up from their conversation with Jim. When she came into the room, their chins were in their palms, pretending to be deep in thought over their next move. They mumbled a greeting as she went to fill the kettle for something hot to drink.

"It's bitterly cold outside," she said, her hand rubbing the back of her neck.

Out of the corner of his eye, Joe watched her, looking out the window with a wistful look. "Are you alright?" he asked.

She nodded. "Bit of a headache. It'll go away. Did everything go okay with the delivery?"

"Sure did. The new rug is really nice. I put weights on the corners to flatten it out. Your yoga ladies will love it." He looked up at her as she leaned against the counter. "Annie, you don't look well," he said, getting up. "Let me make that tea for you."

She met his gaze and nodded. "I'd appreciate that. I think I need to lie down." She twisted her hands around the hem of her sweater. "I hate to ask, but can you stay till the kids get off the bus?"

"Absolutely. Whatever you need." He ran a caressing hand up her arm, watching her face twist into a grimace of agony. "Is it another migraine?" he asked, when she put her hands on either side of her head.

"It started when I was in the doctor's office."

"Why don't you go up and I'll bring this to you when it's ready?" He took her hands in his and kissed them and when he pulled her into his arms, she let him do that too, as if it was the most natural thing in the world which, of course, for him, it was. He felt her relaxing against him, then he took a deep breath, inhaling the scent of her.

The kettle came to a rolling boil and clicked off, disturbing the moment. Joe kissed her temples before letting her go so she could make the tea. Annie's hand went to her hairline again.

"Is your scar bothering you?" Joe asked, forgetting that he wasn't supposed to know about it or how she'd got it. She didn't seem to notice.

"Not really. Well, kind of," she said, a little ho-hum about it. "Maybe it's just because of the headache."

"How did it happen?" Joe's question was daring, and he knew it. He flashed a look in Sam's direction. Sam nodded his encouragement.

"This? Oh, just an accident with the swings when I was a kid. So much blood." She gave a nervous little laugh. "And stitches. They had to shave this side of my head, so I had a punk hair style before it was cool." She tried to smile through her pain, but the effort seemed too much for her.

Sam stood up and took a few steps closer to them. "That's not exactly how it happened though, Honey."

"Yes, it was. Mum took me for ice cream because I'd been off school and missed the end-of-year bus trip. Then we went to the park, and I was so dizzy I barfed all over her new shoes."

Sam laughed out loud. "Yes, I recall having to dish out for a new pair of shoes, but I think you're mixing that up with another day. You got this scar much later than that. Just a few years ago, actually."

Annie squinted, her frown suggesting she was trying to find reason from what he was saying. She glanced at Joe, who was pouring hot water over the tea leaves, then toward the table at their cups.

"Have you two been into the brandy or something? You're not making any sense."

Chapter 24

A contented warmth enveloped Joe as he pulled a blanket over his shoulders and settled into what had once been his chair at their bedroom window. It was dark now, black as pitch, with only a sliver of moonlight casting a golden glow over the bay. He sifted through memories of other such moons and other such evenings that seemed a lifetime ago, now. His hands cupped a mug of hot tea, gathering the memories it brought too, into his embrace.

After a time, he glanced to where Annie lay sleeping. In the soft, golden glow of the lamplight, fingers of darkness climbed the walls to touch the ceiling like trees standing on a shadowy mountaintop. On the nightstand sat a refill of her prescription for her migraines. Joe had given her one, hours ago, when he brought her tea up and she'd settled easily and went almost instantly into a deep sleep. He knew then that she would nap for a while, so he'd taken advantage of some alone time with Noah and Ali and Ryder.

Sam volunteered to tidy the kitchen after supper, while Joe took the kids for a long walk in the woods. They were explorers this time, since that's what Noah and Ryder were studying in school. Noah claimed the name Christopher Columbus and Ryder wanted to be Jacques Cartier, mostly because he and Joe had just watched a documentary about him a few days ago.

"Who can I be?" Ali had wanted to know.

"You can be Roberta Bondar," Joe suggested.

Ali wrinkled her nose. "Who's she?"

"Yeah. What did she discover?" Noah asked, a little sarcastically.

"She was Canada's first woman astronaut," Joe told them.

"Astronauts are *not* explorers!" Noah insisted. "They didn't sail in ships, looking for new worlds."

"No?" Joe challenged. "What is a rocket, then? It's a space-ship. Just because astronauts didn't travel around the earth doesn't mean they weren't explorers."

Ryder shrugged. "Guess I never thought about it that way."

"Guess you never watched Star Trek then, did you? '*To boldly go where no man has gone before*,'" Joe quoted.

Ali picked up a stick and held it up to her eye, pretending it was a telescope. "I'll be that lady," she said, "and I'll look down at you from my spaceship high in the sky." She climbed up onto a rock then and peered through her pretend telescope as Noah and Ryder scoffed at her and went past.

When they'd gone a little deeper into the woods and came to a clearing in the trees, Joe suggested they should turn back as it was getting dark and he only had the light from his phone to guide them if they got lost.

"Can I ask you something?" Noah said as they turned to go back.

"Anything, Noah."

"We know that you're our Dad. Grandpa told us and we saw the pictures. But why did you go away? Didn't you love us?"

"Oh, Noah. Of course, I loved you." Joe found a rock they could sit on, then pulled all three of them close to him. "It wasn't my decision. I went because it's what your mother's doctor thought was best for her. I have always kept in touch with Grandpa and he sent me lots of pictures so I could see how you were growing."

"Mummy is sick, right?" Ali asked, nestling in.

"In a way. Yes," Joe said. He thought of how best to describe it so a six year old could understand. "She has a wall in her memory and it's really tall, so very hard for her to climb over it."

"Can't she just knock it down?" Ali asked.

"Maybe. I hope so," Joe said, giving her shoulders a squeeze. "That's what we all want. It's why I came back. Because her doctor thinks that maybe, if she tries really hard, and if we do our best to help her, she just might."

"What can we do to help?" Noah asked.

"Good question. We can all love her and take care of her and we can be as good as we possibly can so that she doesn't have to worry so much."

"You mean like cleaning my room before she asks?" Noah suggested.

"That would be a big help. Or shoveling the snow, or doing the dishes. There are lots of ways we can help. But mostly, we just have to be patient. Especially when she's a little mixed up and gets these headaches." He looked at three solemn faces with eyes the size of moons. "If you need help with any of this, when I'm not around, talk to Grandpa, okay?"

"And maybe," Ali said, "Mummy will be alright and we'll be a family again."

"What if she never remembers?" Ryder asked.

"I'm not so sure about that yet," Joe confessed. "But this much I know. You and I are staying put here now. Either in Baysville or somewhere close by, so you guys will always have each other, okay?"

"Okay!" Noah slid Ryder a sly smile. "Best friends forever." They said in unison.

Ali threw her arms around Joe's neck. "I hope she remembers so I can call you Daddy and it won't be a secret."

Joe swiped at the tears forming in his eyes. "I can't wait for that to happen. I love you guys so much." He pulled the boys closer, too. "Family hug," he said, as they all huddled together.

Noah gave Joe a kiss on the cheek. "Thanks for telling us everything, Joe. I mean, Dad."

Joe smiled back at him. "I've waited five years to hear you call me that and it couldn't sound any sweeter. I love you too, Noah. And you Ali." He kissed her on the nose. "And you, Ryder."

After a moment while they were all silent, lost in their own thoughts, Joe said, "We should head back, because it's getting late, and I'm sure the calendar on the fridge has a big blue water drop on it for today. I think I can guess what that means."

Noah groaned. "Baths. Yuck!" But he hadn't put up much of a fuss when the time had come and now they were all tucked in their beds and sleeping soundly.

Annie stirred. He slid to the edge of his seat, watching and listening for signs she was waking up, but she didn't. She rolled over and settled again, her breathing almost instantly falling back into sleep rhythm. Joe pulled out his pocket watch and clicked open the cover. Ten fifteen. In another half hour, he'd go downstairs and make up the couch. Just now, though, he wanted to stay with her as long as he could.

His eye caught a curl in the wallpaper, just next to Annie's dresser, and it reminded him of the fun they'd had doing this room over, when they first moved in. They'd slept in one of the cottages for a month, spending their days renovating the house and their nights wrapped in each other's arms. He redid most of the plumbing, as much wiring as he knew how to do, and installed a newer kitchen, which they'd gotten from the ReStore. Annie was a whiz with the decorating side of things and had a keen eye for colours. She made what had been a century-old two story, run-of-the-mill house, with a couple of haphazard additions, look like a modern showpiece while keeping the rustic charm of their surroundings. They combed the second-hand shops for bargains and when they had to, they had dipped into their savings and bought new.

The only thing they ever argued about was the wallpaper in this room. She'd wanted something pink and flowery, and he'd said no to flowers. They'd settled on something neutral that neither of them really liked. At some point, in the recent years, she'd changed it, and he liked this choice she'd made. Shades of green suited this room, whether it was during the day or at night, like now, with the moon throwing shadows across it.

Just as she'd gotten rid of that old wallpaper, she had also wiped all traces of their life together from the room. The only exception were the clothes that still hung in the closet, things he hadn't had room for when he packed up to leave. He'd thought this odd, but Jim seemed to understand.

"You're dead, in her mind, and the clothes are a keepsake," Jim had said. "There might even be a hint of your cologne in them, and that might be comforting for her."

Noah had his dresser now, and a painting of a lake scene had replaced the wedding photograph that used to hang over their bed. Nothing in this room revealed an inch of the man that used to share it with her. He wondered what she'd been thinking the day she took their wedding picture down from over the bed and removed every other trace of him from her life. Hadn't she wanted to keep his memory close? Why had it been so important for her to make a clean sweep and rid him from her life?

She stirred again, and he quickened his gaze in her direction as she attempted to sit up. Joe set his cup on the window ledge and slid forward in the chair. Wait, he thought. Don't startle her. Let her fully wake up first. She sat up and gingerly swung her feet over the side of the bed.

"Oh!" she gave a little gasp when she noticed him sitting there. Then her gaze went past him to the darkness and her hand swiped at her forehead. "What time is it?"

"A little after ten," he said softly. He went to the bed and helped her up, wrapping her in the throw from the back of her chair.

"Come and sit with me. I made you a cup of tea, although it's probably not very warm now."

Annie let him help her to the chair and took the cup from him when she was settled into it. "It'll be perfect," she said, her face glowing in the moonlight.

He wondered if the familiarity of this might jog something for her; remind her of the nights when they sat together, cup of tea in hand, rehashing the events of the day, making plans for tomorrow. It had been a special time, something they looked forward to, something that often led to a night of passion. He held his breath, watching as she breathed in the wafting scent of the tea, then dipped her head to take that first sip. Would she remember? Would this be enough to bring her memories flooding back? And if it was, would she be happy, or sad, or terrified?

"I'm sorry," he said, softly.

"For what?" Her eyes drifted up to meet his.

For everything, he wanted to say. For not being here for you for the past five years. For pushing you to take a holiday you had no desire to take. "If the tea is too cold."

"Actually, I've gotten used to drinking it that way. I almost never get a hot drink these days. Kids, guests, you know…" She let the thought hang in the air between them. A moment later, she said, "Can I ask you something?"

"Anything."

"My kids did something silly, and I just wondered if you helped them. You didn't, did you? I mean, if you did, it's okay, but it's really odd and I didn't think you were the kind of person who would do that."

If she knew she was rambling, she didn't try to stop. His smile was gentle, caring, wanting her to know he was interested in whatever she had to say.

"What is it you think I've aided and abetted with?"

She smiled and tilted her head to one side. "It's not a crime. Just… Well, there's a photo album in the living room and the kids have photoshopped you into the pictures. I guess they want a dad in their lives and maybe they want it to be you."

"Ah. I see. Well, I assure you, I didn't Photoshop anything. I wouldn't know where to start."

"So, it wasn't you?" Joe shook his head, and she sighed. "Well, it wasn't my Dad. He can barely manage his cell phone. Mum did all the computer stuff."

Joe took a daring step. He was treading on thin ice which might crack and suck them both into icy waters at any moment. "What makes you think they've been altered?"

She rolled her eyes and a little pfft sound escaped her lips. "Because my late husband's face has been replaced with yours? It's kind of odd really, because you look a lot like him. You aren't a long-lost identical twin brother of his, are you?" She paused and looked more closely at him, a smile creeping into the corners of her mouth.

He loved it when she was playful, teasing and left the seriousness of a situation behind, even if it was only for a little while.

"I assure you, I have no brother, twin or otherwise. There was only Violet and I growing up, and our parents' best friends who lived across the street. They had a daughter who was a little younger than me, but we were as close as siblings."

She sat back in her chair and sipped her tea, seemingly thinking about the album. It surprised him when she let the matter drop and picked up on the similarities of the names.

"It's funny, don't you think, that my mother's name was Violet and so was your sister's. It's not a common name."

"No, it isn't. But it's a beautiful name and so is Annie. It was my mother's name." Another step onto that treacherous frozen water. When they were younger, they called the girls Little Annie and

Little Vi to keep them straight from their mothers. Would she remember that, too?

"Your mother's name was Annie? That's odd."

The breaking point. The ice was about to crack.

"Why is it odd?"

"Well, I mean, what are the chances that your sister and my mother had the same name and that your mother had my name?"

For a moment, Joe wondered if her headache was coming back. Here it comes, he thought, mentally clinging to the edge of his seat, watching her face for some sign of recognition or breakdown. She shook her head and squeezed her eyes shut.

"I'm confused," she said when she looked at him again. "It's always like that after a migraine. I'm super foggy and sometimes I forget things."

The moment had passed, and he knew they wouldn't come back to it now. She'd diverted the discussion, unknowingly, of course. He'd thought he would probe a little deeper. What was her late husband's name, would she come up with Joe and find that a coincidence too? But it was too late now, for this time at least.

"What kinds of things do you forget?"

"Oh, lots of things. Sometimes I forget whole blocks of time. It just disappears and I have to rely on Dad to tell me what happened."

"Blocks of time? Say five years?"

She laughed and waved her hand at him. "No. Not like that. Like what I was doing just before the headache, or I might forget that I have an appointment or something."

He nodded and took a long gulp of tea. "Can I ask you something?" He ventured.

"Sure."

"Did you love him? Your late husband." There he'd done it. What would she remember?

She sat back and looked up at the ceiling, her face filled with a look he hadn't seen in years. "Yes, I did. Like flowers love the sun, and like dry earth loves the rain." She looked at him. "He was everything. We were soulmates, destined to be together forever. A love that started at a very young age until…"

She was quiet for a moment, looking into her teacup as if the answer lay there among the bits of leaves that had gotten through the strainer.

"There was an accident," she finally said, her voice trembling as if she were in the middle of a violent earthquake.

Maybe she was, Joe thought. Maybe her thoughts were rattling around in her head so violently that memories were getting mixed up between what was real and what was made up to keep the truth at bay. His gaze was fixed on her as he felt the weight of her angst fall on his shoulders. This was wrong. It was too much. When she frowned at him, and tears welled in her eyes, he reached for her hand.

"I'm sorry," he said softly. "Truly sorry. I shouldn't have asked."

Two patches of color rose up on her cheeks and, like a feverish child, droplets of sweat emerged across her brow. But she smiled at him through her pain.

"You're very kind, do you know that?" A half smile formed at the sides of her mouth. "You know what Ali said the other day? She said I should marry you." She blushed and turned her head away to look into the darkness and avoid his gaze.

"Did she?" he laughed. "Why?"

"She said it was because I laugh when you're around. Imagine a six-year-old thinking of such things."

"You have a beautiful laugh, Annie. You have always been beautiful to me."

She turned back to him then and their eyes met and locked and, in that instant, he was sure he saw something. A flash of recognition? A glimpse of their past? A look of hopeful longing for something to come out. Or was he imagining it? But cries came from down the hall that shattered the moment.

"It's Ali," Annie said, pushing the blanket off her shoulders.

Joe stood and pulled it back into place. "You stay here and rest. I'll take care of her."

Chapter 25

On February the 13th, two weeks and two doctor visits since Annie's last migraine, Jim Sullivan thought that Joe and Annie's tenth anniversary, on Valentine's Day, just might spark something more. Over the past few days, they'd all waited and watched, changing nothing in the routine, except that Joe and Ryder were spending a lot of time with Annie and the kids, but only when she requested it.

They'd slid easily into a couple's routine. Ryder took the bus home with Ali and Noah instead of going to the library, and Joe left work in time to help Annie cook dinner. On the weekends, and sometimes during the week too, he and Ryder had been staying over. When the kids went to sleep at night, Joe and Annie went to her room and gazed out the window or at each other, just as they had done in the past. It was so much like old times that Joe was sure one day soon the last pieces of the puzzle floating around in Annie's head were going to slide into place. Their evenings always ended with her going to bed and him making up the couch in the living room.

Until the other night.

They'd been talking about when she and her husband bought the lodge, he gently prying details out of her until she recalled their first big fight.

"It was over something trivial, as fights usually are," she'd said. "Don't you remember? You stormed out in a huff and tripped over the space heater we bought for the office. And then you came back and we…"

And that's where she'd stopped and looked at him. "Sorry, I'm confused." She shook her head. "For a moment I thought…" She gasped, then grinned at him. "Did you put something in my tea?"

A classic deflection. The minute she'd started to realize the truth, she shut down. He'd seen it happen several times in the past few days. She was opening up, beginning to talk more, dig deep for memories.

"Only leaves and hot water, just the way you like it," he assured her.

"I think I need to lie down, but I don't want you to go. Would you stay with me? Just hold me."

"Of course," he'd said. "Whatever you need, Annie. Just let me take care of you." He held out his hands to lift her out of the chair.

"You know, I said before that I didn't need rescuing, but the truth is Joe, sometimes I really do need someone to take care of me."

"I'm here," he'd said. "I'll always be here."

She'd fallen asleep in his arms and he had lain awake for hours, breathing in her scent, feeling the rhythm of her breath and the rise and fall of her body against his. For one night, he'd been taken back in time to when everything was right in their world. It felt unimaginably wonderful. He'd dreamed of that night, of a time when this would happen, but never had it felt so sweet. If only it could always be so.

Now, here they were on the eve of their tenth anniversary. Joe had picked up their groceries—a list Annie had texted him, so they could make cookies for the school Valentine's parties tomorrow. Then he'd picked up the kids from school.

He followed them up the back steps, as they slogged their way under the weight of backpacks, winter parkas and the bags of groceries Joe had divided between them. Inside, he sorted out the chaos after they shed their outer layer before heading for the living room to watch TV, with Max, as always, on their heels. Then he toted their backpacks and the shopping into the kitchen.

"Something smells delicious," he said, coming to kiss Annie as he peered over her shoulder into the pot. "What are you making?"

"Chicken soup. Want to try?" She fished a spoon out of the drawer and scooped a sample from the pot. "Careful, it's hot," she warned.

He blew on the spoon, then sipped it. "Good," he said. "Just a tad more salt."

She wrinkled her nose. "Too much salt isn't good for us."

"Trust me. Just a little more."

She shrugged. "Alright. If you're going to insist. How was work?"

"Wonderful! I put in an offer on an apartment block in Huntsville." He set the backpacks on the counter by the sink, then unzipped the first one and pulled out Noah's lunch container. When he started dumping leftover food into the compost bin, he groaned. "Does this kid ever eat a full lunch?" He felt her staring at him and stopped what he was doing. "What? Did I do something wrong?"

"Nothing," she said with a laugh.

"It's not nothing. You've got a grin the size of a Cheshire cat. Now what's so funny?"

"It's not really funny. It's actually kind of cool." He lifted his brow, waiting for an explanation. "You," she said. "Us. The fact that you and Ryder just fit in here like we're a family. You help with the kids, unpack their lunch stuff, pick them up from school, do the shopping. It's like you're…" she stopped short of saying what Joe wanted desperately to hear.

"Like I'm what, Annie?" he asked, prodding her just a little.

"Nothing, I'm just being silly."

He dropped the containers in the sink and took her in his arms. "You're not silly. I feel very comfortable here, with all of you. It feels like home to both Ryder and me. I hope that's okay with you." Please let it be okay, Annie, he thought.

"I'm happy Joe. I want you to feel like this is home."

"Cookies!" Ali shouted, running from the living room.

"After supper, Pumpkin," Annie said, extricating herself from Joe's grasp and taking her daughter's cold cheeks into her hands. "We'll eat soon, I promise. But for now, why don't you help Joe with the groceries?"

When dinner was over, the dishwasher loaded, and the kitchen tidied, Annie showed Noah and Ryder how to make up the boxes that would hold three cookies. One box for each student in their classes and one for each teacher. Sam went to his room to be out of the 'danger zone,' as he called it, and Joe and Ali got busy in the kitchen. Joe found Ali's apron next to Annie's and tied it on for her. Then he got the mixer out of its corner and plugged it in.

"Now, where's the recipe?" he said, handing Ali the recipe box.

Ali opened it just as her mother came into the room. "You remember which one, don't you, Pumpkin?" Annie asked.

Ali nodded and dove into the cards until her little fingers pulled out the one with the red heart in the top right corner. "Mummy made it easy, see?" She held it up for Joe to examine.

"Clever mummy, isn't she? Can you read it? What's the first thing we do?"

Ali giggled. "I can't read this, silly? I'm just learning."

"Well then, I guess I should help." Joe took the recipe card from her. "Two cups of flour, a cup of sugar, half a cup of butter, a tsp of baking soda, vanilla flavouring ..." He stopped when he felt a tug on his sleeve.

"You have to slow down. And not all the gredients go in at once."

"You mean ingredients," Annie corrected. "Here, why don't you let me do this bit and you two can roll out the dough and cut them into shapes. Ali, can you find the cookie cutters?"

Joe poured a glass of wine for Annie and one for himself, then stood back to watch. It was the simplest of things and yet it was the most marvelous he'd seen in a long, long time. His wife and daughter, in their kitchen, making cookies. What could be more precious than that?

He leaned against the counter, not out of sight, but out of their way as they went to get eggs in the fridge or melt butter on the stove. Annie was in her element, a smudge of flour on her cheek, her hair shimmering in the glow of the kitchen light. When she smiled at Ali and occasionally at him, there was an innocence so pure about her that his breath hitched in his chest and his heart skipped a beat.

She caught him watching her. Each time, she'd smiled back at him, tilted her head to the side the way she did when she was content and happy, and went back to what she was doing. The third time, she set the bowl on the table, everything mixed and made ready for rolling, and came to stand next to him.

"Your turn," she said, pulling him gently toward the table. "My part is done."

His arm went instinctively behind her, and she, just as naturally, nestled in closer to him. "She's beautiful, isn't she?" She said, turning to look at Ali.

"Yes," he said. "She certainly is, and so are you." He kissed her then, unable to resist the urges she stirred in him, and when he felt her respond, he pulled her closer and folded her into his arms. Their kiss deepened, and the desire for something more than just a kiss grew.

"Wow," he gasped as he broke away, making her laugh at the inference of pleasure the kiss had inspired. When he released her, she tilted her head back, exposing her neck and, of course, he kissed it obligingly. Then he kissed her jaw and her cheek, and her lips, one more time.

"Get a room," Noah said, coming into the kitchen. His words broke them apart instantly.

"Where did you hear such a thing?" Annie gasped.

Noah shrugged. "TV. Any snacks? Ice cream?"

"You just finished supper," she cried. Then she looked up at the clock and Joe did too.

It was after nine. "When did that happen? I should get Ryder moving," he said.

"Why don't you just stay," Annie suggested. "We haven't even baked the cookies yet."

"Again? I'm wondering why I pay rent in town." He grinned. Then he whispered in her ear. "Unless you were thinking what I've been thinking."

"Relax tiger. I was offering you the couch." She grinned and pinched his elbow, just a little.

He felt the colour rising to his cheeks. "I know," he lied, thinking of the other night and how wonderful it had been to wake up with her in his arms the next morning. He yanked his mind out of that emotional place to a more practical one.

"I didn't bring any clothes for Ryder for school tomorrow."

"He's the same size as Noah. Jeans and a shirt. No problem." She pressed apples into Noah's hands and sent him back to the living room with a fifteen-minute-till-bedtime warning.

"Okay. I guess we're staying. Again. That means you and I have to get busy, young lady." Joe turned to Ali.

"Just waiting for you, Joe," she said, slapping a pad of cookie dough onto the table.

But they were not finished in fifteen minutes, because the cookies still had to bake. Annie hurried the kids up to bed, while Joe minded the oven and promised to bring a sample to each of them when they were ready.

"Good, that means two bedtime stories. One from Mummy and one from you, while I eat my cookie," Ali said, wrapping her arms around his neck. She kissed him on the cheek, then released him and ran off with her mum.

Joe stood for a moment, smiling after her. She was so like Annie had been when they were younger. Even then, he'd known he loved her, though at that time it was a very different kind of love.

He switched off the oven when he lifted the last tray of cookies out and set them on the racks to cool. Then he made up small plates of cookies; one for Sam, who was in his room reading, the next two for Noah and Ryder, who had built a fort over Noah's bed to sleep in and the last one for Ali, who was snuggled against her mother listening intently to Charlotte's Web. She smiled up at him and patted the other side of the bed. Joe climbed aboard, happy to join them, and set the cookies on Ali's lap.

When Annie was at the end of a chapter, she marked their place and set the book on the night table. "The rest will have to wait for another night. I'm beat." She yawned and stretched and reached out to pull Ali into her arms. "And I know a little girl who is very sleepy, too. I've counted three yawns in the last two pages."

Ali nodded. "I am sleepy. I'm okay to wait. It's a long story."

Annie grinned at Joe over Ali's head, then they both kissed her cheeks, rubbed noses with her, and finally left Ali to curl up with Frank.

"I'll bet you were just as sweet when you were her age." Joe didn't need anyone to tell him that was the case. He remembered exactly what Annie had been like at six, and seven and eight, and every age after that.

"I'm sure my mother would disagree with you if she were here. I'll bet I was a terror." They both reached for the doorknob to Noah's bedroom at the same time.

Joe stepped back to let her go first. "Sorry, I didn't mean to overstep."

She grinned at him. "You didn't. It's fine." But before they went into the room, she said, "You're a little jumpy suddenly. Are you okay?"

"I'm fine. Just, you know, a little unsure of things."

"Things like me, and us, and where this is going? Because I've been thinking a lot about that lately."

"Have you? Me too. I don't want to rush anything. I'd never want to do that."

"I really like having you around, Joe, and so do Dad and the kids." She paused, her hand still on Noah's doorknob. "Why don't you make us some tea and come join me in my room?"

Chapter 26

While their tea brewed, Joe made up a small plate of cookies for them to share. Then he locked all the doors, and said a quick goodnight to Sam, who was reading, with Max curled up at his feet.

At the bottom step, a wave of emotion came over him and Joe grabbed the newel post for support. He took a deep breath as a hundred memories came flooding back to him. He focused on one; the day they took possession of this place, and Annie spinning around and around in the living room, her face alive with mischief. She'd stopped, tilted her face to the ceiling, and smiled.

"Can you believe this is all ours?"

That was eight years ago, but it felt like yesterday to him. Noah was conceived shortly after, possibly that night, possibly on that living room floor because they couldn't wait to walk all the way across to the cottage they'd been sleeping in. He'd found a blanket from an unpacked box marked bedroom, and spread it out over the floor. She'd lit candles and turned out the lights. It was a night he'd never forgotten and one he played over and over in his mind, when Annie seemed far away and out of reach.

His vision faded at the sound of a door creaking overhead. Annie was waiting for him. He skipped the creaky step and went up.

"Open or closed?" he asked, balancing a tray in one hand, his other on the door. She sat in her chair, bathed in candlelight, wrapped in a blanket.

"Closed," she said. "We'll hear them if they need us."

He brought the tray to the table and set it down, handing her a mug of steaming hot tea.

"Cookies too?" she said with a laugh, snapping one up instantly. She watched him settle into his chair and pull a throw of his own across his shoulders. "This room is always chilly in the winter. But I like it. I don't sleep well in a hot, stuffy bedroom."

"Me too. I usually leave my window open just a crack, even on the coldest nights for the fresh air."

They ate cookies until the plate was empty, and the tea was cooling in their cups.

Much had happened in the past few days; a favourable report from Jim, Annie's acceptance of Joe's touches and gestures, the knowing glances they shared when she thought no one else was watching. It felt almost as if their life had picked up where it left off, but there was one big exception. Annie didn't share his memories of the past and she didn't know Joe was the man she'd once loved, married, and had two children with.

"There's something oddly familiar about you," she said, completely out of the blue, interrupting his thoughts.

"Well, I've been here just about every day for the past couple of months. My face must look a little familiar by now."

She giggled. "Not that. No, I mean, I've been thinking about it a lot lately. It's like we've met before or something." She bent to sip her tea. "It might sound kind of silly, but I've been asking the universe to send me someone just like my late husband. Someone who would love me the way he did, love my children, and someone who could appreciate what I'm trying to do here."

"And you think I'm that guy?"

She smiled. "Oh Joe. You are that guy. I know it. You understand what I want to do here. You can see what I've already done, and you have brilliant ideas about what we could still do." She paused. "And then there's the way you are with the kids. I don't have to tell you how much Ali and Noah love you."

He nodded. "I love them too. And I love you. And as for this place… It all makes sense to me. I can see why you were so unwilling to give it up."

She looked at him and took a breath. "I was so angry when you paid off my mortgage, but now I'm glad you did. I'm still going to repay it all one day, but in the meantime, it means I can relax a little."

"Good. That was the idea. I'll let you in on a little secret. My grandfather left me a lot of money. I was his favourite grandson. Well, to be honest, I was his only grandchild after Vi passed away. I thought this place was a much better investment than some company in South America I've never heard of."

"I'm still going to pay you back."

"I think you already have. Meals, time with your kids. I feel like part of the family."

"I'm glad," she said. Then she leaned forward and took his hand. "Because I'd really like you to be part of the family. If you and Ryder would like that, too?"

Joe squinted just a little, trying to catch her meaning, and caught her grinning at him. "Are you asking me to move in with you, Annie Taylor?"

She laughed. "Yes, but maybe not till we've slept together a few times to make sure things in that department are all right."

Oh, they'll be great, Joe thought. Unless she had changed in some way, but he doubted that was possible.

In the early days of their lovemaking, there had been the usual awkwardness, maybe more for them because they'd been neighbours and family friend before they'd become lovers. But once they'd gotten over the initial shyness of those first fumbling attempts to get it right, they'd been so in tune with each other that making love had been like second nature to them. On occasions when one of them was angry, or they'd fallen out of sync in their waking hours, they'd made a point of resolving their differences in that cozy window, and then the make-up sex had been great.

"Well, there's one way to find out," he said, meeting her gaze and raising his brow suggestively. "But like I said before, I don't want to push you into anything you don't want or aren't ready for."

That was when Annie slid out of her chair and let her blanket fall to the floor. She stood before him, naked, unabashedly, reaching out to him. "I'm ready, Joe, if you are."

He let his gaze drink in the beauty that stood before him. The Caesarean scar from when Ali was born was hardly noticeable in the dim light of the room. Time had healed the rawness of the wound, just like it had healed the scar in her hairline from the accident. But had time healed what ached inside either of them? He rose and let his own blanket fall from his shoulders and took her into his arms.

"You're so beautiful," he gasped, trying to control the pounding in his chest. As she nestled against him, her arms went around his neck, he gripped her bottom, as he felt his own desire grow, urging them to a deeper passion. When their lips melded together in a hungry kiss that sent his head reeling, he knew there was no going back this time.

I love you, Annie. There is no one else in this world who could ever be right for me. But we shouldn't be doing this!

Everything in Joe's head screamed that this was wrong, that Annie needed to face the truth before this could be real for either of them. Would this cause more damage than good? What would she think when she realized the truth, if she ever did? Would she be happy they'd made love, or would she be angry? But his passion and his physical need to be with her again outweighed the logic, silenced it and shut it down.

She might have forgotten the last five years of their life, but she hadn't forgotten how to drive him wild with desire. Her hands expertly slid the zipper of his jeans in a slow, teasing motion, and he could barely contain his yearning. She smiled when she found him hard, receptive to her touch, eager. He lifted her up and carried her to the bed.

They tore at his clothing, ripping open his shirt so that buttons flew in all directions, pinging off the windowpane, and the lampshade on the night table. She giggled nervously at their haste, but when he was free of binding clothes, and pulled her beneath him, she wasn't laughing anymore. He moaned at the familiar feel of her body, wanting desperately to be inside her, yet blissfully aware he must take his time. He must please her, let her please him. Then, together, they would know their united ecstasy.

He cupped her face in his hands, kissing her hard, nearly bruising her lips in his need, as she moaned and writhed beneath him. His brain made one last attempt to stop this, but he pushed away the worries. She wanted this. She had asked him to make love to her. This was not something he was pushing her to do.

"Annie!" he moaned when she reached for him again, caressing him, coaxing him, guiding him.

"My sweet and precious Annie."

Part 3

Joe and Annie

Chapter 27

Annie

She woke to find Joe's side of the bed empty, though the dent where he'd laid his head was still in the pillow. If it hadn't been there, she might have wondered if last night had really happened, or if she'd dreamed it. She'd had dreams like that before. Dreams that were so real they took her back to the life she'd had before the accident, orgasmic dreams that made her wonder how such a thing was possible. Was his spirit somehow…? No, that was impossible.

She found her housecoat and slippers where they always were. As she slipped her feet into them, she looked down at the sorry, sad-looking slippers that had seen better days. Maybe it was time for a new pair. New man. New slippers.

She heard soft voices downstairs and her gaze went to the clock. She'd slept through the alarm, or perhaps she hadn't even set it. It wasn't exactly what she had in mind when she got into bed last night. After they'd made love and lay in each other's arms talking into the early hours of the morning, setting the alarm wasn't a priority.

"Shit," she said, hurrying toward the door. "Shit. Shit. Shit." Her hand was on the knob when she remembered she was naked beneath her robe. She couldn't go downstairs like that. Naked under a housecoat meant something had happened and while Ali might have been oblivious, Noah, and probably Ryder, would not. Certainly, her father would raise an eyebrow.

She hurried into the shower, not bothering to dry her hair when she climbed out of it, then pulled on sweatpants and a t-shirt that she'd discarded the night before. As she crept down the stairs, she purposely skipped the creaky one because she didn't want to disturb the conversation in the kitchen. Ali was instructing Joe on how he should make their lunches.

"Make one for Ryder, too," she insisted. "The sandwich is okay for Noah, but he hates plums. But you should put it in. He'll trade it for something he likes."

"I see," Joe said. "Well, maybe we should just give him something he likes, so he doesn't have to trade. What about a banana or a pear?"

The creaking floorboards outside the kitchen door gave Annie away, and when he saw her, Joe smiled. She smiled back, thinking how nice it was to see him in her kitchen, with her daughter, making their lunches. It was as natural a thing as if he'd always been there, doing this every day, except that he didn't know what they liked and didn't. He could learn, she thought. She expected to have to set the table for breakfast but found that not only was it done, but they had all eaten.

"Joe made heart-shaped pancakes," Ali said. "Happy heart day, Mummy!"

"Same to you, Pumpkin. Love you forever." Annie planted a kiss on Ali's nose. "Now, where is your brother?"

"Playing video games with Ryder."

"Can you please tell them to get ready for the bus?"

"I didn't know the rules about video games in the morning," Joe said, when Ali scampered away, and Annie turned back to the lunches.

"It's fine. Sometimes it's the only way to keep the two of them from fighting. She's Little Miss Sunshine in the mornings, but he's Mr. Angry. Most of the time they're great, but mornings can be a struggle." She examined the contents of their lunch containers and lifted out the pear Joe had put in Noah's. "He won't eat this or a banana. Give him one of these." She pulled a container out of the fridge and opened the lid.

"Fruit roll-ups? But aren't they loaded with sugar?"

"Not these. I make them myself. The only sugar in them is what's in the fruit and that's more than enough, trust me."

"I do." Joe grinned at her when she leaned in for a good morning kiss. "I didn't want to disturb you," he whispered, taking her in his arms so they could kiss again, properly this time.

"Thanks. It felt good to sleep in for a change."

"Last night felt pretty good too," he said gently.

She flushed and lifted her chin so she could kiss him on the cheek. She thought about saying, *yes it did*, and *are you coming back for the second act tonight*, but Ali came bounding back into the room.

"We have to get the cookies ready." She stamped her foot anxiously.

"Okay. Okay. There's time." Annie extricated herself from Joe's grasp. "Guess I've been told," she said over her shoulder as she followed her daughter to the dining room.

When they had put all the cookies into one large box, they found Joe organizing the backpacks by the door to the mudroom, and Noah and Ryder searching for mittens to wear. Ali dove into the fracas to put her things on, causing a ruckus in the tiny space and the first big fight of the day with her brother.

Joe sent the boys outside while Annie helped Ali get her things on.

"Are we taking the bus today, Mummy?" Ali wanted to know.

"Don't you always?"

"Joe said he could take us." Ali looked up at Joe. "Right, Joe?"

Annie flashed him a *check-with-me-first* look.

He groaned. "I did say that, but now that I think about it, I don't have a seat in my car for you or Noah, so that wouldn't be safe."

Annie nodded her approval, and Joe breathed a sigh of relief and jokingly pretended to wipe the sweat off his brow.

As they walked to the bus stop, he said, "I could deliver the rest of those to the school. It might be easier than the kids taking this big box on the bus."

"Only if you're going, anyway." She dearly hoped he wasn't. She'd like him to stay and spend the day with her, but she knew he had to work, and he hadn't brought clean clothes with him. Of course, he'd need to go home.

"I have some errands today," he said. "It's no trouble since we live…"

"Right across from the school." She turned to look at him. "Did you sign a lease there?"

"Yes. For a year. I could have gotten a lifetime one, but I wasn't sure this was where we'd stay. I wanted Ryder to get used to the school first, you know, get the lay of the land."

"And what do you think now that you've been here a few months?"

Joe kicked snow from his boots and pulled his coat a little tighter around his neck. "I'm sure Miss Wight is a great teacher but…"

"I've never had any issues with her."

"Well, you wouldn't. You're…"

"I'm…?"

Joe's skin turned pink beneath his two-day shadow.

"Oh…" Annie looked up at him. "It's not like I didn't warn you that she's single." Her lips curled into a smile first, followed by a giggle, then a full-blown laugh.

"What!" Joe said. "Is that so hard to believe?"

"No," she admitted. "Not hard to believe at all, and that's not what is funny. What's funny is the way you blush when you're embarrassed." She linked her arm in his elbow. "It's adorable, and it's really quite sexy."

Joe looked away from her and flushed even harder. Then he laughed. "Okay, you got me. I blush easily. I cry at movies too and sappy TV commercials. Just thought you might like to know."

"I love a man who isn't afraid to show his emotions."

The distant whine of the bus's engine echoed off the embankment.

"Here it comes!" Ali cried, hurrying to give her mother one last kiss goodbye. Then she went to Joe and kissed him on the cheek. "You need to shave," she said, making a face as she pulled away from him.

"Yes, I do," Joe said, laughing and rubbing his jaw as they waved and the kids hurried onto the bus.

Chapter 28

Joe

Joe hadn't made provisions for Ryder to take the bus to school that morning, so they climbed into his car and headed for town. They were well ahead of the bus and stopped at home so Joe could shower and change. He was just doing up the last button on his shirt when Ryder came into his room.

"What are we going to have for supper?"

"Yeah. I know. It's slim pickin's in there. We've spent so much time at Annie's lately, I haven't thought about groceries."

Ryder laughed. "Slim Pickins sounds like the name of a cartoon character." He followed Joe out to the kitchen. "Can we get some marshmallows?"

"I suppose. But we aren't allowed to have any campfires here. You remember the rules?"

"Not for here. For Noah's. He asked if I could spend the whole weekend at his house. It's Family Day on Monday, so we have a long weekend."

"Annie said that was okay?"

Ryder nodded.

"I'll talk to her about it, okay? Maybe you can split the weekend between here and there."

"Okay. Thanks Uncle Joe."

Joe opened up a shopping list app on his phone and made a lengthy grocery list, opening cupboards and the fridge from time to time to check supplies. When Max came out from under the table and nudged his hand for a pat, Joe added dog food and dog biscuits to the list. "Couldn't forget you could we, Max."

Outside, the buses were gathering in the schoolyard across the street. "We better go, Ryder. I see Ted pulling in. Noah will be looking for you."

When the cookies were delivered and the kids settled in their classrooms, Joe headed into town. The hardware store first, a few hours at the office and groceries on the way home. Joe got what he needed at the hardware store and wandered into work a little after ten.

"Nice of you to show your face." Birdie had been George Melville's bookkeeper since day one. She'd been happy to stay on when Joe bought the company and he was glad to have her. She sat behind an old teacher's desk on one side of the room and peered at him over a pair of cheater glasses.

"I never worry when you're here, Birdie," he said with a patronizing smile. From behind his back, he produced a bouquet of carnations he'd bought, a last-minute impulse item in a bucket at the checkout of the hardware store.

"For me?" Birdie teased, exaggerating how impressed she was by his charms. She put the flowers on her desk. "You're far too young and way too handsome to be interested in me. So, you must want something."

"Can't a boss give his best office gal flowers? It's Valentine's Day, after all."

Birdie looked up at the wall calendar behind her desk. "Well, well. I guess you're right."

"Are you telling me your husband doesn't bring you chocolates and flowers?"

"Pfft. My husband wouldn't know a flower if it jumped up and bit him in the nose."

"His loss." He rounded the desk and planted a kiss on her cheek, for which he got a playful slap on the arm. "You should see your face," Joe laughed. "You look like a young girl, again. Every woman deserves to be spoiled now and again, and not just on special occasions."

"I take it you've sent some to your girl," Birdie fished.

"Now Birdie." He shook a finger at her. "You'll get nothing out of me, so stop trying."

Joe went to sit behind his desk, a metal thing that might have been there since the seventies. There were two other desks in the office with computers on them, but there was no mistaking which one was Joe's due to the files and folders, reports, manuals, and an overstuffed inbox that sat on it. He slid some things aside to make room for his takeout coffee and shook his head.

"I guess I should spend a little more time here."

"Yes, you probably should," Birdie chided. "Ryan took a stab at some of that yesterday, but he really doesn't know what you want to do about most of it. I'm afraid you'll have to sort that out yourself."

"No rest for the wicked," he quipped, then dove into the pile of correspondence first, mumbling that everything should be digital to save the trees.

Joe spent the next three hours sorting the piles on his desk, getting in touch with his crew and going over Birdie's entries in the ledger. Birdie was old school with a lot of things, but with their accounts, she was up to date with the computer software; more so than he was. He shook his head at January's statements, not because they looked bad, but because they'd had more work than they could really handle. They were getting backlogged. He could get out in the field and take over some of the plumbing work, but he couldn't be in three places at once. He needed some help, either here in the office or out in the field.

"Birdie, where's the best place to put an advertisement up if you want to hire someone?"

"There are lots of job boards, or you could go to a recruiting agency. Not trying to replace me already, are you? I've got three years left before I retire and I might just have to keep working after that to save my sanity with Ed at home." She got up to refill her cup with coffee. "Who do you want to hire?"

Joe pursed his lips. "This is not for anyone else's ears, you understand, but I've been thinking of hiring someone to run this place. Someone who can take care of estimates, supervise the crews, deal with customers."

"Gee whiz Joe, are you quitting on us already?"

He grinned. "No. I bought Melville's to keep myself busy, but the truth is, I'm too busy. I don't have time for…" Annie, he thought, but he said, "For other ventures."

"Like that apartment block Ryan was talking about?"

Joe thumbed through some envelopes. "Yeah, and other things."

"Lots of people are willing to buy you out, you know. George had more than a few offers."

"I know, but I'm not ready to sell. This is a good company, with strong ethics and a good team. I'd hate to sell it and find out the new owner ran it into the ground."

"Well, I can ask around if you like. I've been in this industry long enough to have met a few people. And if no names come up, we can run an ad, but you might want to tell the boys before you put something in writing. Advertising within the ranks might go a long way to smoothing things over when someone new takes the helm. At least they'd have a chance to apply, even if you don't feel there's anyone suitable."

"Good point. Put a memo out, will you? And call the position, Assistant General Manager, for now."

"You do realize I'm not a secretary. I just do the books and payroll."

He grinned at her. "But you're so much better at these things than I am."

"Hmm. I might have to ask for a raise if I'm going to take on extra duties."

"Consider it done." Joe didn't waste any time. "Add five dollars an hour to whatever I'm already paying you and if you have spare time after your regular work is done, take a stab at some of this filing." He put a hand on the stack of folders he'd just sorted through.

Birdie nodded toward the filing cabinet. "Put your back into it and you'll be fine. In alphabetical order, by client's name."

Joe took the hint and opened the file cabinet drawer. Once he got started, he found it was easy to follow the system already set up. He finished in no time and looked down at the space on his desk. Bare metal, now that was something he hadn't seen in a while. He continued on, shifting the manuals to a bookshelf, and then tackled the correspondence. By three, he was finished and his desk was tidy.

"Well, would you look at that," Birdie said, admiring the now visible surface. "Well done."

Joe smiled. "Feels good to have that out of the way." He stood and reached for his coat from the rack behind his desk. "Thanks, Birdie. If I were thirty years older, you wouldn't be safe working in this office alone."

She flushed and batted her hand at him. "Oh, get on out of here. Sassy little boy. Surely there's some pretty young thing waiting for you at home."

Joe sent her a sly wink and put his finger to his lips. "But don't tell anyone."

He left Birdie with her mouth still gaping open in surprise.

On his way to the grocery store, he attempted to call Annie, to talk about the boys' weekend. For the third time, the call went to voicemail, with Annie's cheery greeting reminding customers of the office hours and the ability to contact them through the internet. At the ding, he left another message; short, to the point, followed by a sincere, *I love you and Happy Valentine's Day.*

The grocery store was a maze of shoppers that made him wonder if everyone had left work early and ended up at the supermarket at once. He wanted to cook something special for Annie that night and he planned to get things to make her favourite dinner, or what used to be her favourite. In one of his earlier messages, he'd suggested she come for dinner to his place, but that message, like the rest, had gone unanswered. When he'd left earlier that morning, they hadn't discussed plans for tonight. It was their anniversary, whether she remembered it or not and he wanted to do something special.

Last night, she'd asked him to move in with her. Last night they'd made love, for what she thought was the first time. Did that count as something to celebrate, or was she having second thoughts? A bit of panic trickled in and lodged itself in Joe's throat so quickly he actually coughed in the middle of the frozen food section. Was that why she wasn't answering him? Had they gone too far? Was she having regrets?

He wedged his way through the crowd at the meat counter, tossed a whole roasting chicken into his cart, and moved on. By the time he found marshmallows for Ryder, visited the dairy counter for the milk, and set a loaf of bread on top of his eggs, he was fed up with the crowds. He checked out with three bags of necessities and a bouquet of roses from a bucket near the till, then sloshed his way through the melting snow to his car.

All the way home, he couldn't help wondering if something was drastically wrong. What would he do next, if she'd relapsed or, if she'd suddenly remembered everything and decided she didn't want their old life back again?

"Jesus," he said out loud. "I'm not prepared for that." And he wasn't. He hadn't because he was so sure this was going to work that he'd barely allowed himself to entertain the what ifs.

Then again, maybe her phone was charging and she hadn't seen his messages. Maybe she'd been busy with guests and cleaning and other things. He reminded himself of how much work it took to run that lodge, even with only a few guests.

When he arrived at the bungalow, Joe relaxed because, to his surprise, Annie's truck was parked in his driveway, and she was standing on his back porch, her hand raised to knock on the door. She turned when he pulled into the driveway.

"Were you looking for me?" he asked, getting out of the car and popping the trunk latch.

"No. I was looking for the mailman." She spun around on one foot and jerked a thumb over her shoulder. "Isn't this where he lives?" No regrets then, he thought as she came down the steps and reached out to help him bring in the bags. "I hope it's okay that I just dropped by. I was curious to see what this house looks like in-side."

Joe feigned a pout. "Oh, so you just wanted to see the house and not me. I'm crushed." He handed her the flowers. "I was going to give you these later, but since you're here now, Happy Valen-tine's Day."

"Oh Joe. That's very sweet. How did you know I love roses?"

No, you don't, he thought. You love gardenias, but I couldn't find any, so you're getting a crappy, last minute, cheap bouquet of roses.

She trailed after him, waiting while he unlocked the door, set his bags on the counter, and took the one she'd brought in, as well.

"Tea?" he asked, reaching for the kettle. "I don't have your famous ones, but these aren't bad." He pulled a tray of packaged teas down from the shelf over the sink. "See if there's something you like."

Joe did some fast multitasking, putting away the groceries and setting their tea to steep, while Annie pulled up a chair to wait.

"I'm being a little daring," she confessed. "The kids will stay with Dad for a little while, on their own."

"I'm sure Sam can manage the two of them. He's getting around well now. I hardly ever see him use his cane."

She nodded. "I'm so proud of him. He really has come a long way." She played with the rim of her cup, running her finger over it and back again, and Joe knew she had something important on her mind.

"What is it?" he asked, leaning a little closer, watching her brows knit together in thought.

"Come home with me," she said after a long pause and a slow, deep breath. "Forever. Give up this house or sublet it or something and move in with me."

He reached out a hand to hers. "Are you sure you're ready for that? I mean, we didn't really talk this through."

"I was never really worried about the sex. I knew it would be great, and it was. But that's not all. The kids love you. Dad loves you. And… and I love you, too. And I know you love me. You tell me all the time and I see it in your eyes and feel it in your touch."

She sighed when he said nothing. He didn't know what to say. Yes. His heart ached for that, but his head kept telling him it was too soon.

"Annie," he said, after a moment.

"Oh, here goes. This is when you tell me you're getting back together with your ex-wife, or you've met someone else, or…"

"No, it's nothing like that. Not at all. There's no one else in my life and there never will be. It's always been you, Annie, always."

"Well, not always. That ring on your finger came from someone." She frowned, looking closer at Joe's ring. "Wait a minute. Where did you get that?" she asked, pulling his hand closer. "That looks like my husband's ring. The swirls on the band are the same. Did one of my kids give it to you? Because if this is some kind of joke, it's not funny." Her eyes flitting from the ring to Joe and back again, and slowly her face morphed into something fierce and angry, turning red as bitterness oozed from her eyes.

"It's not a joke, Annie. The kids didn't give it to me. It's mine. I've had it for ten years." Ten years today, exactly, he thought.

She softened just a little then. "Maybe it's a co-incidence." But the look on her face told him she didn't believe that either. Suddenly, she was pushing back her chair and gathering her things.

"I've got to go," she said without looking at him. Then, in something close to a whisper, she added, "I have to make supper for the kids and get the laundry out of the dryer before it wrinkles and Ali will want two bedtime stories because she always does now and…"

Joe pulled her in his arms, murmuring reassuring words in her ear. "Shh. Shh. It's okay. The kids are fine with Sam. The clothes in the dryer can wait and bedtime stories are hours away." She stiffened against his hold and tried to pull away. Joe released her, instantly, remembering Jim's warnings and not wanting her to feel threatened or that she was being held against her will.

"I should go," she said.

Should, not I have to, Joe thought. "Just wait," he said. "There's something I wanted to talk to you about." He waved in the direction of the living room. "Indulge me for a moment."

"Okay," she said, her voice shaky, her feet even less stable than her words.

He reached out to help her into the living room and lowered her onto the couch, where she immediately pulled her hands away and clung to her own arms.

"I'm not sure I want to hear this," she murmured. "But say what you have to say."

He thought about it for a moment, debated with himself, and finally, he came to the only conclusion that made sense to him. She was fragile, yes. But he knew with such confidence that this was the time to tell he pushed away all doubt and let nothing slip in through the cracks.

"Just a moment," he said, getting up from the couch.

In the drawer of a hutch in the corner, he pulled out a photo album and brought it back to her. On the cover was a photograph, a duplicate of the wedding photo that used to hang over their bed.

"Who do you see in this picture, Annie?"

She looked up at him, then touched the picture behind the plastic cover. "That's me and my husband. Why do you have a picture of us, Joe?"

"Have a good look at him," he said. "Then have a good look at me."

She did as he asked, then slowly shook her head. "It's not possible. You've photoshopped this like you did the other ones. Is this some kind of cruel joke?" She pushed the album away and shrank into her side of the couch. "What are you, some kind of weird creep that goes around seducing widows so you can take over their businesses?"

"What was your husband's name? Do you remember?"

She frowned at him. "Taylor. I'm Annie Taylor."

"No, that's your maiden name. It's your father's name. Sam Taylor. But what's the name on your marriage certificate?"

She shook her head, eyes wild with fear. "I don't have a marriage certificate. It was lost, when we moved, I think."

He opened the album, where their marriage certificate and a photo of them signing it in the church filled two pages. He pointed to their names.

"It's not lost, Annie. Look. This is your marriage certificate. Our marriage certificate. What does this say, Annie? What is your husband's name?"

He watched her face as she read the words, her fingers playing in her lap. He was pushing harder than he should have, and he knew it. But there had been something in her eyes when she'd looked at the ring, then again when she saw the picture. And there it was again, a flicker of familiarity, when she looked up at him. She knew! He was sure of it, even if she wasn't.

"Hewitt? Joe and Annie Hewitt?"

He turned a page to where he'd set in the birth certificates he'd ordered. "And look at these. Noah Joseph Hewitt, and Aline Violet Hewitt. Our children."

She frowned and puckered her lips as if she were working through it all.

"You know, don't you?" he dared to ask.

There was a long pause, while Annie seemed to be considering what he was saying. He watched her face, hoping for some sign of recognition, a sign that said things were falling into place.

Then she looked at him and said, "Are you real or are you a ghost?"

Joe shook his head. "Not a ghost. Just me, in the flesh."

"Real, then," she hesitated, reaching out to touch his arm.

"Yes, very real. You have no idea how long I've waited for you to realize this." He lifted her chin. "We were married ten years ago today, on Valentine's Day. Two years later, we bought Paradise Cove and changed the name to Annie's Lodge. Then Noah was born, and later Ali came along."

She was staring at him, her eyes wild, flitting from the album to him and back again. He could see she was trying to put it all into place, but she wasn't quite sure yet.

He carried on.

"We grew up together. Our parents were best friends. That's why you're named after my mother and they named my sister after yours. It's no coincidence."

She pulled away from him, turned to another page in the album and a picture of Noah's first birthday. Her mother was lighting the candles on his cake. Sam stood on one side of Noah's highchair and Joe on the other.

"You took this picture, Annie," he said, desperately wanting her to see the truth. He pointed to another. "And this one, and this and this and these."

"I don't remember taking them." Her hand traced the lines of Joe's face in the picture, but she did not look up at him. She kept her eyes glued to the page as she flipped to the next and the next. Faces of their family flashed before them; Violet and Ryder, Noah, her parents, Joe's parents and then Joe, covered in sand except for his face.

"This was when we went to Tobermory, before Ali was born," he said, taking a deep breath. Her frown deepened and then a lip curled up on one side, but he could see her smile was grim, and instantly, he was worried. He took the album from her and set it on the coffee table.

"I'm sorry. This was a mistake. You weren't ready and I…"

Her hand reached for his and she squeezed it, like a mother placating a child. It's alright dear, you tried.

"No, It's fine," she said, lifting her other hand to her scar. "Could I have a glass of water?" she asked, thinly.

Another migraine, Joe thought. He should have known.

"Of course. Anything."

He slipped off the couch and went to the kitchen, where he filled two glasses, one for her and another for himself.

When he returned, Annie and the photo album were no longer there and the front door stood wide open.

Joe hurried to the doorway just in time to see her race down the sidewalk in her stocking feet. "Oh Annie."

Chapter 29

Annie

The damp February air whistling through the trees hardly registered as Annie raced out the door and down the shoveled sidewalk. She kept moving, stumbling once, a second time, until finally she came to the street. It was gritty and slushy, and she didn't want to step into that mess, so she crossed the yard, through knee-deep snow, to get to the driveway. She was aware of Joe calling out to her from the door, but she would not go back, not for her boots, not for her coat, not for anything. She yanked open the door to the truck and climbed inside. Safe, she thought as she slammed the lock into place, until she realized her keys were in her coat pocket and she'd left that over the back of the chair in Joe's kitchen.

"Shit. Shit. Shit." She pounded her hands on the steering wheel. "That was stupid." She scoured the truck for the spare keys. Dropped the visor, not there. Checked the glove box, not there. Under the floor mat, not there. And then she remembered she'd given them to Luke, in case of an emergency. But now she couldn't even call him, because her phone was inside too. The school was maybe two hundred feet away, across the slushy road and the snow-filled playground. He would catch her before she made it that far.

Then she saw movement at the back door of his house. Maybe he was going somewhere. To get Ryder at the library. Yes, it must be about that time. Joe came out of the house wearing a warm coat and boots on his feet. He's warm as toast and I'm stuck here in the cold, she thought. What was that in his hands? Her coat, her boots.

"Oh, no!" She shouted through the windshield of the truck. "You're not getting into this truck!"

Still holding her coat and boots, he held up his hands, as he made his way across the driveway. She shook her head wildly. "I don't want them." He was in front of the hood then. "Don't come any closer." Didn't he hear her screaming at him? She cracked the window, just a touch. "Don't come any closer," she shouted through the crack.

"I won't. I'll just leave your coat here and I'm going to set your boots right outside the door, so you can just put them on. Then I'm going to drive away. Is that okay?"

Annie thought about it for a moment, then slowly nodded. "Okay, but I'm not unlocking my door until you leave."

"That's fine. Whatever makes you feel safe." He set her things down exactly as he said he would, then got into his car and drove away.

She waited until he had passed the school and disappeared down the main street of town. Then she took a deep breath. It was okay to open her door, put on her boots, and grab her coat. She was safe.

She stripped off her wet socks and slid her icy feet into her boots. They weren't warm, but they were dry, and that was a start. Next, she grabbed her coat and pulled it around her shoulders, slipping her arms into the sleeves. It was then her teeth began to chatter, and she realized just how cold she was. She felt for her keys and found them exactly where she'd left them, her phone in the other pocket. When she pushed the starter, the engine roared into life. Still shivering, she cranked the heat to the max and headed for the main road and the bridge that would take her home.

When her feet began to thaw, it seemed as if her mind did too. She looked over at the photo album on the passenger seat and thought about the pictures in it and the marriage certificate with her name on it. The photographs she was in with him and the kids. What kind of cruel joke was this? And why was he doing it? Was he some kind of lunatic who preyed on innocent widows or something? He had everyone fooled. The kids and her father. But not her. He was not going to play this game with Annie Taylor. Fingers gripped the steering wheel as she negotiated the bends on Echo Lake Road. There hadn't been any new snow for days, but the grit and salt made the road slushy and sometimes that was worse than new snow. She felt the tires slip a little at the turn that led to the bridge and knew she had to slow down. The last thing she wanted to do was careen down the embankment and into the lake.

It was dark, that deep in the woods, where there were no streetlights and nothing but her headlights to guide her. A flash in her review mirror told her someone was following her. Was it him? Had he decided to come after her? She pushed her foot down on the accelerator, just enough to put some distance between herself and the car behind her. A half mile further, it turned off onto another road. Not him, she sighed with relief.

She was at the last hill before she came to the lodge, when another pair of headlights flashed in her mirror. Annie's white knuckles squeezed even harder on the wheel, her eyes darting for the edges of the road, praying she would make it home before... Before what? Before he caught up with her? And what would he do if he did? She wasn't about to find out. Annie put her foot to the floor and willed her tires to grip the road. They clung to the grit and sped her forward. She turned into her driveway and the car behind her carried on up the road. Annie parked and rested her head on the steering wheel.

She was home. She was safe.

Chapter 30

Joe

"Why aren't we going in?" Ryder asked when Joe didn't follow Annie's truck into the driveway. "I thought we were going to have supper and hang out for a while."

"Not tonight. I just wanted to make sure Annie got home alright."

Ryder thumped the back of the seat and crossed his arms over his chest.

"Sorry bud. It's just not a good night," Joe said. "Annie has one of her migraine headaches."

"Yeah, I get it. It's just…"

"I know, Ry. Maybe another time." And maybe not, but he wouldn't say that just now. Joe didn't want to think too hard about the future he might have just ruined. He thumped the steering wheel, angry at himself for what he'd done. At least she was home, safe. Now all he could do was wait and hope.

They followed the Ring Road all the way around to the junction at Echo Lake Road, then headed for home. The minute they were in the door, he asked Ryder to set the table, then Joe went to his bedroom to call Sam.

"I'll call you back in a while," Sam said in a hurried voice once Joe explained what had happened. "I promise."

When they hung up, Joe felt the disconnect, as if it were six months ago and he was a hundred miles away. He had to trust Sam to let him know what was going on and to take care of Annie.

He sat on the edge of the bed, heaving a mental kick at himself for pushing her so hard and for Jim Sullivan and his crazy notion that all of this was the right thing to do. Joe had been ready to believe him, that Annie would find a way through the fog and they would put their lives back together again. But had he just pushed her over the edge?

"The mind is a strange place," Jim had said, when they discussed this last fall. "It keeps things tucked away, hidden from the rest of the world, and sometimes from ourselves. I can't tell you why she's shutting you out, Joe. But in every case I've had, like Annie's, they have all come around, eventually."

"All?"

Jim had done a funny thing with his lips then and sat up straighter in his chair. "Well, all but one. But he had a lot of childhood trauma, too. Annie doesn't have that. From what she tells me, she had a happy childhood. Everything was fine until the accident."

That bloody trip to Florida and the accident had been the cause of it all. Joe paced the room, wondering if he should use the cell phone number Jim had given him for emergencies. Was this an emergency? Annie hadn't been like this since that first day in the hospital when she woke from the coma and hadn't known who he was. She'd been terrified of him, crazed to the point of shouting accusations until the nurse came in and gave her a sedative.

Pacing the room, deep in thought, Joe caught Ryder's reflection in his dresser mirror. "Come in Ry. What's up?" Joe sat on the bed and patted the place beside him.

Ryder came closer. "It's really nothing. I know you're busy."

"Not too busy for you, bud. Tell me what's bothering you."

Ryder gazed out the window for a moment, and Joe gave him space to put his thoughts together.

"It's kinda past supper time, and I was thinking. Could we get some burgers and fries for supper?"

That was a simple question to answer. "That's one I don't have to think too hard about. Of course. Grab your coat. Let's get out of here."

Joe was grateful for Ryder's suggestion and couldn't believe how hungry he was until his burger was set in front of him. He ate the double patty, bacon and cheddar, *heart attack waiting to happen* burger, then wolfed down the fries hungrily. Ryder finished his too, though he didn't seem as ravenous as Joe had been. He talked about school, once Joe opened up the conversation, and told him he'd scored three goals in floor hockey that day.

"That's great! I'm proud of you. Next fall, we'll get you signed up for hockey. I promise."

Ryder smiled. "Thanks Uncle Joe. I'd really like that."

Ryder was tucked into bed and sound asleep when Joe got Sam's call, just before ten that night.

"How is she?" Joe asked.

"Sleeping. I've convinced her to see Jim tomorrow, even though her appointment isn't until Monday. It didn't take much, really. She's pretty confused. Did you actually show her your marriage certificate?"

"Yeeeah…" Joe raked one hand through his hair and gripped his phone with the other. "I know. Stupid right? But she was asking questions, and we seemed to be moving forward, so I thought maybe… To tell you the truth, I wasn't thinking, not logically, I suppose. I was desperate."

"Well, don't be so hard on yourself. It just might have worked. She was looking at her album and she had a lot of questions about people, so I got out a couple of mine, and we went over them together. She remembers everyone, Joe. She even mentioned you, but in the past tense. Joe as her late husband."

"Because I'm responsible for that damned accident. I couldn't keep her safe, Sam. She hates me. I'm such a jerk."

"No. I don't think so. She loves you. At least she loves the man she married. She's just not sure that you and he are the same person. Her mind can't work out how you can be dead and alive at the same time. And that's where she's getting confused."

"Well, I'm pretty confused too."

"I know you are. Try to get some sleep and do your best not to worry. These things have a way of working out."

"Thanks. And hey, I love you, by the way. Not sure I tell you that enough. You've been a rock through all of this."

"So have you. It'll all work out. You'll see."

Chapter 31

Annie

"Come on, kids. Ted will be here any minute." Somehow, she'd slept through her alarm again. She hadn't done that since Joe had stayed over. But that wouldn't happen again. That had been a mistake. Joe wasn't the man she thought he was.

She couldn't deny she missed waking up with a man next to her, or that she enjoyed the warmth of his body spooning hers in the night. She missed the scent of a man's cologne that lingered on the pillow and a man's things in the bathroom. And if truth be told, she missed the time after the kids went to bed, sitting by the window and talking about their day. Most of all, she missed the way a husband and wife were together, the security you felt when someone loved you that much and you loved them back. But she wasn't about to let a crazy man into her life to have those things.

Was he crazy?

Hadn't she felt these things with Joe, or was she remembering her husband and the way they used to be and trying to recreate that with someone else? She tugged at the memories, always coming back to the similarities between the two. How is it that there are so many things about them that seemed the same? Their eyes were the same colour, their features too. And they both had a slightly receding hairline. Was Joe telling the truth? Was he really her husband, and she'd somehow shut out a gigantic block of time? The migraines made her forget things, yes, but could she have forgotten that much?

This was what Dr. Sullivan had been trying to tell her for a while now. They'd even tried hypnosis a few times, hoping to bring out whatever deep-seated memories were keeping her from the truth. This much she knew for sure. It all centered around the car accident. That's when he'd died. And later, when she woke from the coma, her children had no father and Annie had lost the love of her life.

She'd seen it happen, seen them working on him when they took her away in the ambulance. One of the attendants pushed her down when she struggled to go to him.

"You can't help him," the woman had said, laying an arm across Annie's chest. "You're bleeding everywhere. We need to take care of you."

And that's when someone had said, 'he's gone. Might as well get the next one.' That's the last thing Annie remembered before blacking out.

Later, when she woke from the coma, she was in a Toronto hospital, alone, except for her parents, sitting anxiously by the bed. For weeks, they kept her away from her children; the doctors insisting on tests, tests and more tests. Endless counseling sessions for grief and shock and things she couldn't remember any more.

Now, though, she had some questions. Things she'd never thought to ask before. She would see Dr. Sullivan and maybe together they could figure this out.

She set the table for breakfast and started making the kids' lunches. Outside the kitchen window, the snow was melting in the tire tracks down the driveway and along the path between the lodge and the house. Soon, they would have to take the fishing huts off the lake. She made a mental note to call Ben and ask when he was free to help. Maybe Luke wouldn't mind coming out, too.

Sam sauntered into the kitchen, poured himself a coffee, and stood next to her, staring out the window. "Have to get those huts off the lake," he said, repeating her exact thoughts. "I'll call Ben later this morning."

"I was just thinking the same thing," she said. Then suddenly, she turned to him. Completely out of the blue, she asked, "Why wasn't there a funeral?"

"A funeral for who?" he asked.

"After the accident. We didn't have a funeral. Or did you have one when I was still in the hospital?"

Sam put down his coffee cup and took her in his arms. "Oh, darling girl." He kissed her forehead. "You still don't know, do you?"

"Know what?"

"There was no funeral because no one died." She frowned at him and started to say something, but he stopped her. "Joe is your husband. Those photos weren't doctored up. That marriage certificate is real."

"How do you know about that?" She shot at him, pulling herself out of his grasp. She wrinkled her face at him, as if she were seeing something ugly and terrifying. "You've been talking to him."

Sam nodded. "Yes. He's worried about you, Annie, and so am I."

She turned back to making lunches, stuffed Noah's into his backpack and zipped it up. "There's nothing wrong with me. I'm fine. I'm just fine. I wish everyone would just stop pestering me."

"Alright. Alright." Sam held up his hands and backed away.

"Ted's coming. Ted's coming." Ali raced down the stairs, past the kitchen and into the mudroom. When Annie came in with their backpacks, Ali was pulling on her coat and shoving her feet into her boots. "Mummy hurry. Ted's coming. I heard the bus."

It was a mad scramble, but they made it up the drive just as Ted was pulling up.

"Morning, Annie," he called out. "Morning Aline. Noah."

The bus pulled away, with Annie waving at Ali's face pressed close to the glass. "Want to switch places today?" she said half out loud to her daughter. The problems of a child seemed so minor to her just now. But she wouldn't wish this confusion on anyone else, especially Ali.

Annie pulled her coat tighter over herself and when the bus disappeared around the bend in the road, she headed back to the house. She would do the laundry, make the beds, clean Raven's Nest Cottage after the guests leave and then she would go to Huntsville.

Chapter 32

Joe

Jim Sullivan's office was located next to a busy bakery and the block of abandoned apartments that Joe had recently purchased. He glanced up at the sold sign in the window and his heart swelled a little, knowing that soon he would send in a demolition crew and work would begin. Ryan Whitmore, a young up-and-comer in the company, was keen to take charge of the project. He was well liked by his crew and everyone at Melville's, but Joe had concerns about his work ethic. It seemed as if sports, his friends, and hanging out at Hank's bar always took priority over putting in overtime when they were in a crunch. Being the lead man on an apartment block project would mean a lot of overtime. Ryan would have to prove to Joe he was ready for that kind of commitment.

The door to Jim's office swung wide on freshly oiled hinges, unlike the last time Joe was there and it had creaked and groaned in resistance to his pull. He'd mentioned it to Jim and offered to take care of it for him, but Jim wouldn't hear of it. He had a "guy" for things like that, Jim had told him.

"Mr. Hewitt." The receptionist behind the desk smiled at him.

Her name always escaped him, but her friendliness never did. She had a billboard kind of smile that made him think of the one at the edge of town advertising for the local dental clinic.

"Dr. Sullivan called me and said it was urgent I come in," he said, approaching the desk.

She picked up a blue file folder. "Right this way. He's waiting for you."

No waiting. Joe liked that. No sitting in uncomfortable straight-back chairs, reading old magazines and staring at even older landscapes on the walls. He followed her down a short corridor to Jim's office.

"Mr. Hewitt is here," she called out, when they went inside. Light from the adjoining bathroom cast a glow into the room, and Jim came from it, a glass of water in his hand.

"Hello Joe." Jim said, waving him toward a chair. Then he dismissed the receptionist. "Thank you, Pamela. I'll let you know when to make that call."

Pamela. Why couldn't Joe remember that?

"You've redecorated," Joe said, settling into one of the leather wingback chairs opposite Jim's desk and crossing one leg over the other.

"Gotta spend the client's money someplace," Jim joked. "Otherwise, my accountant gives me grief." He settled into the chair next to Joe's and turned it a little so they were facing each other.

"I did a really stupid thing, didn't I?" Joe asked, looking at his hands in his lap. As usual, Jim didn't answer right away, so he went on. "I'd give anything to have yesterday to do over again."

The idea of a do-over had played in his mind all day. He wouldn't have gotten up so early, would have stayed longer in bed that morning with Annie curled up in his arms. Later, when the kids had gone to school, he wouldn't have gone to work at all. Instead, he would have spent the entire day with her, doing whatever she wanted to do, and he certainly wouldn't have shown her the damned marriage certificate. But there were no do-overs in real life. What happened, happened and he couldn't change that now.

Jim tented his fingers and tapped the tips of them on his chin, deep in thought. "You think you pushed her too hard?"

"Don't you? She had questions. I thought maybe she was putting things together." Joe fidgeted, twisting in his chair, watching Jim's face, waiting for the verbal slap that was about to come.

Instead, Jim dropped his hands to the arms of his chair, crossed his legs, and looked at him in an almost paternal way. "Let's do something different, shall we?"

"O… kay." Joe dragged out the word with a degree of caution, wondering what was coming.

"Tell me about the accident, Joe."

Joe's gaze squinted across the space between them. "You already know about the accident."

"Humour me. I'd like to hear it again. Let's start with that morning. As I recall, you left Charlotte, North Carolina, right after breakfast on day two of your journey, drove for a few more hours, and then stopped for lunch and fuel. Is that correct?"

"That's right."

"When you got back in the car, who was driving?"

"I was."

"And where was everyone else?"

"Ali and Noah were in the middle row, in their car seats, of course. Violet and Ryder were in the back. Annie was in the co-pilot seat. She liked to navigate."

"Is that when it happened?"

"Not long after that stop, yes. We had a truck behind us for a while. He was a good distance back, but as we were going down a steep hill, he came at us fast. We were sandwiched between him and the cars in front and a line of cars on our left. Nothing but the ditch on the right. We thought he would take the runaway, but he missed it and his front bumper caught us and sent us into a spin. That's when the shit hit the fan." Joe took a deep breath. "Then the truck jackknifed and most of us ended up in the median or the ditch or up the embankment and into the oncoming traffic." Joe heaved an annoyed sigh. "But you know all this."

Jim nodded. "You were knocked unconscious, weren't you?"

"I was. When I woke up, the first thing I heard was a lot of moaning and crying, and that's when I saw Annie. Her head had smashed against the window and she was bleeding. God, the blood was everywhere. I tried to open the door, but we were penned in by other cars."

"You went to the hospital in an ambulance, didn't you?"

Joe nodded. "Yeah, I went with Annie when they took her."

"Are you sure about that?"

Joe nodded, then frowned. "No, that's wrong. She went in another ambulance. The one that took the kids."

"Okay, and while you were in your ambulance, what happened?"

"What do you mean?"

"I mean, what happened to you? Were you hurt? Broken bones?"

"No, I was okay. Just a few scrapes.

"Are you sure about that?"

"Yes, I'm sure! What is this third degree treatment all about?"

Jim pointed to Joe's chest. "Unbutton your shirt for me, please."

"What for?" Joe didn't even try to keep the annoyance from his voice.

Jim just grinned at him. "Humour me. I like hairy chests."

"Fine." Joe undid his buttons and spread his shirt open. "Happy?"

"Where did you get this scar?"

"A hockey injury, when I was a kid. Some guy crashed into me and his skate cut me."

"Are you sure?"

Joe did his shirt back up again. With a smirk running across his face, he looked at Jim. "Why is this so important?"

"Think, Joe. If you need a reminder, I have your medical records here." Jim reached for the blue file folder Pamela had brought with her. "Says here that when they were loading you into the ambulance, your heart stopped."

"No. That's not possible. I…"

"The attendants got it going again. But later when you got to the hospital, it stopped a second time. That time, the surgeon had to cut you open to massage your heart."

"No. That was someone else. I was fine. I…"

"Annie wasn't wrong, Joe. You died, twice. The first time it happened, Annie was watching. She saw you die, saw the EMTs look at each other after trying to revive you and heard one of them say, 'he's gone but we can't pronounce.' That's when Annie slipped into a coma."

"No, that's not possible. I wasn't…I…"

Jim held up a file folder. "Want to read the reports for yourself? Here you go." He dropped it in Joe's lap. "It's all there. Everything I've just told and more."

Joe rubbed the scar on his chest through his shirt. "No, it's not possible. I…"

"No? Then why do you see a cardiologist twice a year?"

"Because I…"

"Because your heart stopped, Joe. In the accident."

"But I don't understand. I thought…"

"Let me ask you one more thing. One more detail about the accident that also has escaped your mind. Who was driving the car when the accident happened?"

"Me. Of course it was me."

"You're sure about that?" Jim pushed on relentlessly. "When Annie's head hit the window, and the glass smashed, was she in the co-pilot's seat, as you called it?"

"Yes. Of course. I told you. She liked to navigate."

"Then why is Annie's scar on the left side of her head?"

Chapter 33

Annie

It took Annie less than ten minutes after Jim's receptionist called to get back to his office. She'd only gone to a café around the corner after her session. Earlier, it had taken two hours of probing, another hypnosis session and a lot of in-depth exploration, to get to the bottom of it all. But she'd been determined when she left the house that morning with the photo album tucked under her arm that something in her memory wasn't right and she would not rest until it was sorted out. Something was locked in tight, refusing to allow her to admit the things everyone else had tried to tell her.

The marriage certificate, Joe's ring, the name on the kids' birth records, using Hewitt when she'd registered them at school; it all made sense if she and Joe were married. He didn't seem to be the type to play an elaborate ruse involving her father, the kids, and neighbours and friends. And for what? She decided he must be right, but why couldn't she remember their marriage? When she thought of her late husband, the image that came to mind was cloudy, blurred at the edges as if he stood in a dense fog. Why had she blocked him out of any memory of her past, and why didn't she realize that he and Joe were the same person?

She recalled coming out of the coma. Seeing her parents standing at the side of her bed, smiling, hopeful, wary. There was a man, a stranger, someone she'd never seen before, who smiled down at her and wanted to touch her face and kiss her and sit with her. They insisted he was her husband, but he couldn't have been. Her husband died in the accident. She vividly recalled the paramedics' faces when they shook their heads and looked at her with compassion in their eyes. That's the last thing she remembered. After that, everything went black.

When she first woke from the coma, she couldn't remember the accident at all. Months and years of therapy and they still hadn't gotten to the bottom of it all. Until recently, she had recalled nothing more than what people had told her, except that her husband had died. But in the last few weeks, as she dove deeper, she'd begun to piece flashes of memory together and it came to her that if she hadn't been so anxious to get out of the mountains before nightfall, they wouldn't have been going too fast when the truck came up behind them. At a slower speed, they might have had time to take the runaway. She'd confessed this to her doctor earlier, and that was when Jim began to probe a little deeper. In hypnosis, he was able to take her right back to the day and the moment it happened.

"Who is driving?" he'd asked.

"Me. I'm at the wheel and the truck is coming at us fast. There's nowhere to go. What do I do? He's going to hit us! He's not taking the runaway. Then he told *me* to take it. But I froze. Too late."

"What happened next?" Jim had prodded.

"He reached over and forced the wheel toward the cars on our left. They swerved too. But it was too late. The truck hit our back end, anyway."

When she'd gotten the words out, Annie opened her eyes and looked at Jim. "I killed him. It's my fault."

"It wasn't your fault, Annie. It was a faulty brake line on that truck. The trucking company took responsibility. It was all over the news. Millions of dollars paid out to people like yourselves. But the good news is you're all safe. You all survived."

Annie shook her head. "Not all of us."

"Yes, all." Jim opened the photo album. "Look again, Annie. Look at that man in the pictures and tell me who you see."

Annie bent over the pages, her fingers caressing Joe's face. Then she looked up at Jim. "Joe's my husband? He didn't die?"

That's when Annie began to sob uncontrollably, and Jim had taken her into his arms. Eventually, he led her to the couch and urged her to lie down, then gave her a mild sedative to help her relax. She slept and an hour later, when she woke, she remembered everything they'd talked about. In the past, a difficult session had led to a headache and a complete memory lapse, but this time she had remembered it all.

Joe was alive! And she remembered him.

Now she hurried down the hall, past Pamela's desk, not waiting to be announced, and burst through the door. Joe jumped out of his chair as she flew across the room.

"You're not dead!" she cried as he pulled her into his embrace.

"No. I'm not dead," he said, tears flowing down his cheeks.

"I'm sorry. So sorry. It's all my fault. I was driving, and I thought you were dead."

"Shh. Shh. It wasn't your fault. Nothing was." Joe cupped her face with his hands and kissed her through both their tears. "It's alright now. We're both alright."

After a few minutes, Jim let out an exaggerated cough. "This is such a happy occasion, I hate to break it up. I'd like to schedule a follow-up in two weeks' time. I'm sure you're both going to have questions."

"I have one now," Annie said. "Why did I create this ridiculous illusion?"

"You each had a version of the truth that allowed you to come to terms with your guilt. In Joe's, he blamed himself because he'd encouraged and almost forced you to take the trip. Afterwards, his need to take care of you made him block out the severity of his own injuries. He didn't remember that he'd died and been revived. In your version, Annie, you felt responsible for the death of your husband. Medically, Joe died, so yes, it was a real death. You just didn't know he'd been resuscitated. When you woke from the coma, you didn't recognize Joe because, in your truth, he was dead. And because you'd convinced yourself that his death was your fault.

But now you both know the real truth, the one the medical records and the news reports of the accident tell us. Go home. Get to know each other again. Talk about this with Sam. We'll meet again in two weeks' time."

Joe shook Jim's hand. "Thank you for everything. I don't know what we would have done without you."

"I'm happy I could help."

As they headed down the corridor, back toward the front door, Joe said, "School will be out soon. Should we pick up the kids?"

"Yes. Let's. Then we can get your things and Ryder's. I'd really like it if the two of you came back home."

"There's nothing I'd love more, but only if you're sure."

"It's the first thing I've been sure about in a long, long time. I love you, Joe Hewitt. I want us to be a family again."

"I'd like that too. But there's something else I'd like. I want you to take it easy for a change. Sleep in, in the mornings. Let me get the kids to the bus, take care of the customers, deal with the bills."

"But…"

"No buts. You've been taking care of everyone else for long enough, Annie. From now on, let me take care of you."

Epilogue
A few months later…

Joe pushed his feet into a pair of boots that sat in readiness at the back door. Someone's pounding had woken him at an ungodly hour. It was Sunday; a day to lie in bed a little longer, curl up next to Annie and watch the sun rise over the lake. It was not a day to be bothered by guests who'd lost their key, or needed directions to somewhere, or wanted to know if they checked out early, could they get a refund?

Spring had come to Ril Lake, but the mornings were cool with temperatures still in single digits. With his housecoat knotted over his pyjamas, Joe opened the back door to see one of their cabin renters standing coatless in the dewy May morning. Joe peered beyond the man to the lake behind him, where a pinch of the sun was just peeking over the horizon.

"Good morning, Mr. Westfall. What is it this time?" he asked, crossing his arms over his chest. It was the third day in a row the man had come up to the house with a complaint. Joe was fed up with his daily grievances and was ready to throw him and his family out, lock, stock, and nylon sleeping bags. He'd pack up the car himself if it would get them off the property any sooner. How on earth had Annie had the patience for this?

"The space heater isn't working," Mr. Westfall said, rubbing his hands together, pretending to be freezing.

"Well, you're in luck," Joe said, nodding toward the horizon. "The sun will be up in about half an hour and you won't even need one."

Joe heard a rustling behind him and saw Mr. Westfall glance over his shoulder into the mudroom. Annie pushed the hair out of her eyes as she came to stand next to Joe.

"Problem, Mr. Westfall?"

"It's like I was telling your husband, the space heater in our cabin doesn't work."

Annie looked at Joe and said, "That must be the same one that was in the Gibson's cabin last Christmas." Joe shrugged and rolled his eyes as Annie turned back to Mr. Westfall. "We'll take care of it. Might be a faulty wire or something." She handed him a leaflet from a stack on the washing machine behind her. "Take your family out for breakfast at the diner in town. There's a coupon inside for twenty-five percent off."

Mr. Westfall reached up to take the leaflet and reluctantly nodded. "You'll fix the heater then?"

"First thing. As soon as my father is up." Annie smiled and reached out to close the door. Mr. Westfall headed down the stairs and back to his cabin.

"Well, Mrs. Hewitt," Joe said, pulling her into his arms. "At least you're not giving them free breakfasts anymore."

"They just need a little help. Everyone needs someone to take care of them now and again."

The End.

Thank you!

Thank you for reading my story. I hope you enjoyed it and if so, please leave a review for me wherever you purchased the book.

It takes more than just an author to create and publish a novel.
Yes, the author creates the story and the characters, but there are others whose influence is vital to the final product. Beta readers, proofreaders, editors, members of writing/critique groups and instructors all have some input into the books you read.
I am grateful to everyone who has had a hand in the completion of this novel. Specifically, this time, my thanks go to Janice Barrett (friend and author of Authorized Cruelty), Joanne Cannings, friend and travel companion, and my editor and sister Judith Rose. All three have given freely of their time and provided me with constructive feedback, which has resulted in this incredible story.

If you are interested in becoming an Advance Reader, for future projects please, contact dmr58@hotmail.ca

About the author

Margery Reynolds is the pen name of Dale Margery Rutherford, the daughter of an Ontario peach farmer. She is the mother of three, grandmother of two, and now lives in Edmonton, Alberta. Her personal reading choices lean toward historical fiction, but she also enjoys light romance, cozy mysteries, and the occasional suspense.

Her years of cottage rentals in the Muskoka Region of Ontario are what inspired the Ril Lake stories. She has also published short stories and is working on a historical fiction trilogy based on a group of Abolitionists in upstate New York and their journeys from the south to the Niagara River to bring runaway slaves to freedom.

Margery is also keenly interested in tea as a natural remedy for many of life's ailments. Having previously owned a bookstore and tea shop in Niagara Falls, Ontario, she has developed many blends, including her Ril Lake blends, which are available to order.

You can follow Margery on Facebook at

https://www.facebook.com/authouroffiction

visit her website at

www.margeryreynolds.ca

or Substack at

https://margeryreynolds.substack.com

or send her an email. She'd love to hear from you.

dmr58@hotmail.ca

Manufactured by Amazon.ca
Acheson, AB

13430809R00173